She says she wa... ...r
thinks she does... ...g..~ .~ ~...~. ..~ ~~p..~s
that she isn't entitled to one, not automatically, not
under the Prevention of Terrorism Act, but that he will
think about it when they are at the station.

'Who are you?' she asks him.

'Chief Inspector Shaw, Anti-Terrorist Squad,
Scotland Yard.'

'There's been a mistake,' she says.

'Then we'll get it cleared up soon.' He calls all his
men to heel. 'Come on. Let's leave the SOCOs to it.'

They take her downstairs. The sun is setting somewhere over Oxford. The sky is white with little pewter
clouds. The mean, red-brick block of flats, with its stairs
that smell of urine and its peeling green front door, looks
like paradise suddenly, and Maire is being escorted out
of the garden by angels with flaming swords.

About the author

Susan was born in the Chilterns and brought up in Oxford. After reading French and English at London University, she worked as a freelance computer consultant for many years.

She is now a full-time writer and lives in West London with her solicitor husband and cat.

The Seventh Victim

Susan Kelly

CORONET BOOKS
Hodder and Stoughton

British Library Cataloguing in Publication Data

Kelly, Susan
The seventh victim
I. Title
823.914[F]

ISBN 0 340 60995 8

Printed and bound in Great Britain by
Cox & Wyman Ltd, Reading, Berkshire

Hodder and Stoughton
A Division of Hodder Headline PLC
338 Euston Road
London NW1 3BH

The Maguire Seven . . . were never credibly members of any IRA gang. The 'intuition of innocence' was universally felt by those who had dealings with them. Here were seven people whom 'everybody knew' did not commit the acts for which they were sentenced. Yet against them stood strong scientific evidence . . .

The Times *Leader, June 26th, 1991*

For Francis, as ever,
with all my love

Acknowledgements

I would like to thank Una Padel whose study *Insiders: Women's Experience of Prison* (with Prue Stevenson, Virago, 1988) and whose personal help on the telephone made Part Two of this novel possible. I also made use of *Proved Innocent* by Gerry Conlon of the Guildford Four and Chris Mullins' *Error of Judgement: the Truth about the Birmingham Bombings*.

SK

Foreword

Outrage

The Hope and Anchor in the centre of High Wycombe is as full as it ever gets at half past ten this warm Friday evening; and that's full, as the serious drinkers stockpile the last few pints in the run-up to closing time. Workers from Parker Knoll's gather here. Freed from their week's drudgery, they are schoolboys let home for the holidays, although Friday is also the night they bring their wives with them. It's the night the single mothers find a couple of pounds for a baby-sitter, 50p for their first gin and lime, do each other's hair and come along to chat up the soldier boys from the local barracks with their steady jobs, fit young bodies and generous ways.

The Hope is the right sort of pub: not so smart you feel unwelcome, not so squalid you have to mind where you put your feet. Mick Brady's band plays here most Friday nights: all the favourites – 'Knock Three Times on the Ceiling If You Want Me', 'Tie a Yellow Ribbon round the Old Oak Tree'; no punk.

Toni Giordano, the young landlord, is second-generation Italian and looks it. He's twenty-eight, not overly tall, but slim and tanned and vibrant. He's sexy and he knows it. He strayed out this way from Friern Barnet five years ago, liked it, stayed and took on this tenancy. He's worked hard. Catering is in his blood and he's put a lot of effort into his bar meals. He serves *osso bucco* as well as steak and kidney pie. On Friday nights he doesn't stop. The food is Italian, the band Irish, the music American: nations intermingle. Chrissie Giordano – pretty, lively and popular – is a local girl. She likes being his co-worker as well as his wife and it means she can keep her eye on him. After three years of marriage, they still exchange glances and the odd surreptitious squeeze in passing. Her two sisters take it in turn to help behind the bar. Toni and Chrissie have just spent a few thousand doing the place up on a bank loan: new plum velvet cushions on the seats, the latest in microwave technology out back. The changes have lost them a few grumbling regulars but they've more than made up for it with a new – younger – crowd.

Windows shatter for half a mile around just as Chrissie opens her mouth to yell: 'Last! Orders! Please!'

Corporal Jack Carmichael of the Second Buckinghamshire Rifles, recently returned from a six-month tour of duty in Northern Ireland, is in the gents at the time and just zipping up – eager for one last pint before the towels go on – when all the opaque windows fly in at him in a shower of tiny silver sparks like Guy Fawkes Night.

He lurches out through the swing door, back into the saloon bar – more shocked than hurt despite a few minor cuts on his face. He opens his mouth to say 'Christ! That could have taken my prick off', and realises he's the only one of his drinking party still standing. The air is thick with dust – the unsuspected innards of tables and chairs and the debris of that occult space beneath the floorboards. Those who are still conscious are choking.

Chrissie Giordano is screaming with the pain of the shards of glass in her left eye, through which she will never see clearly again. Her sister, Marilyn Piper, who was collecting up the soldiers' glasses when the bomb went off at their feet, is dead.

The phone behind the wrecked bar isn't working but Carmichael finds an unvandalised box in the bus station next door and calls an ambulance first, police second. The police say they are already on their way – they have had 999 calls from all over town.

He runs back to the pub, bullies the walking wounded out to a safe distance in case of a second explosion. He lays the others down on the floor, making them as comfortable as he can, their heads on plum velvet cushions which hardly show the blood.

Smoke gets in his eyes and ears as he gives the kiss of life to Private James Scott who has had a leg blown clean off and has just stopped breathing. Today is Scottie's twenty-second birthday, which is why they were all out celebrating at his expense.

People go on screaming, minutes after the disaster. Outside, Toni Giordano is doing his best to stop people leaving the scene before the police arrive, while trying at the same time to minister to his injured wife and to keep her from learning too soon the news about Marilyn. On the forecourt, on a frosting of broken glass, two tough-looking men pick a fight with each other over nothing – each needing to prove to himself that he is not afraid. Disgusted bystanders drag them apart. They stand teetering a few yards at bay, blaspheming, swinging their arms in aggressive futility. Women are crying. Toni, looking at what is left of his business and his home, wants to join in but it is not in his heritage.

Sirens whine out in the street and Carmichael hears the noise of well-serviced brakes. Soon, a voice says, 'Let's have you out to the ambulance now, soldier, you've done a great job.' He doesn't believe it: he was the senior officer here, the oldest; he has failed his men, his friends, his brothers in arms. Kindly hands lift him off Scottie and take control. The wounded man's chest begins to rise and fall in regular rhythm once more.

As he heaves himself to his feet, swaying slightly, Jack Carmichael becomes aware that Scottie's civvy clothes are covered in minute threads of black nylon and strands of black plastic – the remnants of a cheap woman's handbag. No, he corrects himself automatically, a woman's cheap handbag.

No: a cheap woman, a worthless woman.

Part One

Life Destroyed

One

This is the last time Maire lets anyone persuade her to go on a blind date.

'He's a nice bloke, Maire, in insurance, about thirty. He'll buy you a nice meal, at least. When did you last have a nice meal out? Steak, a bit of Black Forest gateau, a bottle of vino. You can't remember the last time, can you? What have you got to lose?'

Sandy's nasal whine had nagged and coaxed until it had seemed easier to say yes and get it over with. Maire sees now that Sandy is mistaken. She does have something left to lose: her self respect.

So she is angry this humid night, angry with herself for being here. A groping oaf, that's what this Brian has turned out to be in the five minutes since she met him outside the cinema as arranged – a gross bull of a man with thick, ogling glasses and ugly, sweaty clothes. As for the nice meal, there has been no talk of that, nor does he want to see the current film. He doesn't expect to spend more than the price of a couple of drinks on a cheap lay for the evening.

He leads her down the road to the Hope and Anchor, his hand sticky on her bare arm.

In spite of her short stature and slender build, Maire is a hard woman to overlook and several men in the bar turn to glance, then look away, then back again for a more considered appraisal. She is not, in any conventional sense, pretty, but her Black-Irish looks are unusual and striking and she stands out here among over-made-up women, and girls with bleached hair, tight skirts and high heels. She has put on a skirt tonight – since this is, after all, a date – but it falls demurely below her knees and is cut full enough to cover them even when she sits. Her legs are bare and her shoes are flat black pumps, like ballet shoes. She wears a blue cotton shirt and is braless, not to tantalise but because her tiny breasts need no uplift and money for clothes must be carefully allocated. She keeps her dark curls short, giving no frame to her bare, tense face but highlighting her sharp cheek bones and her well-made ears with their gold studs.

She is not aware of scrutiny but finds the crowd disturbing. Back home, a few years ago, she had been a great one for the 'Crack' – that love of company, conversation and laughter which is the cornerstone of Irish social life – but that had been among family, among friends she had known all her life. She stands looking round. The band puzzles her: the faces are almost familiar – with their russet hair and ruddy cheeks, their short and stocky bodies – but the music is not. She clutches her roomy shoulder-bag against her protectively as he guides her towards a corner seat.

He asks her what she's having. Her voice, with its Celtic aspirates, is never loud, but she has no difficulty in making herself heard when she needs to, her low pitch sneaking in beneath the noise of these serious drinkers. She asks for an orange juice. His face creases up in disapproval like a florid prune; it should be rum and Coke, port and lemon – something to get her giggly, amenable.

He can't get her name right, keeps calling her Nora. 'It's Maire,' she says each time, 'Maire O'Neill,' and he says, 'What sort of a name is that?' 'It's Irish,' she tells him, 'like Brian,' and he looks puzzled. She wonders if Brian is his real name or just one he has chosen for the evening since he is as obviously married as if he had 'Sold' tattooed on his forehead. He is just as obviously not thirty, and she amuses herself by counting the wrinkles of fat round his wrists to date him, like the rings of a tree stump.

Lonely is not a word she ever allows herself to use, but it is a half life – this being at home all day with no company but that of a child, however beloved that child may be – a half life she has been living for five years. Sometimes she thinks she has forgotten how to talk: has lost the ability, even the will, to converse with intelligent adults, to chafe, to exchange quotations, little grown-up jokes. Was that why she agreed to this evening's folly: in the vain hope of a little human contact?

They have nothing to say to each other. 'Not very chatty, are you?' he remarks at intervals. Then he complains about the heat, tugging at his loosened tie, running a finger inside his nylon shirt collar, stroking his redly glistening neck. For something to say she asks him about selling insurance and he responds with a list of the places he's been lately – Reading and Swindon, Newbury and Marlborough – and grumbles about the landladies at the B & Bs he stays at and the roadworks on the M4.

So she is stuck in the Hope and Anchor when she could be at home playing snap with Roisin and saving herself the two-fifty for the babysitter. She silently curses Sandy, who will not understand that any woman can be happy on her own. A single woman of twenty-three, according to Sandy, especially one with an illegitimate child on her hands and no money but what she earns stuffing circulars into envelopes on the kitchen table, must be in want of a man – any man. Who is Maire to be so fussy?

Wasn't it a man – Connor – that had put her here in the first place, had put an end to her lovely plans for Dublin and university the following year? She had gone to Dublin, all right, at the age of seventeen, but only to catch the boat as so many had before her. Abortion had not been an option, not for her. She had spent a few months in Liverpool, surviving on the dole until the birth, then headed south, because someone had told her that the living was easier in the Thames Valley. She had happened on this dull, ugly, prospering town, rapidly eating up the green valley with its glass and concrete shopping centres, its multi-storey car parks, and had not had the strength to search further.

She had never heard from Con although she had written to tell him about Roisin, sent him a photograph of her, all red and new.

Shortly after ten-thirty, she knows she can't stand any more, that she will stifle. The pub Brian has chosen – the sort of place, she imagines, where he isn't likely to run into anyone who knows him – is overflowing now with raucous human life. A group of soldiers at the next table is almost drowning out the band, shouting offensive comments with their leering, beery mouths at any woman who happens to walk past, stripping her bare with their eyes.

'Just going to freshen up,' she tells Brian. He looks like the sort of man who will be shocked if a woman says she's going for a pee. He nods permission. He moves his knees so that there is just enough room for her to squeeze past, so long as he gives her a moistly helping hand.

The women's toilets are some distance away, leading off the lounge bar. He had been too mean to take her in there, saying that the saloon was cosier and that she would enjoy the band. The geography is ideal for her purpose; she isn't going to waste any time in explanation or recrimination. She pees, since she really does need to, washes her hands, dries them on the least wet patch of a roller towel which won't roll, walks out of the door which leads from the lounge bar into the street and heads for the neighbouring bus station where her bus is just closing its doors. She breaks into a run and they open for her.

'Bye, Brian,' she murmurs, leaning her hot forehead against the cool of the window as she waits for the bus to get underway. 'Thanks for a horrid evening.'

She knows he will wait a good ten minutes before he goes to look for her, will assume that women always have arcane rituals to perform in front of the mirror – that she is making herself pretty for him, putting on lipstick to make a greasy pink ring round his cock in the back of his car later. Then he will not be able to believe that she has walked out on him. He will spend another ten minutes looking for her, asking after her, becoming more and more bellicose, making himself a figure of fun. She will be home by the time he gives up and leaves, cursing his wasted money, muttering, to salvage his pride, that she wasn't much to look at anyway with her flat chest and unpainted face and tousled black hair.

Roisin will be awake, despite the late hour, despite the threats and bribes of the babysitter. She always waits up for Maire on her rare evenings out, like the worried mother, and it's Friday, after all, and no play school tomorrow.

Maire doesn't hear the explosion, although half the town does. Her little council flat, high up on the north-eastern slope of the valley of the almost dried-up river Wye, is out of earshot.

Two

Roisin is restless the next morning, as if she knows. Normally Maire works at the kitchen table on Saturdays, at least during the morning, while she sits quietly in the corner, leafing through the pages of *Thomas the Tank Engine* or whatever the library has to offer that week, querying the odd difficult word. She is always quiet and good, sometimes even a little solemn.

But not this Saturday; this Saturday she wakens Maire shortly after half past six, explaining that she has tried very, very hard to go back to sleep, demonstrating how she has screwed up her eyes and sucked her thumb, pressing her comfort blanket to her nose and mouth, willing sleep in vain. She burrows under the blankets like a mole, her thick black hair scratchy against Maire's bare limbs, demanding stories. Stories are one of their things.

So Maire tells her about Lir, King of the White Hill. Of how he married Niamh – the daughter of Aillil of Aran – who was like the beauty of winter: like a tree hoared with frost or the stretch of snow along a mountainside as far as your eye can see. Of how she gave him four children, two sets of twins, three boys and a girl.

'Finola,' Roisin says, counting on her fingers, 'and Aedh and . . .' She gives a look of comic despair.

'And Fiachra and Conn,' Maire reminds her.

'And she was the oldest – Finola – and could tell all her brothers what to do.'

Her mother laughs. 'Something like that.'

She tells how Niamh died giving birth to the last two. Of how Lir then married her younger sister, Aoife, who was like . . .

'Like the beauty of autumn,' Roisin interrupts.

'Yes: russet and gold and cream and hazel.'

'What beauty am I like?' she wants to know.

Maire looks at her. She is tiny for her five years, wiry, with black hair and eyes, and skin like milk, fresh and warm from the cow. She resembles Maire, as if Con had no part in her making.

'Winter,' she decides. 'Like Queen Niamh.' The child looks thoughtful and says that winter is the saddest season because everything is dead and cold then. Maire hugs her and says that in the depths of winter, spring – with its new hopes and promises – is only just round the corner.

She tells her again of how Aoife was barren and grew, over the sterile years, to hate her stepchildren. Of how she exhausted her spite, finally, in turning them into swans with a spell that could not be broken for nine hundred years but, in sudden remorse, let them keep their human voices to sing music sweeter than any music ever heard on earth. Of how they lived out their nine hundred years of purgatory and were freed . . .

'"Never wavering",' Roisin breaks in. 'You missed out "never wavering", Mim.'

Maire ruffles her hair. 'What a tyrant you are! All right: *never wavering* in their love for each other, until they were freed from their spell in time – ancient lady and old old men as they then were – to be baptised into the new faith and be buried in one grave.'

'More!' Roisin cries. 'More stories.' So then Maire tells her about how Luke Skywalker and the Princess Leia fought the Evil Empire and destroyed the Death Star with the help of the Force, and then her imagination is full and it's time for breakfast.

It has rained heavily in the night, sweeping away the humidity to leave a dry, bright, late summer's day. Since Roisin will not settle, Maire gives herself a holiday from filling envelopes and they put their swimsuits and towels into a plastic carrier bag and take the bus down to Wycombe Rye where there is an outdoor pool, where the air echoes with the screams of over-excited children, making the most of their last week of freedom before school resumes.

Maire chooses not to swim – the chlorinated blue water no

substitute for the chilly, fishy swimming hole back home – but settles down in her modest one-piece swimsuit, on her towel, on the grass, where she can keep an eye on Roisin without crowding her, as she splashes fearlessly in the children's pool. She sees her talking to another little girl, examining her bloated water-wings in puzzlement; Maire hopes she will make a new friend. Her self-containment is troubling at times and she blames herself for it. It is for her daughter's sake that she puts up with the likes of Sandy who has a girl of the same age. Sometimes Maire feels that Roisin is older than she and, looking into her dark eyes, she senses deep reserves of wisdom.

She sees the other child walk away, hurt – embarrassed by the new plastic wings which had been her pride just moments before. Neither Maire nor her daughter has the gift of tact. She watches her next accost a boy who is the owner of a big blue beach-ball, and they begin to toss it desultorily back and forth between them. She lies back on the grass and looks at the sky. They will stay all day, she decides, get their money's worth, eat greasy burgers and chips in the glass canteen – hoisted high above the pool – as a special treat. They will have fried onions and ketchup and sickly Pepsi – all the things that are usually forbidden – and to hell with caution.

She has her sketchbook with her and for a while she amuses herself drawing outlines of the strange and exotic birds that come to mate on this island. There are the vultures, all male, who splash each other and jump on each other until pulled up – for a few minutes – by the lifeguard's whistle. She draws their noses long, like Pinocchio, like tearing beaks. Then there are the birds of paradise, all female, strutting their multi-coloured plumage to tease the vulture boys. There is commotion, as a provoked punk vulture throws a green bird of paradise in at the deep end, wetting her feathers and making her scream. The lifeguard throws him out and the bird retires with her companions, squawking in outrage. Maire smiles and draws.

Two women come and flop down on the grass a few feet away. One is plump and dyed blonde, the other a skinny redhead with a bad dose of sunburn. They fan themselves with their hands and take no notice of Maire or of anyone else except when the redhead shouts to a cross-looking boy that he should stay out of the deep end or she'll give him what for. The blonde takes out a cosmetic bag and begins to paint her claws a cruel red.

Maire closes her eyes and tries to move away into her own world, but snatches of their conversation keep drifting across with the breeze: 'Outrage . . . IRA . . . Girl blinded' . . . 'Only just done the place up'. Then the red-headed woman says very loudly that hanging is too good for the bastards and if it were up to her . . . Then she lowers her voice and Maire doesn't hear what she would do to them, whoever they are. They begin to talk about the Jeremy Thorpe scandal instead – giggling and nudging each other as people will who expect their politicians to be more virtuous than they.

Maire wonders what they are talking about. There has been a new bombing campaign on the mainland recently and she supposes that there has been yet another explosion in London which is thirty miles away and might as well be three hundred as far as she is concerned. But their words have reminded her, unexpectedly, of home.

Donegal, where Maire comes from, is in Ulster but in the Irish Republic. People don't understand when she tells them that: they think Ulster is synonymous with the six counties of Northern Ireland. She has to explain that the ancient kingdom of Ulster was nine counties, three of which are now in the Republic, and they shrug their shoulders since, for them, the distinction between Ulster and the North is as nothing. The border with the North was a few miles to the south – perhaps twenty minutes' drive – of where she grew up.

If you're not Irish yourself it can be hard to understand the attitude of the ordinary people of Ireland to the IRA. Maire supports their aims and deplores their methods, which is what everyone says in their rational moments. But she remembers how her Uncle Tommy used to get drunk on a Saturday night and when he was drunk he would sing. It never seemed to occur to him that he might not. Her father and her Uncle Francie had to hold him up at the microphone since he was too drunk to stand up; but not too drunk to sing.

He would always start with the same song – the one with the refrain that goes:

Every man will stand behind
The men behind the wire.

For hadn't his own mother's brother been shot by the Brits in 1916, as he never tired of telling them, and hadn't he, a peaceable farmer, a duty to keep the old man's memory alive? And suddenly the whole pub would be on its feet, cheering and clapping. Then he'd sing about how they were all off to Dublin in the green (in the green), where the helmets glistened in the sun, where the bayonets flashed and the rifles crashed to the echo of a Thompson gun. Then he would down a last pint of stout and round off with the National Anthem in Gaelic – a language he didn't speak, coming of a generation which preceded its compulsory teaching in school – and there wouldn't be a dry cheek in the house. Even Maire would wipe away a tear, telling herself that it was just that it was such a damn good rousing tune.

Uncle Tommy was the one – and there's one in every family – who would go to Dublin twice a year to make his confession, not trusting to the discretion of Father O'Donnell.

For some reason that chorus keeps going through her head this afternoon: Every man will stand behind the men behind the wire. It mingles with the complacent voices of the two women and with Roisin's gentle but determined pleas for a second ice-cream which she knows is not allowed out of concern for her teeth.

Gentle but determined: that may sum Roisin up. Maire gives in. To hell with caution; everyone deserves a day off.

Three

They have been watching the flat all day.

Maire barely has time to put the bathing costumes in soak and get the kettle on for a late tea before they are hammering on the door.

They are very polite and very firm and very jumpy. As soon as they've flashed their warrant cards at her, they are searching every room in the flat: flinging the doors open, pressing themselves against the hall wall as they do so; checking cupboards, under beds, calling to each other – 'Nothing here', 'All quiet here'. It doesn't take long – not in a three-roomed council flat, on the second floor of three, with neither cellar nor attic.

One of them says, 'Well, no one's been in or out this afternoon, that's for sure.'

Two of them are armed. They hold their guns pointing ceilingwards against their cheeks. She can see the shoulder holsters under their flapping jackets. They are the ones who fling doors open. She has never seen an English bobby with a gun before, thought it was not allowed. Meanwhile, a woman searches her. That doesn't take long either – she wears only a skirt, pants, that same blue shirt and a pair of plimsolls.

Then she and Roisin sit in the kitchen with the policewoman who, like the men, is not in uniform but wears a Marks and Spencer cotton skirt quite like Maire's own and a neat blouse. She answers no questions but says in a neutral tone that the Chief Inspector will speak to her in a minute.

Roisin is excited and jumps round the room la-la-ing a tune which Maire recognises, belatedly, as 'The Men behind the Wire'. She must have been humming it on the bus home.

One of the men calls the WPC out for perhaps half a minute.

When she comes back she asks, 'Is there anyone who can look after the little girl for a few hours, Miss O'Neill? Your mother? A sister?' Maire explains that they are all away off in the West of Ireland, then remembers to ask why she needs anyone to look after Roisin when she is here herself to take care of her. They want her to come in for questioning, the young woman says. About what? About the bomb blast, the deaths, at the Hope and Anchor last night.

'What!' Maire can't take in what she's hearing. 'The Hope and Anchor? But that's impossible. I was there last night myself.'

'We know,' the WPC says quietly.

When she can think again Maire says that Sandy might take Roisin for a couple of hours. She's not on the telephone and nor is Sandy but the policewoman uses her radio and Sandy is deposited on the doorstep by car within fifteen minutes. She looks pale and rather plain and Maire realises that she has been caught in the middle of putting on her Saturday-night face for the world. She is a harassed-looking woman with thick legs and prominent teeth. She is Maire's age and also a single parent; they have nothing else in common.

She has her little girl with her and Roisin agrees, a little reluctantly, to go round and spend the night at her friend Cheryl's house, as a special treat. Sandy goes off with a girl in each hand. She doesn't meet Maire's eye as she says, 'Say good-bye to Mum, Rosie.'

She realises that she has never been parted from Roisin for a single night.

More people arrive – technicians encased in clean white overalls and wearing latex gloves. The most important man, the one all the rest call 'Sir', who is also the tallest, tells her that she is wanted down at the local station initially. Initially? she repeats stupidly and he says she might be moved to London later. He arrests her formally, reciting the words of caution she has heard so often on television – about anything she says being taken down and given in evidence – but never expected to hear applied to herself.

She says she wants to see a solicitor since she knows, or thinks she does, that she has a right to one. He replies that she isn't entitled to one, not automatically, not under the

Prevention of Terrorism Act, but that he will think about it when they are at the station.

'Who are you?' she asks him.

'Chief Inspector Shaw, Anti-Terrorist Squad, Scotland Yard.'

'There's been a mistake,' she says.

'Then we'll get it cleared up soon.' He calls all his men to heel. 'Come on. Let's leave the SOCOs to it.'

They take her downstairs. The sun is setting somewhere over Oxford. The sky is white with little pewter clouds. The mean, red-brick block of flats, with its stairs that smell of urine and its peeling green front door, looks like paradise suddenly, and Maire is being escorted out of the garden by angels with flaming swords.

She gets into the back of a dark blue Austin Princess with a man on either side of her. There are no marked police cars, no men in uniform with tall hats; they are not conspicuous. No curtains twitch – not even those belonging to Mrs Roote, the elderly widow on the ground floor, who seldom neglects her post. The men are all in jeans and casual jackets – they might be setting out for a night at the disco were it not for the handguns. Instead they drive to Queen Victoria Street where the police station is. She has passed it many times on her way to the library a couple of doors along, but it has never registered. They pull straight into the car park past the sign marked No Entry and take her in at the back door with a policeman on each arm. The tall man, Shaw, goes ahead, opening the door with a plastic cardkey and a rapidly punched code number. The woman constable comes after them. They make a little procession.

Four

Maire remembers what her grandfather used to say: that the reason the sun never set on the British Empire was that God didn't trust an Englishman in the dark. She follows the Englishman, Shaw, along a brilliantly lit corridor until they come to a big room like a lobby with people everywhere and a desk where a man sits in uniform, his jacket draped over the back of his chair.

'One to book in, Sergeant,' Shaw says. 'Miss Maire O'Neill.' There are other people waiting in this custody area: a sulky young rastafarian, a bored prostitute. Maire jumps the queue; no one objects.

As she is booked in, searched, her belongings catalogued and labelled, she notices several uniformed bobbies stopping to stare at her and her companions. They are the star turn. Shaw's eyes follow hers and he frowns and they all dissolve instantly away into the bowels of the police station. She signs something: a list of the humble contents of her pockets. She asks again to see a lawyer and the Sergeant looks at Shaw who says that they will send for one as soon as she has seen the doctor.

What doctor, she asks?

Sergeant says that the boffin has been notified and is on his way and should be here in about an hour and a half.

'Has everything been fixed up as I asked?' Shaw asks.

'We've given him the collating room,' Sergeant says. 'It'll be a bit cramped but it was the best I could do at short notice.' Shaw sighs and says that it will have to do and Sergeant looks irritated and replies, 'We're not geared up for this.' He hopes, *with all due respect*, that Shaw realises that this is not a Category-A set-up.

The Chief Inspector takes Maire gently by the arm and leads her deeper in, to a cell where, he tells her, she must wait until she has seen the doctor.

What doctor, she asks?

The cell is a bare concrete box. It is painted, in chilly gloss paint, a duck-egg blue. The floor is concrete and the overhead light remains switched on at all times. There is one window, very high up and with bars. This is to be her home for the next three nights – the place where she hardly sleeps. By way of furniture she has a wooden sleeping-platform with a mattress – a grubby, greasy slab of rubber two inches thick. She sits on it now, tucks her feet up under her. She sits there alone for almost two hours, with nothing to look at, nothing to do. The spyhole in the door remains open and every five minutes a constable stares through it. Halfway through her time the constable changes and an older man gives way to a nervous, fresh-faced boy. She feels almost silly. She tries to engage him in conversation for something to do, calls out to know his name, offers her own. He ignores her with a wooden discipline.

Then Shaw comes to fetch her again, tells her the doctor is here at last. What doctor, she asks? He takes her to a small room where a folding table is set out. A man in a white lab coat sits there, bobs up to shake hands with Shaw then sits down again. He is an ascetic-looking man with a small pointed beard and a slightly Slavic cast to his features. He is not introduced to Maire. He has a young woman with him. She perches tensely on an upright chair at the far end of the room with a notebook on her lap. They look at Maire without curiosity.

'Can we get on?' White Coat asks impatiently. It is Saturday evening and he had other plans. Beneath his lab coat, he is in evening dress.

'Ready when you are,' Shaw says.

He sits Maire down at the table opposite White Coat who takes a pair of surgeon's gloves from a sealed bag and puts them on his hands. He tears open a flimsy cardboard box, extracts some cotton-wool swabs, wipes them over the gloves and puts them to one side.

He says, 'Control samples,' to Shaw, who nods.

'Right hand,' he says to Maire. Note Book begins to write as she holds out her hand. White Coat regards it dispassionately like a specimen for vivisection; he is not interested in Maire or her crime. He is not interested in people, only in Science, in facts.

He uses more swabs on her palms, the backs of her hands, between her fingers. They are slimily wet and smell of dentists' waiting-rooms. He puts each one in a transparent bag as he goes along, sealing and labelling it and calling out things to Note Book: Sample A – right-hand palm; Sample B – right hand between thumb and first finger.

When he has done with the swabs and both Maire's hands feel clammy and alien to her, he takes a wooden nail-pick and scrapes her short, workmanlike nails out on to a tissue which is also bagged and labelled. The whole business takes perhaps ten minutes. Then he says to Shaw, 'That's it,' and nods at Maire grimly as if to say that she may have her hands back now. 'If that's all, I'll be back off to London. You'll have the preliminary results some time tomorrow.' Shaw thanks him politely and he packs up and is gone, with his handmaid, in an instant.

'Who is he?' Maire asks.

'He's a forensic scientist from RARDE. This way, please.'

'What's a rardy?' she asks, rising to follow him.

'R.A.R.D.E.' He spells it out for her. 'It's the Army Research Establishment. They do all the testing for explosives – nitroglycerine and so on – anything used in making bombs.'

'And you expect to find something like that on my hands?' It is almost laughable except that they all look so deadly serious. 'I've never touched any explosives in my life.'

'We shall see, shan't we?'

She reminds him about the solicitor and they go back to Sergeant who telephones someone called the duty solicitor and says he will be here within the hour.

Shaw takes her to an interview room. He is still scrupulously polite, sends one of his men for some coffee for them both. He is playing this one by the book. They sit and look at each other without speaking until the coffee comes.

All policemen look tall to Maire, but Shaw must be six foot two, quite thin. She thinks he is about forty-five although he has a lot of grey in his short dark hair, which might make him look older than he really is. He isn't her idea of a policeman:

she is used to the plump, beery-faced Garda at home, breaking up fights at closing time and lending a hand with the harvest if it's needed. His dark eyes are watching her. His long thin face is composed, unsmiling; his nose is a shade too short for it, his lips unexpectedly full and pink. The lips part as she waits and he says, 'May I call you Maire?'

'I suppose so.'

'I need to get to know you, Maire, to find out what makes you tick. How old are you? Nineteen? Twenty? I have a daughter not much younger than you.'

'I'm twenty-three.'

'Twenty-three. Why do you let yourself get mixed up in this sort of thing? You, with your whole life ahead of you?'

'I'm not mixed up in anything,' she says, and they relapse into silence. He is wearing a grey suit like any bank clerk or civil servant, a pale blue shirt – well ironed – a blue striped tie with a little crested tie-pin. There is a thick gold band, worn dull, on his ring finger – a family man with a daughter not much younger than Maire.

The door opens and one of the other men comes in with three mugs of coffee on a tray. He is more like her idea of a policeman: burly, with the ruddy complexion that speaks of high blood pressure and a taste for drink. He wears jeans and a black leather jacket as if he is there to do the rough. Shaw gets up and takes two mugs without comment, gives her one, sugars and stirs the other.

'Interview with suspect, Maire O'Neill, begins at 10.57 p.m.,' he says, 'DCI Shaw and DS Croft present.' He turns to his prisoner. 'Where are the others?'

'Who? What others?'

'We're watching every port, they won't get back to Ireland. Tell us where they're hiding out. A safe house in London? Oxford? I need the address.'

'I don't know what you mean.'

'We know you're not a ringleader,' Shaw says, moving restlessly. 'Just tell us what happened.' He passes behind her and puts his hand on her shoulder in a gesture of reassurance, calling on her to confide in him. It is the hand with the wedding ring.

'Was it a boyfriend, Maire?'

'I haven't got a boyfriend.'

'I expect you get a bit lonely, don't you? Single mother. Was it the little girl's father?'

'I haven't seen her father since before she was born, for whatever business it is of yours.'

Shaw sits down opposite her again and shifts his tactics slightly; his suspects never know what to expect next and are thus wrong-footed. Now he is the stern father, speaking in sorrow, not anger.

'I don't like bullying women, Maire. You're a sensible girl and we'll get on fine if you'll just stop messing me about. You met a man recently, isn't that right? Someone from back home? Michael? Patrick? Jimmy? He was nice to you, bought presents for the little girl, took you out, made you feel special.'

'This is pure fantasy,' she tells him coldly. 'I live very quietly with my daughter. I haven't got a boyfriend. Ask the neighbours. Ask Mrs Roote on the ground floor – she's the self-appointed concierge for the block.'

'And then this man – this Jackie or Terry – asked you to take the bag to the Hope and Anchor last night. You have got a black plastic shoulder-bag, haven't you? We found it in your hall. It was a bag just like the one which contained the bomb.'

'Then it can't have been my bag,' she points out, 'since it must have been blown to kingdom come.'

'So he gave you a new bag for the purpose, but he'd have bought one very like the one you already had.'

'I got it at Murray's sale for four pounds just after Christmas. There were a hundred like it. A hundred women in the town have one just like it.'

'But they weren't all at the Hope and Anchor last night – by their own admission.' He speeds up, ticking off the evidence against her on his fingers. 'They didn't all run off, claiming they were just going to powder their noses, half an hour before the blast. They weren't all seen running very fast away from the pub . . .'

'I was running for my bus,' she protests, hardly able to believe what she is hearing. 'It was just closing its doors, so I ran to catch it. I'd have had to wait half an hour for the next one.'

'So Denny, or Danny, gave you this new black handbag, told you to leave it under a table near the dartboard, in the saloon where the soldier boys always went, then to get out fast. That's what happened, isn't it? Isn't it? That was all you knew – all you needed to know.'

The problem is, Maire thinks, that it all sounds so perfectly plausible, even likely . . .

She has just turned fourteen. It's Wednesday afternoon which is always games afternoon at her school and she is meant to be practising the discus with Caitlin Sweeney, her best friend.

Caitlin is a wild one – big for her age, already full-breasted. Her talk is all of boys and the films and pop music. It's 1969. She has bought a mini-skirt and smuggles it out of the house in her satchel and changes into it when she's out of sight, knowing that her father would half kill her. She sometimes persuades Maire to go mitching – playing truant – with her, and they get the bus into Donegal Town – a tenth the size of an English market town – and Caitlin parades round the Diamond showing off her heavy white thighs and hoping some boy will offer to buy her a coffee.

They make an odd couple of intimates: Caitlin robust and florid and gingery and looking seventeen and Maire skinny and pale and flat like a twelve-year-old boy.

Today Maire has refused to go mitching, has not got the bus fare, will not risk thumbing it. They are in a corner on their own, out of the eye of Miss Toomey, the games mistress, and Caitlin – who considers herself too grown-up for school sports – is playing the fool. She whirls round in preparation for a throw but then, instead of letting go, she goes on spinning round and round and round until, giddy and giggly, she loses her hold on the discus which flies off in a mad erratic arc and lands just short of the long-jump pit where Miss Toomey is coaching the school athletics team.

'Oh God!' Caitlin squeals. 'Oh Jesus, Mary and Joseph! Someone's for it now.'

Miss Toomey snatches the discus up from the ground and comes striding across the grass towards the two girls.

'Who threw this?' she demands, still several yards from them. She looks from Maire to Caitlin and back again. Maire looks

at Caitlin who stands there smiling, as innocent as the Holy Virgin herself. Miss Toomey thrusts the discus under Maire's nose. 'Maire O'Neill! What do you mean by throwing this in that dangerous way? You could have killed someone!'

In her indignation, her outrage, at this unjust accusation, Maire cannot speak but stands there staring as Miss Toomey grows angrier and angrier, her coarse-veined cheeks reddening with every new second of silence.

She will not dignify the charge by a denial. Qui s'excuse, s'accuse. Protestations of innocence sound cowardly to Maire's ears, like lies.

'And you haven't even the grace to apologise!' the games mistress snaps finally. 'You can stay in for two hours of detention after class today. Maybe that'll teach you to be more careful next time.'

She flings the discus down on the ground, turns and walks away, her ugly great hockey boots churning the fresh mud with their studs. Maire looks at Caitlin again; Caitlin shrugs, as if to say that life is like that and that there's Justice for you.

. . . Now, indignant, outraged, Maire sits staring at Shaw, who remains coldly calm. She knows that he takes her silence for guilt but she could not open her mouth to deny it if he was threatening to hang her there and then.

'Actually you might consider yourself lucky,' he says after a pause. 'He could just as easily have slipped the explosives in your bag – your Christy or Gerry – and left you to go up with the rest of them. I've known it happen. They've no one to testify against them then. He had some conscience, at least, your Sean, your Connor . . . Ah!' He is on his feet again, excited, triumphant. 'Connor! That got a reaction at last, didn't it? So that's the name he gave you. Connor what?'

'Connor was my daughter's father,' she mutters.

'What? I didn't hear that.' She repeats it more loudly. It is as if he has stripped all her clothes away from her, leaving her exposed, and is now making a start on her skin.

'Was it him?' he asks.

'Don't you listen? Don't you people ever listen? I haven't seen him since before she was born.'

'What is she? Four? Five?' Maire nods. 'And you still react

like that to his name after all these years? Pull the other one, Maire.'

She leans back in her chair and closes her eyes. She does not answer him. She can't explain to him about Con, the only man she has ever known in that way, who was like brother and father and husband all in one, whom she had trusted and loved.

'Speaking of the little girl . . .' His voice seems to come to her from far away and she opens her eyes again and sees that he is pacing up and down at the far end of the room. 'If you go to prison, what will become of her? Eh, Maire, have you thought of that? Children's home? Orphanage?'

He is well under her skin now.

'That's wicked,' she says. 'It's not right – threatening my innocent child.'

'Found your voice again?' He sits down once more. 'I'm not making threats. I'm asking a practical question. You wouldn't want her in jail with you, even if you could take her, which you couldn't, and you may be an old woman by the time you get out. You're cut off from your family. You have to think of these things.'

She shall understand the enormity of her predicament. If it kills him, he will make her understand that she has no other choice.

He sighs and shakes his head and says sadly, 'It's not you I want, Maire. I don't want to lock up romantic, muddle-headed girls. I should be able to offer you a deal if you'll only name the people who provided the explosives and give evidence against them. But it's you or him. You must see that . . .'

The door opens and Sergeant from the front desk puts his head round and says, 'The duty solicitor is here, sir.'

Shaw says, 'Interview suspended at 11.12'. He leans across the desk and says quietly, 'It's war, Maire, and not of our declaring.'

'Nor mine,' she says.

Five

The duty solicitor is called Roberts – he doesn't seem to have a first name. He's a little ferret of a man she thinks must be more used to conveying houses than to advising dangerous criminals. He regards her from the first with nervous horror. He assumes her guilt and he's supposed to be on her side.

He immediately picks up on what Shaw has said about betraying her accomplices in exchange for lenient treatment. It's her best hope, he says, will mean a lesser sentence. She points out that she has been arrested on suspicion of murder and that the sentence for murder is a mandatory one: life imprisonment. He pauses, then says it might mean a lesser charge, but she's shaken him, this surly, black-eyed girl straight out of the bog, shaken him with her obvious intelligence and her grasp of the seriousness of her situation.

She hears him talking to Shaw next, out in the corridor, saying half-heartedly that he had better charge her soon or let her go. Shaw replies that he is holding her under the Prevention of Terrorism Act and is in no hurry. He will hold her for a week without charge if he chooses.

'She'll be up in front of the magistrates for committal in a day or two,' Shaw says. 'Or three, or four – or when I'm good and ready.' Roberts says unconvincingly that he will be asking for bail and Shaw laughs in his face.

'If I let her out on bail, she'll be back in Belfast and gone to ground by midnight tomorrow,' he says. 'No magistrate will hear of it.'

'I don't come from Belfast,' she shouts through the half-open door. 'I've never been to Belfast. I'm from the Republic.'

Precisely: a Republican, an IRA supporter. She can't win –

if she comes from the North that makes her, as a Catholic, an IRA sympathiser; if she comes from the South that makes her, by definition, a fellow traveller.

She won't run. Where would she go? This is her home. Donegal isn't real to her any more. The shabby Palace Cinema on Frogmore, that's real. The Cornmarket, the only bit of the town which even looks old; the High Street with its Woolworth's surreally topped by a huge red lion – these are the landmarks by which she navigates, the boundaries of her life. This is the only home Roisin has ever known. Her friends are here. She starts school next week. People don't, can't, just disappear.

She dismisses Roberts, he is no use to her. She doesn't want him sitting in on her interrogation; he embarrasses her. He says he will be at the magistrates' court when the time comes. After that, he will fix her up with someone more suitable, a criminal lawyer, someone with experience of this sort of work. She is a nasty smell an inch below his nostrils; he wants to wash her off – disinfect the spot – as soon as possible.

Chief Inspector Andrew Shaw is not a bad man; nor is he a bully, although it can suit him to appear as one in the interview room. More than anything, Maire O'Neill saddens and exasperates him. What he would really like to do is to pick her up and give her a good shaking, but that is not possible. He is telling the truth when he says that it's not her he wants but the real criminal, the instigator. He will never understand women: the ones who let their men beat them up time and again and still won't testify, the ones who will protect and alibi a rapist or murderer. You won't find men sacrificing themselves to save their wives' skins. Maire O'Neill, it seems, is willing to go to jail for her boyfriend. So be it.

Shaw is relatively new to the Anti-Terrorist Squad but disillusion has come upon him fast. He is involved in a war he does not believe he can win. The Irish Republican Army is like some battalion from ancient myth: every time a soldier is cut down, ten more rise up to take his place. He is learning to know his enemy: the impressive discipline, the loyalty he commands. This quiet girl is not as unlikely a recruit as she may seem to the man in the street. She is orderly – unobtrusive, as sleepers must be. The IRA has no time for hoodlums and tearaways, polices its Catholic areas of Belfast with a punitive hand.

Shoot the women first.

That had been rule number one at his Interpol-led course last year. He could still see the lecturer from German Special Branch, leaning forcefully on his lectern as he emphasised this maxim to exchanged looks of surprise and concern among his audience. Years of tangling with, among others, Bader-Meinhof, had taught him that the women were more ruthless, more dedicated, more deadly, than the men.

He recognises that Her Majesty's Government would like nothing better than to withdraw its young men from Northern Ireland and wash its hands of the place. With the economy moving into recession, endless trouble with the trade unions, Britain the sick man of Europe – Northern Ireland, with its high unemployment and its endemic poverty, may be the millstone that drowns a sinking government. But he also knows that withdrawal is not politically acceptable and that both major parties will insist on their commitment to the Union in their forthcoming electioneering.

Meanwhile he is a man with a job to do and there seems little left for him to do now but to charge her. That may bring her to her senses. But once he has charged her he can no longer question her and his hope of catching her confederates trickles away. But he is under pressure to bring his case to court quickly, to remind the public, in a possible election year, that the government is controlling these outrages, that law and order has not broken down as the Conservative opposition would have it. These buts seem mutually exclusive and he is unsure which path to follow.

He will keep trying for the moment, and she must remain in custody, of course, if only for her own safety. The speed of her arrest must have shocked her accomplices; he would not give much for her chances if she was given bail. If they don't get her, an appalled public will.

Shaw takes up the interview where he left off. It is late and they must soon stop for the night. He is about to play his trump card.

'You left the Hope and Anchor half an hour before the bomb went off last night, Maire. Is that right?'

'I left at half past ten,' she tells him. 'I don't know what time the bomb went off.'

'Of course.' He smiles without parting his lips, registering respect of the fact that she hasn't fallen into his trap. 'It was just as they were calling last orders, just when the place was at its fullest. Your friends gave no warning, you know. Even the Birmingham bombers phoned through a warning.'

He opens his briefcase and takes out a large brown envelope and removes something from it.

'Since you had already left, you didn't see the results of the explosion.' He hands what she now sees is a black and white photograph across the desk to her, face down. 'Take a look.' She turns it over and examines it; she is beyond horror.

'That's Private James Scott,' Shaw says, pointing. '"Scottie" to his pals. It was his birthday. He was twenty-two – younger than you, Maire. He lost his right leg and most of his hand. It's not a colour photo, of course, but you can still make out the pools of blood.' He points again with the end of a pencil. 'See the darker stains on the cushions he's lying on? That's where the blood gushed out, pints of it. Have you ever seen anyone lose a limb like that, Maire? The blood just spouts out like a strawberry fountain.'

Maire looks at Scottie's face – boyishly hairless, childishly plump. He is obviously, blessedly, unconscious, although his mouth is still screwed up with the pain he must have felt for a few seconds before his body applied the best anaesthetic it knew.

'Poor boy,' she says, and puts the photo down.

'He's going to live,' Shaw says. 'He was on the operating table most of last night; every soldier in the barracks was at the hospital giving blood. They knew it could have been any one of them.' He looks at the boy again, lying there in a mound of his own shattered flesh. 'If it were me, I'm not sure I'd be very grateful for that.'

'No.'

She agrees with him. She has never seen death as the greatest enemy and she sees now why they have taken away her shoe laces and her belt.

'You're a cool one,' he says to her, and any compassion she may previously have seen in his face is gone.

'Has it occurred to you,' she asks, 'for one second, that you may have got it all wrong? "I beseech you, in the bowels of Christ, think it possible you may be mistaken."'

She has studied her Irish history: she knows about Cromwell.

She thinks she sees doubt there, fleetingly, in his face; but then that, like compassion, is gone.

Six

On Saturday night, shortly after half past twelve, two young men are leaving the High Wycombe Irish Club by the back door. They are Sean Cleary and Patsy O'Feigh, nineteen and twenty-one respectively, and they are part-time barmen at the club. They have just finished washing the glasses and cleaning the bar and are locking up for the night. The bulb above the door seems to have blown again and Patsy makes a mental note to replace it the next day. Everyone else has gone and Sean wonders briefly whose is the blue transit van parked in the alleyway and thinks perhaps it belongs to the band who may have gone in search of some late-night fish and chips.

As he turns the key, Patsy hears a low whistle from behind the van and spins round just in time to take a punch straight in the face, sending him staggering back against the door. Sean, with reflexes like a whippet, dodges round the van and starts to run towards the nearby car park, but this move has been anticipated. His way is blocked by a gang of about seven men and youths, all wearing balaclavas or scarves to hide their faces, and he is swiftly knocked to the ground.

Both boys are badly beaten: kicked in the kidneys, in the groin, in the head; used as punchbags. Their faceless assailants are silent and the whole business is carried out like a brutal five-minute ballet, the quiet of the night punctuated only by the moans and sobs of the two Irish boys, the panting of their aggressors and the thwack of blows.

A second whistle brings the torment to a halt. Only then does one of the men speak.

'That's for the boys at the Hope and Anchor. We'll bring knives next time.'

'We'll torch this place next time,' another corrects him roughly. 'With all you Paddies in it.'

With a final kick deep in each set of groaning ribs, the men pile into the van and depart. Sean has passed out. Patsy tries to memorise part of the registration number as the van drives off but his mind will not obey his will.

The following morning the police have to be called as worshippers leaving early mass at the Catholic church on Amersham Hill are subjected to a barrage of stone-throwing and chants of 'Paddies go home'.

Mick McGrath, who will not see sixty again but is a game scrapper, raises his fists against the mob.

'Come on, then, just you come on. Cowards! Bullies!'

His friends, with wiser counsels, drag him away.

Chief Inspector Shaw, against his better judgment, is forced to go public and explain that an arrest has already been made in connection with the Hope and Anchor bombing. He calls for an end to this civil disobedience. Even so, many Irish people are afraid to turn up for work on Monday morning for fear of reprisals.

The torturer works on the assumption that the tortured has something to tell. The man on the rack is admitting nothing; allowing that he has nothing to admit would make the torturer's job untenable. Enough pressure – that is the secret, or so he tells himself – always one more turn of the screw.

Shaw's technique is to go over the same ground again and again until Maire is sick of it and thinks he must be too. The next morning, he begins again. He questions her for two hours, then they take a break. She is given tea, cola, sandwiches, fruit, chocolate bars, fried chicken – whatever she asks for within reason – and a chance to go to the lavatory and stretch her legs.

Then she is back in the same room – tiny, anonymous, windowless, airless, as it is – on the same chair, at the same table, with the same two policemen and listening to the same questions. Shaw returns seemingly refreshed each time, picking up – not where he had left off, that would be too obvious – but where he had started on the previous two-hour session, as if those questions had not already been asked and answered a dozen times.

Who is the man, the boyfriend? What's his name? Where did she meet him? She replies once more that there is no such person, wishing all the time that there were, so that she could answer Shaw's questions, make him happy, make him *stop*. It is just him and her, in truth. The Sergeant doesn't intervene. He is wallpaper.

In the middle of the afternoon, the Chief Inspector is called out for a few minutes. He returns to tell her that Dr Kurowski – whom she takes to be White Coat – has reported a positive result on his preliminary test. There were still traces of nitro-glycerine on her hands last night.

'That's impossible!'

'There's no wriggling out of it now, Maire.'

By the evening of that second day, the Sunday, she is more than ever worried about Roisin. She tells Shaw she will not say another word, nor eat, nor rest, until she knows where her daughter is, who she is with, that she is all right. Shaw says finally that she is staying a second night at Sandy's and that a social worker will be moving her to a council-run children's home the following morning.

'Children's home! She'll hate that,' she protests, 'I'd rather she stayed at Sandy's.'

'I dare say you would, Maire, but Sandy isn't willing to keep her any longer. You can see her point of view.' She wilts in her chair, defeated. She can see Sandy's point of view: she doesn't want to keep the child of a dangerous terrorist in her house, corrupting her own daughter. Not Sandy.

'Now,' Shaw goes on, 'if you'll just give me that name, an address, a description, a photofit, we can have you out on bail in a day or two and you can take the little girl home.'

She dreams for a moment of pleasing him. She understands at last why people confess to things they haven't done. She can make a plausible statement, surely, he has given her all the guidelines she needs. She is a practised storyteller. She can put an end to this agony.

Yes, she can say at any moment, *yes; you're perfectly, brilliantly, right, all of it. His name is Tommy, Tommy Mahon. He's five foot six with tufty red hair and blue eyes and a ruddy complexion. And a beard, oh yes, I almost forgot, a little red-gold beard.*

He said he was a Kerryman, the son of a dairy farmer twenty miles from Tralee. He wore jeans and a denim jacket and a black sweatshirt and boots that needed a clean. He drove a blue Ford Cortina, not new, L reg, a bit dented. He said he was a brickie, moved around, went where the work was.

I met him at the Irish club up by Queen's Road one night in June. We danced. He bought me a drink, made me laugh. He was warm and generous. He gave me a new black handbag. Roisin liked him. He played games with her and threw her up in the air until she squealed with excitement.

Yes, I can do you a photofit that'll match a thousand Irishmen and then I'll be off home.

She shakes her head.

'We can offer protection, you understand,' Shaw says, encouraged by her long pause for thought. 'Against reprisals.'

He thinks it is fear that keeps her silent, not ignorance. He thinks that she will speak if she is only offered a new identity, a new life far away where 'they' can't find her. And all the time the only protection she wants is from him.

A policewoman has fetched a change of clothes from her flat – a clean pair of jeans, a woollen jumper, fresh socks and underpants, a dressing gown and slippers. She has no pyjamas which are, like bras, an item of expenditure she cannot justify to herself. She has her hairbrush, toothbrush and flannel. She has asked for other things: for some cold cream for her sensitive skin, aerosol deodorant, some books. But Shaw says she won't be allowed to take them to prison with her and will not send his WPC back again. She is not paid to run errands for Maire.

Seven

Shaw takes her before the magistrates on Tuesday. She is being held on a specimen charge of the murder of Marilyn Piper.

'It's a pity, Maire,' he says, as they wait for the van. 'I thought we could do business.'

Word has got round and a rabble two or three hundred strong has gathered outside the courthouse despite a steady drizzle. A dozen policemen hold them back and fight a path through for Maire and her escort. Women carry placards with 'Hang the Bitch' lettered on them in red. The paint is running in the rain and the words bleed spikes. Maire has Shaw's raincoat sheltering her head. A woman spits at her as Shaw helps her out of the back of the van. She misses and her yellowish spittle hits the van door and trails in a shiny line down towards the handle, like snail slime. People are taking photographs and shouting questions.

'We should have sent a decoy,' Sergeant Cross grumbles. 'Some bugger's been talking.'

She peers round helplessly as Shaw grabs her arm and says, 'Come on! For God's sake, come on!' But she is mesmerised by the grotesques surrounding her. She sees a throng of creatures as though reflected in fairground mirrors: too tall, too fat, too thin, too squat to pass as human – their faces ugly with hatred. Shaw has almost to drag her into the courthouse to shouts of 'Murdering Bitch'. One man – youngish and pale and meek-looking, with an improbably long moustache – throws a stone in her direction, then bolts as a uniformed constable moves to arrest him, other grotesques deliberately impeding his pursuit.

It is from among such people as these – this lynch mob – that a jury of her peers must be found.

The court sits *in camera*. They are not kept waiting. It is not necessary for the police to present all the evidence for the prosecution to the magistrates; they have only to convince the bench that there is a case to answer. Shaw is a more senior officer than they are used to, distinguished and persuasive with his black handbag and his fleeing girl. He shocks them with talk of dead women and mutilated men and dazzles them with gas chromatography and the rest of the RARDE repertoire which will soon prove guilt beyond a doubt. The matter is settled in a very few minutes. Roberts will not let Maire speak since her accent, he claims, will negate any good she can do herself. He does not waste anyone's time by asking for bail.

She is remanded in custody pending trial in a higher court. They take her out of the back door where the van awaits, but the press is ready for this tactic and one of them is quick enough to get a clear photograph of her as she leaves the building, despite the speed with which Shaw moves to cover her face. The picture appears on the front page of all the daily papers the next morning and is sold to many of the weeklies too. The young photographer who was so fast off the mark is well rewarded.

The law-abiding Irish community of High Wycombe heaves a sigh of relief and goes back to work.

The tabloid newspapers have already sharpened their knives for Maire: she is the baby-faced killer, the girl next door with death in her pocket. She is an unmarried mother – the hypocrites of Fleet Street underline this fact – gave birth to a bastard daughter at seventeen; she is immoral. The reader is left to infer that she lives on Social Security, is a foreign parasite.

The perennial debate on hanging for terrorists resurfaces. Hasty polls show that seventy per cent of the population now favours restoration of the death penalty. The Leader of the Opposition, Mrs Margaret Thatcher, promises a free vote on the issue when her party is returned to power. She will herself, she says, be going through the Yes door.

Maire will now await trial at the convenience of the Director of Public Prosecutions. The van returns to High Wycombe police station but only to drop off DCI Shaw who will follow it back to London in his own car. When Maire realises that he is getting out here, she lurches forward without warning and seizes him by his neat lapels. One of the uniformed men grabs her by the hair to drag her off but she feels no pain.

'Let go of her,' Shaw barks, and the man releases her in sullen confusion. 'What is it, Maire? Have you gone mad?'

'What about my daughter? What about Roisin?'

'A social worker will be appointed. It'll be seen to.'

'I don't want it "seen to". I want you to see to it. You. Understand?'

'Very well.' He removes her failing hands from his suit and readjusts his tie. 'I will see to it personally.'

'I don't trust you.'

'Is there anyone you trust better?'

There is no answer she can make to this. The van door is opened from outside and Shaw climbs down. 'See you in court,' he says.

The van pulls up the steep hill to the M40 motorway and heads east towards London. The traffic is heavy and it is almost two hours before it arrives at its destination, a bleak residential area of north London and an even bleaker building. In a state of flux – part Victorian stone, part red seventies brickwork – Holloway prison opens its twelve-foot gates to admit yet another remand prisoner.

Eight

Maire is handed over to a prison warder at the gate and signed for. The warder grumbles that they have not been given enough notice of her arrival and are already over-crowded on the remand wing. She leaves her sitting on a bench in a locked waiting room, no bigger than a cubicle, for just over two hours until someone is willing to see her. Finally she is led into a reception room where a warder sits at a table with forms and files and pens and two others stand by in case of trouble.

They take from her the plastic carrier bag which contains her change of clothes, hairbrush, toothbrush and flannel. They are disappointed that there is nothing there they can reasonably confiscate. A list is made and Maire is told to sign it. When she tries to read it through first, she is shouted at. She signs.

They tell her to strip.

Maire is shocked. Her upbringing has left her uncomfortable about nakedness which is a private thing for family and lovers. She cannot expose herself under these harsh fluorescent lights in front of these grim faces. The woman at the desk tells her to get a move on and one of the others approaches her.

She is not a tall woman and is somehow squat. Fat, though not flabby, she fills out her uniform and the buttons strain over her shelf-like bosom. Her hair is short and shapeless and steel-grey. She is about fifty and looks as if she has never smiled, never eased her facial muscles into anything but a cold stare.

'She's a first-timer,' the third woman says, but the squat woman silences her with a look.

'Seems you need some help,' she says, and begins to unbutton Maire's blouse. Maire shies back and starts to tear off her clothes, not pausing to undo unnecessary buttons or hooks, throwing them to the floor.

'There, I thought you could manage it really.' The squat woman steps back and surveys Maire who is now naked, wrapping her arms about her torso, covering her breasts, her cheeks unnaturally red.

'Nothing much to hide,' she says with a leer. 'I shouldn't bother. I've seen better tits on a boy.'

'First-timer,' the woman at the desk echoes. 'She'll learn.' The third woman picks up the clothes, riffles quickly through the pockets, then lets them drop again.

The squat woman picks up Maire's file from the desk and begins to read through it, her lips moving slightly. It's a thin file but she takes her time. She whistles surprise and inspects Maire more closely. 'Nasty bit of work, aren't you?' she says. 'Still, it makes a change from the usual shoplifters and prozzies who can't pay their fines.' Maire's feet are cold on the linoleum floor. She feels the beginning of a cramp in the arch of her right foot. Her big toe twitches in pain.

'My name is Miss Turnbull,' the squat woman says. 'I'm in charge of the remand wing. You address me at all times as "Miss", clear?' Maire nods. 'Say it.'

'Yes, miss.'

'And you stand up whenever one of us comes into a room. Clear?'

'Yes, miss.'

'When I said strip, I meant strip. That goes for the jewellery too.'

Maire removes her ear studs and her cheap watch. The only other jewellery she wears is a silver ring on her right hand. She wants to keep it. She asks humbly. A little ring, narrow and smooth, cannot do any damage or harm, to herself or others. But it's against the rules. Maire asks to see a copy of the rules.

'Troublemaker, eh?' Turnbull says, pleased. 'Bend over.'

Maire bends. She has been telling herself for days that nothing worse can happen to her and each time she has been proved wrong. She takes the opportunity to rub her throbbing foot. The warder goes behind her and peers.

'You on drugs?'

'No! No, miss.'

'Alcoholic?'

'No, miss.'

Turnbull straightens her up and turns her round, holding her by the meagre flesh of her upper arms in a pinching grip. 'If you are on drugs or booze, you'd better say or you'll soon be sweating it out. Any medication? Tranquillisers? Anti-depressants? Any history of mental illness?'

'No, miss.'

'Not mad or sad, then. Just bad.'

She looks deep into Maire's eyes. They are clear and healthy, her pupils tiny with the brutal lighting and being forced to look so closely at something she already loathes. She sees that Turnbull wears a bright red lipstick, clumsily enhancing her ugliness.

'All right,' Miss Turnbull says finally. 'You can put your dressing gown on.' She pulls the shabby towelling robe from the carrier bag and throws it across the room. Maire struggles into it. The slippers follow and the pain of her arch abates a little in the fluffy warmth. She gathers up her clothes in her arms.

'Now you wait to see the doctor,' Turnbull says.

'I'm not ill,' Maire says.

'Not a doctor yourself, are you?' Turnbull derides her. 'The doctor will tell you whether you're ill or not. Then we'll give you a bath.' She wrinkles her nose. 'You stink!' Maire bows her head. She is willing to believe that she stinks. No bath or shower was made available to her while she was being held in the police cell.

She waits another two hours until her name is called to see the doctor. She is with him for less than five minutes; he takes one look at her and says in a bored way that he has never seen a healthier specimen. He checks her hair perfunctorily for lice and gives her two white pills.

'What are these?' she asks, bewildered.

He shrugs. 'Tranquillisers, of course.'

Liquid cosh.

Maire doesn't argue; for the first time in her life she is grateful for her convent education which taught her that arguing with those who have arbitrary power over you is a waste of breath.

She puts the tablets in the pocket of her dressing gown. She will flush them down the loo first chance she gets.

She is taken for her bath in a cold bare room with no lock on the door. The other warder is with her now, the one who pointed out that it was her first time. She tells Maire her name is Mrs Palmer. She is middle-aged, plump; her hair is short and grey, like Turnbull's, but arranged in soft curls around her motherly face. She hasn't the bleak, dead look about her that Miss Turnbull has. She is Miss Turnbull's deputy.

'Make the most of it,' she tells Maire, not unkindly, 'you'll only get one of these a week.'

She stands and watches as Maire bathes. The bath is only half full and the water is a little above tepid. There is no soap; prisoners must provide their own from their frugal wages or their own resources. Maire splashes about hastily and her right foot seizes up again in the water, making her gasp. She would like to wash her hair but has no shampoo.

She dresses again. Women prisoners no longer wear uniform, a recent concession. Her clothes are crumpled and stiff with wear but they are hers and they cover her vulnerability. She walks stiffly up and down the room, trying to ease her convulsed foot, almost grateful for the physical pain which is occupying her thoughts, stopping her from dwelling too long on the nightmare of the last seventy-two hours.

Mrs Palmer takes her to a single cell and locks her in. In all the hours she has spent on the reception process, she has missed the evening meal and Mrs Palmer says something will be brought to her in an hour or so.

'Room service tonight,' she says, and laughs.

Maire sits on the bed. She sees that it isn't made up, that a clean sheet and pillow case are lying folded under the blanket. She makes the bed. The sheets are heavily starched and scratchy. She walks to the end of the cell, a distance of about eight feet, stands there a little while, crosses to the window, looks out. She is quite high up, on the first floor, and can see over the external wall. There is a road there, a dual carriageway, street lights, cars: blessed signs of life.

There is more lino on the floor and a small rug by the bed, the sort of rug normal people keep in their bathrooms. There is a closet for clothes and a washstand with an empty bowl, a bucket underneath. Can she really be expected to use that, like an infant at its toilet training?

It's nearly eight o'clock. She would have coaxed Roisin to bed by now, told her a story. She would be sitting in the kitchen, drinking tea, reading – she wasn't, isn't, much of a one for the television. Sometimes she would listen to the radio though, very quietly since the walls of the flat were, are, thin and Roisin is a light sleeper. How can Roisin be expected to sleep in some awful council dormitory?

She must stop or she will break down. She looks out of the window again. She has nothing to do, no book to read; she cannot even tidy her cell; there is nothing but her few clothes in the plastic bag. She takes them out of the bag and hangs them up, very slowly, in the closet, trying to shake out some of the creases.

There is a fumbling at the door, a key turns. Mrs Palmer pushes the door open and another warder brings in a tray. There is a jug of warm water for the washstand and a meal consisting of tepid soup and sandwiches. The warder crashes the tray down on the bed and leaves.

Mrs Palmer says, 'Night night. Sleep tight.'

She smiles very gently, almost vacantly. Maire shivers as she watches the door close upon her again until morning.

After she has eaten, she spends some more time gazing out of the window. It is dark now and she watches the cars chasing along the road, balking at traffic lights, then resuming their race. A faint mist has descended on the yellow street lamps and diffuses the headlights in an eerie haze. Ethereal people are entering the pub on the corner.

Although it's still early there seems nothing to do but to go to bed. She undresses slowly. She cannot decide whether to wash her face or clean her teeth first, since she must do both in the same cooled water. In the end she just splashes a little water over her cheeks before brushing vigorously without toothpaste. She pees in the bucket, gets into bed, lies on her back staring at the ceiling.

Half an hour later a woman begins to scream on the floor below her which is, she later discovers, C1, the psychiatric wing.

Maire waits for something to be done, for the noise of cells being unlocked, help being offered; nothing happens. Finally she pulls her pillow over her head to shut out the continuous, hoarse, desperate howling.

Nine

Since Maire has not been convicted of any crime, she is allowed certain privileges, one of which is that she need not work for her keep. This is a mixed blessing: work in Holloway is drudgery, consisting mainly of scrubbing floors which are already clean, but it passes the time. She is kept locked up in her cell for twenty-two hours a day. The other two hours are spent on eating, exercising in the yard and 'association', in which she sits around with a dozen other remand prisoners hearing them exchange complaints and banalities. The food is often cold; it's stodgy, to fill them up, and bland to offend no tastes. She has been allowed access to the library and occupies her time with endless reading.

She may have daily visits, rather than the monthly ones meted out to convicted offenders, and after two days she is called out of her cell in the middle of the afternoon to be introduced to her probation officer.

Trish Murray is a girl of about her own age, small but energetic with a sweet face which almost disappears in the tangle of her streaked hair. She is lopsided by an over-stuffed bag hanging from her right shoulder. She is a lot tougher than she looks, has to be, and streetwise in a way that Maire can never hope to be. She shakes hands as she introduces herself, smiles; she is trying to make no judgments.

'I may be sort of part of the system, okay?' she gabbles. She dumps the bag on the floor, pulls up a chair across the table from Maire and straddles it, tossing back her hair. 'But I don't take sides. Really. You're innocent till they prove different and little Rosie . . .'

'You've seen her.' Maire stretches forward eagerly. 'You've seen Roisin?'

'Seen her, talked to her. She's well, and as happy as she can be in the circumstances. She's in a place called Fairlawns. It's okay. Really. As these places go, it's one of the best. They've told her there that her mother is sort of ill and won't be able to look after her for the time being.' She shrugs. 'I don't believe in lying to kids myself. Really. I would've told her the truth, but it's done now and it's no use getting her head all sort of messed up with different stories.'

'When can I see her? I can see her?'

'Ye-e-e-s,' Trish says, 'there's nothing to stop you.'

'Then I must see her, at once . . . soon.'

Trish looks round the room. Maire follows her gaze. She understands then what Trish is trying to say: that this forlorn room is no place to bring a sensitive child. How will she comprehend or bear Holloway: the clanging of doors, the impatience of warders, the noise of unhappy women? Maire is torn between her own urgent desire to see her child and that child's best interest.

'Cheer up,' Trish says. 'They got another room, with sort of toys and stuff, which ain't so bad. It's just a question of making sure they understand that they gotta give us that room, okay? Cause otherwise they'll put you in here just for a laugh, like, sort of out of spite. Really. I've seen it.'

She hauls the bag up on to the table. 'Before I forget. You're allowed stuff, you know? Stuff you can have brought in on remand.' She produces a chemist's bag which proves, to Maire's joy, to contain toothpaste, soap and shampoo. 'These are just the sort of basics, of course. What else d'you need?'

A radio, Maire suggests diffidently. Trish nods: no problem. Her own books. Her photos, especially those of Roisin.

'I should be able to pick your gear up from your flat any day now,' Trish says. 'The copper, Shaw, he says they're nearly finished and then I can get access. Just have to hope they haven't done too much damage, too much sort of trampling underfoot.' She giggles.

'Who pays for all this?' Maire asks.

'You get an allowance. Oh yeah, before I forget, don't worry 'bout your flat. They'll pay your rent for up to a year while you're in here. Really.'

'Who will?'

'Social Security.'

'You mean that after the trial, if they let me out, I can just go back home and pick up where I left off?'

'Yeah. I guess so. Sort of.' Trish looks doubtful again. Toni Giordano has told the press that if, by any stupid miscarriage of justice, that murdering bitch gets away with it, he'll do for her himself.

Trish gets up to go; she is a young woman always in a hurry and it's a long walk back to Caledonian Road tube station. She heaves the bag up, over her left shoulder this time and staggers two paces. Maire wants to reach out a hand and hold her back. She is a lifeline.

'I'll be in touch in a few days, with your stuff. Really.' Trish speaks kindly, recognising the other woman's need.

'You'll be sure to find me at home,' Maire says.

Trish smiles at the tiny joke. 'That's the way. Don't let them break you. And you'll be hearing from your lawyers, of course. They've appointed that young QC to handle your case, Steven Hale, you know?' Maire shakes her head. Trish grins a grin of feminine complicity. 'He's a dish. Really.'

'And you'll see about Roisin?' Maire is not interested in successful young QCs, dishy or otherwise.

'I'll liaise with her social worker, soon as I get back, but they can't keep her from you – not if you're sure.'

'I'm sure.' She sees now that this place cannot hurt Roisin so long as there is enough love to cocoon her; that it cannot hurt her either, unless she lets them break her.

Maire sits waiting, seated at the table, not attempting to leave until a warder sticks her head round the door and demands to know what she thinks she is doing, lounging around here like Lady Muck. She gets up then, docilely, and allows herself to be shepherded back to her cell.

Ten

Steven Hale, in his fortieth year, has the world at his feet. Since rising early to the eminence of QC five years ago, he has made a name for himself in some high-profile trials, pleading for the defence. It doesn't pay well on legal aid but he more than makes up for that with his civil work, and there is more to success and ambition than money. He is a brilliantly persuasive advocate and knows it. In a profession where age adds dignity, he is a mere boy, and has nothing but an increase of wealth and fame to look forward to. He will certainly be a judge one day, if he chooses. The envious call him arrogant.

He is photogenic, being tall and lean with just a sprinkling of white salt in his black-pepper hair. His clothes are not perfect – the English mistrust a man who dresses too well. He has an elegant wife and two attractive children. He was at the front of the queue when charm was being – unfairly – shared out. Maire, normally impervious to personal charm, particularly of the male variety, is captured at once by his enthusiasm and warmth and begins to hope again.

He is brought to see her at Holloway by her new solicitor, George French. Mr Roberts, who does not feel qualified to handle a crime so monstrously outside his experience, has passed her on and she is glad of it. French has briefed a good many criminal cases, including murder; he is brisk and optimistic and inspires confidence. She can see her legal advisers every day if she, and they, so choose, and in private. Soon she feels that she has known them both for a long time, that these are old friends she is receiving in her parlour.

They have broken the worst news to her. RARDE have finished a whole battery of tests on the swabs taken from her hands at High Wycombe police station on the night of Saturday, August 26th, and declared them all positive. They are adamant that nothing but nitroglycerine could produce these test results and that it must have been directly handled. Maire is at a loss; she cannot begin to offer an explanation.

'The big problem with scientific evidence as technical as this,' Steven Hale explains, 'is that all the best forensic scientists work for the government. They're not impartial; they present their findings in the light most likely to lead to a conviction. If we are to attack their findings, we must have our own scientists to offer a different interpretation of these tests to the jury, or at least allow us to question their conclusions.'

'How can it be?' Maire holds her small white palms up in front of her face and stares at them as if she has never seen them before. 'How can they have found traces of nitroglycerine on my hands?'

'I'm not a scientist,' Steven says. 'It may well be that – whatever RARDE says to the contrary – other substances can produce the same test results; or that you could have got the traces in the pub that night, by handling something the real bomber had already handled – the back of a chair, an ashtray, a towel.' He speaks with confidence and authority and Maire feels her stiff back begin to relax.

'There is a man who may do for us,' French adds. 'A Dr Fletcher who used to work for the Home Office, dealing with explosives, but is retired now. Our expert will be as good as theirs.' He does not tell her that Dr Fletcher is seventy or that his experience is neither recent nor a hundred per cent germane. He's the best offer they've got at present.

'We have to move quickly,' he goes on. 'The Crown wants to bring this case to court as soon as they can, to mollify the sense of public outrage that always follows one of these bombings.'

'The sooner the better.' Maire glances round at the thick stone walls of the Victorian house of correction.

'We're looking at early next year,' French says. 'February or March.'

'You call that soon!' Maire speaks bitterly. 'And I'm to stay locked up here all that time, with my daughter in some bloody orphanage.' She does not often swear, was brought up not to, but the idea of Roisin lost and bewildered in some council-run home is more than she can bear.

'It's soon enough, believe me,' Hale tells her. 'We have to put a case together.'

'Have you spoken to my neighbour?' Maire asks eagerly. 'Mrs Roote who has the flat below mine. She's an old widow woman with nothing to do all day but watch people come and go. She'll tell them this murdering "boyfriend" of mine is just a figment of their imagination.'

Hale and French exchange glances. They have spoken to Mrs Roote as have the police. Neither side intends to call her. She is not a good witness: she gets flustered, contradicts herself; means well. Yes, she has seen men coming and men going but, now she comes to think of it, they could have been for young Tina on the second floor, above Maire. Or perhaps just friends of Paul and Sue in the flat opposite. Although some of them were sinister-looking men, could easily have been terrorists. What does she mean by sinister? Oh, their eyes were too close together or their hair over-long or their clothes a little shabby perhaps, she's not sure. Did she ever speak to them on the stairs? She can't remember. Did any of them have an Irish accent? Yes. No. Her colour is up by now and her hand goes to her throat repeatedly in a nervous clutching gesture. She begins to stammer slightly. The jury will not believe her, whatever she tells them.

'Sandy,' Maire suggests. 'My friend. I would have told her if I had a boyfriend, wouldn't I?' She would not previously have described Sandy as a friend, but she needs friends now.

Steven Hale tells her gently that Sandy has disowned her, told the police that they were never close and that Maire did not confide in her; which, after all, is true.

What about the man, the groper who called himself Brian. He won't come forward in case his wife finds out he had a date with a woman in a pub. He must be tracked down, she tells them, subpoenaed. French explains that Brian Swinnerton has indeed come forward, is giving evidence for the Crown. He had left the pub only minutes before the bomb went off, could easily have been killed or maimed himself. He will have his revenge.

'Then is there no one to speak for me?' Maire asks. 'No one on my side?'

'We're on your side,' French says, smiling.

'Chin up,' Steven Hale says as the two men prepare to leave, repacking their bulging briefcases with expert hands. 'We'll have you out of here. They've no evidence, no real evidence – it's all circumstantial or open to scientific interpretation. I'll make mincemeat of all their witnesses, you see if I don't.'

It is easy to see why those who do not like Steven Hale call him arrogant.

The high heavy gates of Holloway have closed on them for a short time only. They will go home now to their wives and children, to privacy and a good supper.

'Chin up.'

Eleven

Trish reappears ten days after her first visit with the artefacts Maire has asked for. She has brought a transistor radio. It is not Maire's own radio; Trish explains that she may not have short-wave. The 'allowance' has bought a supply of batteries since she may not run it off the mains. She has a bridge to the outside world at last. Trish has also brought a book of first-class stamps in case Maire needs to communicate with her lawyers urgently. She seems to think of everything.

She has struggled gamely on the Tube with a box of well-read paperbacks collected from the bookcase in Maire's bedroom at home. It also contains Maire's sketchpad and all her coloured pencils. She has brought all the personal papers she could find: postcards, documents, photographs. The snaps are few since Maire has no camera of her own and has to beg pictures from others; most of them are of Roisin.

But of the little girl herself, she can obtain no more than a promise. School has started. The social worker doesn't want her unsettled any more than she is already, doesn't want her anodyne lies about Maire's illness to be exposed. Trish admits, under cross-examination, that Roisin is sleeping badly, will not make friends with the other children at Fairlawns, is being cheeky and unco-operative.

Maire agrees politely that Roisin must not miss school and asks for a weekend visit. The social worker is not prepared to bring her at weekends, it seems, has children of her own who see little enough of her. There has been a hearing; the little girl is a ward of court. Maire has no rights now; it is the council, not she, who is *in loco parentis*. She is ready to weep. Trish – overworked, warm-hearted Trish – volunteers to bring Roisin

69

herself, if they will let her. Soon. Really. Next weekend.

Next weekend brings not Roisin but – the next best thing, perhaps – a note in her curiously unchildish handwriting, couched in her precociously fluent idiolect.

I love you, Mim. I hope you are better soon and come back for me soon. I don't like it here much tho we have ginger cake for tea on Saturdays. We played rounders on Beeches Field after supper yesterday. Our team won.

Maire has never shed tears easily. She sucks them back now, pins the note to her cell wall with the pictures and keeps waiting. If there is one thing prison teaches you, it is patience. Roisin is beginning to adjust, Trish has explained, is sleeping better in the dormitory. They will let her come soon.

Maire does not dare to hope the following Saturday, she has been disappointed once too often, but she is taken this time to a different room – somewhere the warder refers to as the Ivory Tower.

She enters the room alone and the door swings to behind her. Trish is sitting on the window sill, leaning on her ever-present shoulder-bag; she is laughing. Roisin is on the floor near her feet, absorbed in some alphabet bricks, trying to make the most exotic word she knows, which is 'Bungalow'. She glances up as Maire comes in and says, 'This is the nastiest hospital that ever was, Mim.'

Maire dare not touch her for a second in case she dissolves into the walls. It is Roisin who gets up and comes to her. She puts her arms round Maire's waist and buries her head against her stomach which is as high as she can reach. She is trembling. Maire's hand rests on her child's matt-black hair, grown a little longer than usual. She holds Roisin away from her, to look at her. It has been more than three weeks; already she has forgotten little details, like that determined curl of the lip which no photograph of this small, impish face has ever captured. Her breath smells faintly of ice-cream and she knows that Trish has been cajoled.

For a few seconds they are as alone in the world as a pair of new lovers, then Trish breaks the spell with a well-meaning: 'I wish I could leave you alone together. Really. But someone has to be here and better me than an ugly old warder. Just treat me like sort of part of the woodwork.'

'Re-al-ly?' Roisin draws the word out, mocking her.

'Really. Really. Really,' Trish says.

She gazes resolutely out of the window. The other two sit down. Roisin is a little awkward now. She is rocking back and forth on her chair in the unconscious way she does when she is distressed.

'What's the matter with you, Mim?' she asks. 'Why are you in hospital so long? Debbie's mum was in hospital having one of her breasts off and she was only in ten days. Debbie's my best friend at the new school. She tells me everything, like about her mum, because it's a secret. Where are the doctors and nurses? Are you having one of your breasts off, Mim?'

Maire shakes her head. She looks at Trish. Trish mouths, 'It's up to you.' Maire takes Roisin on her lap.

'This isn't a hospital, Rosie, darling. I am not ill. I'm here because some people think I did a very bad thing.' She hesitates.

'And did you do the bad thing?' Roisin wants to know, going straight to the point, as usual.

'No, but I must stay here for a while until I can prove that I didn't do it.'

'How long?' Roisin's face screws up with sadness.

'A few . . . weeks.' She has sympathy for the social worker suddenly. It is so hard to tell children the truth when you know it must hurt them. 'There's a nice man called Mr Hale who is going to tell people that I didn't do the bad thing, that it's all a mistake. You must be brave.'

'Can't he tell them now? Today?'

'They won't listen to him yet. They have to get a lot of people together, twelve people to hear what Mr Hale has to say and . . . believe him.'

Trish mimes applause. Roisin says simply, 'I'm glad you're not ill.'

The visit proceeds; they talk, play with the bricks and a teddy bear. Maire is relieved that everything is so normal, that Roisin can cope with it all.

'Before I forget . . .' Trish says, as they prepare to leave an hour later. She rummages in her bag, produces two large bars of milk chocolate. 'I know the food is slop in here.'

'It's not that bad actually,' Maire says. 'There's plenty of it; it reminds me a lot of what we used to eat at home – in Ireland,

I mean, my parents' home.' Lots of potatoes, dumplings, pie crusts. Not much fruit or fresh vegetables.

'Well, you're allowed to have food brought in while you're on remand,' Trish says, 'so make the most of it and save this for the night starvations. Here.' She hands one bar to Maire and gives the second bar to Roisin who accepts it eagerly. 'Junior gannet.'

'She's not allowed much chocolate . . .' Maire begins her protest then tails off. Let the poor child have a little chocolate at least.

'They say chocolate makes you happy,' Trish says. 'Really. It's got something in it, affects the happy hormones in the brain . . . or something like that. I read it in *New Society*. It's true. Really.'

She takes Roisin by the hand. 'I'm glad the visit went so well, Maire. I can bring her up every three weeks. Come on, Rosie, time to go back to dear old High Wycombe. Time for an exciting ride on the Underground.'

But Roisin begins to howl pitifully. Her face is contorted with rage, puce with misery. She screams that she doesn't want to go, leave her mother; that she hates Fairlawns, that she wants to stay here; that she will do a *bad thing* so that they will send her here with her mother. She throws her chocolate bar to the ground and stamps on it. A warder comes in to see what all the fuss is about. Unfortunately it is Miss Turnbull.

'I knew you were trouble, O'Neill,' she says. 'Since I first laid eyes on you.'

She has to help Trish to carry Roisin out, kicking and biting. Little Trish struggles, trying to cope with her bag and an hysterical child.

'I'm sorry,' she shouts over her shoulder. 'Sorry. Really. She seemed okay.'

There are no more such visits – Maire's decision, not Trish's, not the social worker's, not Miss Turnbull's; Maire's.

Twelve

'*I*t is out of the question!'

Maire is furious, shouting.

'How dare you go behind my back like this! I won't hear of it.'

Steven Hale has just told her that he has been to see Roisin at Fairlawns, talked to her for over an hour, wants to put her on the witness stand to testify that her mother did not, at any time, have a man friend in the flat. Her reaction takes him by surprise; she has been so calm throughout, so accepting.

'I must say, Steven,' French says in his dry way, 'that you've been a bit high handed. You might have talked it over with us first.'

'It just came to me yesterday,' Steven says a little sullenly. He doesn't want Maire to realise how desperate he is becoming. 'I wanted to talk to her first, to see if it was at all possible before I mentioned it.'

'She's *five*,' French points out.

'You haven't met her, George. She's intelligent, responsible. I agree most kids of that age would be hopeless witnesses. That's why I went to see her, on the off-chance that she might be the one five-year-old in ten thousand who would help to get her mother off. And I found a very grown-up little woman. I'm sure she would want to do anything she can to help.'

'I won't hear of it!' Maire says. 'She's been through enough. I will not expose her to an ordeal like that.' French makes soothing noises, but Maire can see only too clearly in her mind the screaming, rigid figure of Roisin being bundled out of the Ivory Tower by Trish and Turnbull. 'I didn't even know a child that age could testify,' she finishes lamely.

'Oh yes,' French says. 'Technically. Most certainly. They can give sworn testimony if the judge is satisfied that they understand the nature of the oath; if not, they can give unsworn testimony. But I can't help thinking, Steven, that the jury wouldn't take much heed of what she says. She would not be exactly an unbiased witness and you know what juries are like about uncorroborated unsworn testimony.'

'You haven't met her,' Hale repeats. 'The jury will lap her up. She's very articulate and her love for her mother is . . .' he clenches his fist in the air, seeking a word '. . . palpable.'

Maire erupts into unashamed tears.

'Now see what you've done,' French sighs.

Steven Hale produces a pale blue linen handkerchief which doesn't look as if it was ever intended to be used.

'This is all academic,' she says, when she's wiped her eyes and blown her nose. 'I won't allow it.'

'Do you want to spend the next twenty years in jail?' Steven demands. He knows he is being brutal, but he has been unable to turn up anyone better than Dr Fletcher to contest the damning forensic evidence and he knows, in his sinking heart, that Fletcher will not do.

'That's it!' she rounds on him. 'You're sacked. Do you hear me? Fired.'

'All right, that's enough.' George French is a small, skinny, bespectacled man in late middle age, but he has a quiet authority. He doesn't raise his voice; he doesn't need to. 'Sit down, both of you, and calm down.'

They exchange resentful looks, but obey him.

'Steven,' he says. 'I think we will start with an apology from you for going behind Maire's back.'

'You hired me to get her off, and now you're trying to stop me doing it.'

'I'm waiting,' French says.

'I apologise,' he says stiffly.

'Maire?'

'All right. I accept your apology.' They glare at each other.

'So we are agreed,' French says, 'the little girl is to be kept out of this.'

'Don't mind me,' Steven says, 'I'm just the hired help.'

Thirteen

Maire is on remand for five months in Holloway. It seems a long time to wait for the due process of law to rumble into action, but she learns that it has nothing to do with the seriousness of the charge and that many a young woman is held just as long awaiting a trial for shoplifting which may well end in a non-custodial sentence. She would probably have waited longer had not the government, now inexorably nearing the end of its term of office, been eager to make a public example of her.

Christmas is the worst time.

The thing that strikes her most about prison, the memory that she will carry with her all her life, is not the violence, the bullying, the lack of hygiene, the cockroaches – but the pettiness. It is as though rules are invented for no other purpose than that the women may be punished for transgressing them.

For five months she goes about her daily routine like a zombie. Up at seven, slop out, tidy the cell, breakfast, back in the cell reading or listening to the radio until lunchtime; then more reading or a visit from Trish (alone) or French and Hale; exercise, association, evenings that go on without end; early bed.

Trish brings her apples, oranges, grapes; decent conversation. She is the closest friend Maire has had since she left Donegal and Caitlin Sweeney. She is not, as Maire had thought, her own age, but almost thirty. Her background is solidly middle class – she had grown up in Kenya where her father was a judge, been to boarding-school. The accent, the tricks of speech, the streetwise lope, are later acquisitions, although none the less authentic for that.

The five months are up now. It is late February 1979. The

case will be heard at the stone and concrete mass of the Central Criminal Court. Mr Justice De Freitas presides.

'We could have drawn worse,' Steven Hale says.

On the Monday morning they take her to the Central Criminal Court in a Category-A prison van very early in the morning so as not to disrupt the rush-hour traffic. They speed through the sleepy streets of north London with a police escort, sirens going, not stopping at red lights.

Early risers on the pavement stare and ask themselves who this important person can be. They cannot see in, although Maire can see them, since the van has one-way windows. Their curiosity is not satisfied until the first editions of the London evening papers hit the stands at about ten o'clock.

'High Wycombe Bomber in Court Today.'

There is already a small crowd in the Old Bailey despite the early hour. One man defiantly waves an Ulster Unionist flag with its blood-red hand.

She is taken up endless flights of stairs to the Category-A cells, which are at the very top of the building, to await the opening of her trial.

Fourteen

The Clerk of the Court reads the indictment. It is a slow business since there are many counts to answer.

'Maire Deirdre O'Neill, you are charged that on the night of the twenty-fifth of August 1978, at High Wycombe in the county of Buckinghamshire, you did murder Marilyn Susan Piper. Are you guilty or not guilty?'

'Not guilty.'

'. . . That you did murder Jonathon Paul Simmons . . .'

'Not guilty.'

The judge sits in his red robes and wig in Court Two at the Old Bailey, listening to the rest of the counts with half-closed eyes. There is a sword on the wall behind him, symbolising Justice, but also – to Maire's eyes – Death.

Steven Hale – also in wig and gown – sits in the well of the court. His junior is behind him, almost invisible behind a pile of law books. French is just behind them. Steven, who normally wears contact lenses, today has two pairs of glasses, one on his nose and one on the desk in front of him. He uses them as theatrical props: switching from one to the other, waving them at a witness to drive home a point. Hale is objecting to a number of the jurors. He objects now to a military-looking man with a copy of the *Daily Telegraph* under his arm. The man looks pleased; the *Telegraph* may have been specially purchased and displayed for the purpose.

Mr Justice De Freitas sighs heavily. He is in his early sixties and has been a high-court judge now for five years. He has a reputation as a mild and fair man, which is why Steven told Maire that they could have drawn worse, but his temper has deteriorated since Steven last appeared before him. He is nursing – all unknown – the bowel cancer which will kill him in less than two years. The early ravaging of his digestive tract inclines him to irritability. Diarrhoea makes for frequent adjournments. He will not see a doctor but soothes his discomfort with sarcasm.

'Are any of our jurors going to meet with your approval today, Mr Hale?' he asks.

It seems unlikely. Hales is not sure that Maire can have a fair trial, given the amount of publicity surrounding the case. The jurors have read in their newspapers about Maire O'Neill and the slaughter at High Wycombe; the tabloids have long since summed up for them.

Maire sits in the dock – a slight, unthreatening figure, with a woman police officer on either side of her – as prospective jurors are summoned and stood down. Hale has theories about juries, theories which are ahead of their time. Ten years from now, American lawyers will employ psychologists to gauge the current mood of the jury and adjust their questioning accordingly, but that science is still in the womb. Steven knows what he wants, however: not too many women – they are the more vindictive sex and less willing to make allowances for youth and vulnerability; as young a jury as possible – young people may more readily accept, and make allowances for, political idealism.

The trial may last some time. Many of the people summoned are anxious to extricate themselves. He lets two young men in casual clothes pass unchallenged, then a young woman wearing a CND badge, then objects to two middle-aged men. They now have half a jury. De Freitas looks at his watch. By the time the jury is assembled, he adjourns for lunch.

Fifteen

The Prosecution – in the rotund shape of Barney Winch-Gore, QC – sums up the events of that fateful Friday night for the jury. The facts are incontrovertible and he goes through them ponderously. There was an explosion at the Hope and Anchor public house: an act of terrorism which killed six people, maimed one and injured countless others. It was caused by a bomb made of nitroglycerine and concealed in a large black synthetic leather bag – a woman's shoulder-bag – which was placed under a bench, at some point during the course of the evening. Photographs of the devastation are circulated to the jury with a caveat that they may find them distressing. No warning was given, Winch-Gore explains, and no one has ever plausibly claimed responsibility.

What is at issue, what the jury is there to decide, is whether the accused, Maire Deirdre O'Neill – they all turn and stare at her – planted the bomb in the Hope and Anchor that night. The Prosecution will prove, beyond a reasonable doubt, that Maire O'Neill had recently handled explosives; will prove that she had the means, the motive and the opportunity to cause that explosion, and will call evidence upon which the Prosecution invites the jury to find her guilty of murder.

He goes on to tell the court how he had hoped to call Private James Scott, who lost a leg in the explosion, as his first witness. Sadly, Private Scott is not well enough to attend. He is, Winch-Gore explains, in a psychiatric hospital, receiving treatment to help him come to terms with his mutilation. The court murmurs its sympathy.

Instead they hear first the evidence of Corporal Jack Carmichael, who recreates for them the carnage of the night of the bomb. He looks tired, has difficulty sleeping since the tragedy, is making plans to buy himself out of the Army. The jury likes him: he is young, tall, good-looking, holds himself upright, speaks clearly and civilly, calls the judge 'My Lord' and the QCs 'Sir'. He is not an imaginative man – it is not a quality demanded of soldiers – and his account of the tragic evening is simple and dignified with no redundant embellishment or needless speculation. When he recalls his distress at first seeing his young friend Scottie with his leg blown off, the jury winces in shared grief, although it has already seen the pictures. Carmichael has given the victims a human face.

He had assumed at the time that the bomb was the work of the IRA. Steven Hale objects – the witness's assumptions are not evidence – and is upheld. The facts then: he and his men had recently returned from Northern Ireland where he had seen the human debris of similar atrocities; it was in the handwriting of the IRA. They had been vigilant over there but had dropped their guard, it seems, since coming home. The court murmurs again: this is a brave and chivalrous young man who has been risking his life for democracy in Ireland and who walked out of August's hell alive only by the merest luck.

It is not in Steven's interest to try to discredit this witness who has already won the hearts of his listeners. He asks Carmichael merely if he had noticed Maire in the pub that night. Is he aware of her having approached the table where he and his friends were drinking, or the bench upon which some of them were sitting and beneath which the bomb was concealed, at any time during the evening? No, if she had come over to that corner, he had not noticed her. Steven is satisfied. He has no further questions.

Carmichael looks doubtfully at Maire now; she is not his image of a mass-murderer, this unflurried girl who listens to him with her head held high. He has read about her in the papers, but he warms to her in person and he prides himself on his judgment of men, and women. She looks like somebody's daughter, somebody's sister, although he has learnt in Belfast not to trust a friendly face or a cooing voice. His mind is open.

The judge thanks him, praises his courage and cool-headedness. He steps down.

*

DCI Shaw is the next prosecution witness and enters the witness box the following morning. Although he has long since abandoned any religious beliefs he might have had as a child, Shaw takes the oath, since he knows from experience that juries don't like atheists.

He fills in the gaps in Carmichael's evidence, relating how the remains of a black mock-leather bag had been found under the bench on which three of the dead soldiers had been sitting, how it had been tested in the Metropolitan Police's laboratories and found to have been used to conceal the explosive. The handbag was a 'Miss Jones' bag, manufactured in their thousands by Price and Son of Lancaster and sold in all main department stores. He reads what Maire O'Neill said on her arrest: that she does not deny owning such a bag and carrying it on the night of the bombing.

'I believe that Miss O'Neill was acting under the instructions of a man, with whom she probably had some sort of emotional or sexual relationship . . .'

Steven Hale rises to object. This is pure speculation. Shaw replies that a man was seen entering and leaving O'Neill's flat in the months preceding the bombing and that a neighbour, Mrs Tina Grace, who lives in the flat above O'Neill's, will be giving evidence to this effect later. Steven asks to confer with his client and the court adjourns for ten minutes. Maire is looking bewildered. To Steven's hurried 'Who is this man?' she replies, 'I have no idea.'

'No man ever came to your flat?' She shakes her head. 'Ever? Milkman? Bread man?'

Maire gives a little gasp. 'He's talking about the envelope man.' Steven looks puzzled. 'I worked at home putting circulars into envelopes and addressing them from a list. A man came twice a week to pick up the ones I'd done and deliver the next batch.'

'So he wouldn't have been with you more than a minute or two each time?'

'Sometimes he would have tea, or coffee, if it was that sort of time.'

'What was his name?'

She thinks hard. 'Roy? Ron? Ray?'

'All right. Leave it to me.'

Steven persists in his objection. If Mrs Grace's evidence is to be referred to by DCI Shaw, then the court must hear it first and he must be allowed to cross-examine on it. The judge agrees and, as Mrs Grace has not been called until that afternoon, adjourns the court. Steven hides a sigh of relief and goes to confer with his client.

'She always seemed a nice enough woman,' Maire says, 'Tina from upstairs.'

But Tina is distinctly hostile towards Maire when she comes into the courtroom that afternoon. She is a divorcee in her mid-twenties with one child, a boy of about two. She is, in her commonplace way, an attractive young woman – ash-blonde, well made-up, nicely, if cheaply, turned out.

Since her husband's abrupt departure about eighteen months ago, soldiers from the local base, along with airmen from the USAF base up the hill, have been her most constant, and enthusiastic, escorts. She likes a good time – dancing, a few drinks, the odd London nightclub – and servicemen know how to enjoy themselves. Here today, gone tomorrow; they don't need much time to get acquainted. She didn't know any of the men killed last August, wasn't in the Hope herself that night; but she could have done, might have been.

She has exchanged a few banal words with Maire since she moved in above her a year ago. They have few points of contact but her neighbour was quiet – no late-night music, no screaming matches – and had been willing to babysit for her a few times. She shudders now at the thought that she had left little Jason with a murdering terrorist. Who knew what might have happened?

She takes the oath and turns her baby-blue eyes on the judge who tells her not to be nervous and to try to speak up. She explains that she is a divorcee with a toddler and therefore, in the absence of her errant husband, dependent on the state. So she doesn't go out to work and is usually to be found at home in her flat by day.

Twice a week, on Tuesdays and Fridays, she would see this man come to Maire's flat.

'How did you know it was the defendant's flat he was going to?' Winch-Gore wants to know.

'The walls are quite thin. I could hear him ring her doorbell and her go and answer it. I could hear him say things like "Hello, my love, and how are you today?"'

'And how long would he stay each time?'

She is not so sure of this. Apparently the walls were not thin enough for her to hear him leaving also. But she knows that the man drove a transit van.

'He was nothing special to look at: sort of medium height and build, brownish hair, casual clothes.'

The Prosecution has no further questions.

'Mrs Grace.' Steven rises to his feet. He removes his glasses and holds them away from his face, giving her the full benefit of his handsome brown eyes. 'Did you at any time look out of the window when you heard this man's van arriving?'

'I might have done, once or twice.'

'And would it not be true to say that his van had the words "Cressex Circulars" painted on the side?'

'It may have done.'

'Did you notice if the man was carrying anything when he came into the block of flats?'

'He usually had a big box, a cardboard box, which he brought in with him.'

'And what did you infer from that?'

'I object. The witness cannot possibly guess at what was in the box.'

'The witness may answer the question.'

'I thought it might be presents, for her . . .' she indicates Maire '. . . or the kid.'

'A great big box of presents, every time he came?' Steven turns to the jury. 'What a generous man!' There is a ripple of laughter in the courtroom. 'Did it occur to you, Mrs Grace, that the man might be visiting Miss O'Neill on business?'

'Well . . . I don't know, I'm sure.'

'Did you know that Miss O'Neill supported herself and her child by doing piecework at home? That she would address and fill envelopes for mail shots?'

'I suppose so.' Tina sniffs. She had thought Maire a fool for working when she could just as easily have claimed the dole. Or else claimed the dole and worked on the side.

'And it didn't occur to you that this man might be delivering and collecting these envelopes in his transit van, in his big cardboard box?'

'I never thought.'

'No, Mrs Grace, that much is obvious.' The laughter swells again as the young woman reddens in anger. 'What does the greengrocer call you, Mrs Grace?'

'Eh?' The question catches her off balance and her gentility slips.

'You do shop at the greengrocer's, or the butcher's? You do go to the newsagent's? What do they call you when they serve you?'

'I don't see the point of this line of questioning, Mr Hale,' the judge interrupts.

'Please, My Lord. All will become clear. Do they call you "Madam", Mrs Grace?'

'I don't know. I don't notice.'

'Or is it "Love" perhaps? "Love", "Darling". That's what tradesmen call young women, and not so young ones, isn't it?'

'It might be.'

'So when you heard the delivery man address Maire O'Neill as "My love", you didn't really take it as a term of endearment, did you?'

'Perhaps not.'

'I have no further questions.'

French leans forward as Steven sits down again and murmurs, 'Well done.'

Sixteen

Shaw is recalled the next morning. He is annoyed at Steven's easy demolition of Tina Grace. Silly little scrubber; she'd come to him with her 'evidence', hadn't told him the half of it. Looked as if she'd got it in for O'Neill for some reason. Some women's quarrel, no doubt.

'I need hardly remind you that you're still on oath, Chief Inspector,' the judge says. Shaw shakes his head impatiently. He passes quickly over the rest of his evidence. He tells the jury of the arrest of Maire O'Neill following interviews with the man she had ditched in the pub that evening and the bus driver who saw her running hell for leather away from the pub. He agrees with Steven that no admission of guilt has been obtained.

'Did your office receive any telephone calls after the bombing?' Hale asks.

'Only the usual cranks.'

'Cranks?' the judge queries.

'After any atrocity, My Lord, there are always false confessions, sensation-seekers.'

'And you had many such after the Hope and Anchor tragedy?' Steven persists.

'Half a dozen, but none of them had the right code word.'

'Could you explain to the jury about the code words?'

'Certainly. The police agree a series of code words – passwords, if you like – with the IRA. That way we can sort out the real warning calls from the hoax calls, and the real claims of responsibility from the false ones.'

'Did any of the callers give a code word at all?'

'One of them,' Shaw admits, 'an out-of-date one.'

'Did it have the ring of authenticity otherwise?'

Winch-Gore objects to this and is upheld.

'You must admit, Chief Inspector,' Steven says, 'that your case is flimsy in the extreme.' Shaw will admit no such thing. He flourishes his glasses and hooks them on to his nose. He raises his voice, presses forward into Shaw's space.

'I put it to you, Chief Inspector, that you have no evidence against Maire O'Neill. I put it to you that you were under pressure from your superiors to make an arrest in this case; *any* arrest. I put it to you that you are under pressure from your masters, in this election year, to get a conviction at all costs . . .'

Shaw is impassive, not even trying to reply to any of this. Fat Barney Winch-Gore, on the other hand, is bobbing up and down like a cork on the sea, objecting and objecting. Steven Hale does not even pause to draw breath. Finally De Freitas bangs hard on his desk with his hand, stopping him at last.

'Mr Hale! This is outrageous.'

'I agree, My Lord. It is outrageous that this innocent young girl . . .' he gestures towards his client '. . . should be made a political scapegoat in this way.' He sits down. 'I have no further questions.'

French scribbles a note and passes it to him. Steven reads, 'Lord Olivier, eat your heart out.'

After a fifteen-minute adjournment which is ostensibly to give the jury a break but is really to let tempers cool and to allow the judge to retire, Winch-Gore calls Brian, who strides into the courtroom, looking about him with a defiant air. He takes the oath loudly, holding the Bible up in front of him as a talisman. He stares contemptuously across the room at Maire.

He is Brian Swinnerton, insurance salesman, of Clifton, Bristol? He agrees that he is. Does he recognise the woman in the dock? Yes, she is the woman he met last August who called herself Nora. Can he tell the court, in his own words, about the night of Friday, August 25th last year?

Steven rises and says that the Defence is not disputing that Miss O'Neill was in the Hope and Anchor on the evening in question. Winch-Gore says he believes this witness's evidence to be germane. The judge rules that it shall be heard.

'Spiteful-looking little oik,' Steven mutters.

Brian characteristically runs a finger round inside his collar

– he is literally hot under that collar. He values his own life highly, highly enough to present himself voluntarily to the police and make a statement under the strict understanding that his wife need not hear of it. Unfortunately it seems that only he, and not DCI Shaw, strictly understood this.

He explains that he had felt sorry for the girl – yes, the accused – a not very attractive young woman, a single parent, obviously lonely. He had asked her for a quick drink out of pity and she had suggested the Hope and Anchor. Pity? Yes, he had felt sorry for her. He glares across the courtroom again at Maire and is taken aback to see her smiling at him.

She is smiling at the thought which had just come to her that Brian is not committing perjury, that he *believes* that his version of events is the true one. He would pass a lie-detector test. He has rewritten history. She is not, in any case, smiling *at* him, only vaguely in his direction, since that is the way she happens to be facing. She is unaware of how she has disconcerted him. The jurors, following Swinnerton's eyes, are also startled to see this young murderess smiling dreamily in the face of her horrific crime.

Swinnerton goes on, prompted by Counsel, to agree that she had a black shoulder-bag with her that night. He tells how she disappeared not half an hour before the explosion, lying to him. He is not sure if she took her bag with her or not; he is inclined to think, now he comes to picture the scene, that she was not holding that bag as she left the bar. This speculation is the evidence the Prosecution holds so crucial. Steven objects to it and is upheld, but the jury has already heard it.

He had waited ten minutes for her, asked around the two bars, then left and gone back to his car. Driving away, he had been halfway up the High Street when he had heard the bang. He says, indignantly, that he could have been killed.

Hale rises to cross-examine and questions his account of events. Swinnerton is an unreliable witness and an unpleasant man and he wants to make sure the jury appreciates both these points.

Is it not true that, far from running into Maire O'Neill casually and asking her for a drink on the spur of the moment, the meeting had been deliberately set up by a third party, a woman called Sandra Bathgate who works as a typist in one of the firms he does business with? He looks at him over the top of his glasses like an elderly schoolmaster daring an inky boy to lie.

Swinnerton blusters that he cannot see what difference it makes and the judge tells him sharply to answer the question and to remember that he is on oath. He agrees that it was a blind date and avoids looking up in the public gallery where his wife is sitting. Hale looks triumphantly at the jury who cannot see, either, what difference it makes.

Is Swinnerton sure that it was Maire O'Neill and not he who chose the Hope and Anchor? Quite sure. He may not be deliberately lying; it may be that his memory is poor on this point. He is being asked about things which happened almost six months ago.

'Are you in the habit of arranging to meet young women when you are away from home on business?' Steven asks him.

He admits that, yes, he may be grateful for a little companionship from time to time. There's no more to it than that. The life of a salesman, on the road for five or six days a week, forty-seven weeks of the year, trying to earn an honest living to keep his wife and children, can be a lonely one. What harm can there be in taking a girl for a drink and a chat?

Steven Hale has no further questions. He is pleased. He does not think Swinnerton has made a good impression. He did not see Maire's ironic smile; he may have been the only person in the courtroom who didn't.

Seventeen

The next morning Winch-Gore calls his *pièce de résistance*, his forensic expert. He wants him to testify early in the day while the jury is alert and receptive.

He swears by Almighty God that the evidence he will give will be the truth, the whole truth and nothing but the truth.

'You are Dr Pavel Kurowski, Senior Forensic Scientist at the Royal Armament Research and Development Establishment at Woolwich Arsenal?'

'I am.'

Dr Kurowski appears regularly for the Prosecution in important trials and knows what to expect. He is a small, ascetic-looking man with his neatly pointed beard, studious in appearance, quietly spoken but authoritative. His suit is good but slightly shabby, his tie that of the Royal Society. He stands with his well-manicured hands on the rail of the witness box, leaning slightly forward. He is exactly the jury's idea of what a boffin looks like.

'You were in charge of the tests on the swabs taken, by yourself, from the hands of Maire O'Neill at High Wycombe police station on the night of Saturday, August 26th last year?'

'I was.'

Most of the jurors pick up their notebooks and pens to write down the gist of what he says. Dr Kurowski has spent several weeks testing the O'Neill samples and what he has to tell them today is already a selective gist, a summing up of hundreds of hours of work in a morning. He knows what he thinks is relevant and his lies are lies only of omission.

'Please tell the jury in your own words the nature of the tests you have carried out?'

Kurowski turns to face the jury and addresses them directly.

He is interrupted frequently, mainly by the judge asking for clarification, but this – interruptions apart – is what he has to say.

'Firstly I carried out what is known as a Greiss test.' He spells it. 'This is what we call a screening, or presumptive, test. Should it prove negative, then no further tests need be carried out.

'The swabs were soaked in ether and the resultant liquid poured into three identical, uncontaminated bowls, one of which is kept for control purposes. I added caustic soda to the first bowl, followed by the Greiss reagent. Nitroglycerine-like compounds will turn the liquid pink within ten seconds.'

'And what was the result of this test?' Winch-Gore asks.

'The liquid turned pink. The result was positive.'

The jury nods. A positive result. This is not as hard to follow as they had feared.

'I then poured the reagent only into the second bowl. If nitroglycerine were present I would expect that liquid to stay clear, which it did.'

'And how certain were you then that the substance found on Miss O'Neill's hands was indeed nitroglycerine?'

'Ninety-nine per cent certain. The only other substance I know of which produces this same result is also a constituent of explosives.'

'Ninety-nine per cent certain,' Winch-Gore repeats for the benefit of the jury. 'But you went on to carry out other tests too, didn't you, Dr Kurowski?'

'I did. I next carried out a thin-layer chromatography test. For this, I took a glass plate coated with silica sand and measured the rate of movement of the sample up the plate. Different substances have different rates of movement, you see.'

At this point Mr Justice De Freitas asks, on behalf of the baffled jury, that this point be clarified, and the scientist hands round photographs of the glass plate in action and graphs showing the expected results of different substances. De Freitas says that he sees and nods to Dr Kurowski to continue.

'The TLC test shows that the substance tested is nitroglycerine of the type used in commercial explosives. So that there should be no shadow of doubt, I then used the facilities at

Aldermaston to carry out a gas chromatography – or mass spectrometry – test as well.'

He explains how this test breaks the substance down into its component parts or ions, allowing each part to be separately analysed and the three ions which make up commercial nitro-glycerine to be identified. This test also produced a positive result.

The most conscientious of the jurors have listed the three tests by name and placed a large tick next to each one. Three positive results, no less.

'In your opinion,' Winch-Gore asks, 'your *expert* opinion, is there any substance, other than nitroglycerine, which could have produced these results.'

'I know of no other substance which would give these exact results,' the scientist replies promptly.

'You are certain?'

'Quite certain.'

'You may, if you wish, make a note of that, members of the jury,' the judge says in case they haven't got the point. 'Dr Kurowski is quite certain that the substance tested, the substance found on the defendant's hands after the bombing, cannot be anything but nitroglycerine.'

'I wish I could be half as certain of anything in this life as that,' Steven Hale hisses to his junior, as he rises to cross-examine. He wishes he could find a way of conveying to the jury that all they are hearing is one man's opinion which would not be admissible in court were the witness not an 'expert'.

'Is it possible, Dr Kurowski, that the defendant's hands could have become contaminated with explosives other than by handling them directly . . .'

'Quite impossible,' Kurowski says firmly. He was being cross-examined while Steven Hale was still studying Politics and Law at the LSE.

'For example,' Steven perseveres. 'Supposing someone who had been handling explosives were to wipe his hands on a towel, or wrap them round a beer glass. If a second person were then to come along and also use the towel or handle the glass, might they not pick up the substance thereby?'

'I have never known a case of such a thing happening.' Dr Kurowski is a man who likes certainties. Steven has had the bad luck to meet one of the few forensic scientists prepared to give a straight answer to a straight question.

'The results I achieved in my laboratory could only have come about if the defendant had been kneading the explosive . . .' he demonstrates a wringing action with his hands '. . . as one does in order to make a bomb.'

'Is it not possible, Dr Kurowski, that nitrocellulose – a quite innocuous compound found in varnish – could produce the results you obtained?'

'Not at room temperature,' he replies. 'It would have to be heated to 60 degrees centigrade. That's 140 degrees Fahrenheit, in layman's terms, and I think I would have noticed if the room was as hot as that.' The court titters and Kurowski smiles at Steven, his lips red and thin inside his beard. He knows he has won the exchange.

Steven says, 'No more questions,' and sits down, feeling that he has succeeded only in reinforcing in the jurors' minds the certainty of Maire O'Neill's guilt.

Eighteen

The Prosecution keeps its slow, relentless course throughout the first week of the trial.

The bus driver testifies how he saw the accused running away from the pub as fast as her pounding feet would carry her. He agrees, under cross-examination, that she might simply have been running for the bus but thinks it unlikely since the bus was not due to leave for another five minutes. He does not think to mention – or has forgotten after all these months – that he had been having trouble with the doors and had been testing them as Maire rounded the corner; no one thinks to ask him.

An army of technicians, Scenes of Crime Officers, give details of their findings at the pub. The bomb consisted of eight to ten pounds of explosives – quite small by recent standards but adequately deadly – detonated by an alarm clock, an Ever Ready battery and half a screw. No trace of explosives was found at Maire O'Neill's flat although they took the floorboards up and the back of the TV off.

Toni Giordano is an angry and vengeful witness, his manhood threatened by a disfigured and half-blind wife. The jury is less interested and excited now than it was on Monday and concentrates less hard. They are looking forward to the weekend.

Silvie Crewe is Roisin's social worker and is looking for a new job. It had seemed the right caring profession to take up when her own youngest child started school; she had enjoyed the training course. Three years later, she is willing to consider anything that is not an emotional drain – an emotional sewer.

This Monday morning, in the second week of the trial, she

is in a meeting with the rest of the child welfare team. She nibbles at her nails as they make laborious decisions about yet another little boy on the at-risk register; there is not much nail left and she gnaws at the skin down the side of the cuticle, drawing blood.

'Roisin O'Neill.' The senior social worker, who is chairing the meeting, pronounces the name as it is written. 'Silvie, one of yours?'

'Rho-sheen,' Silvie corrects her automatically. 'Short-term fostering?' she hazards. 'Until the position is clarified. Perhaps in a home with no other children. She's the sort of child who will benefit from individual attention. Put her in a crowd of other, rowdy, kids and she just withdraws inside herself.'

Silvie does not like Roisin much – considers her a precocious little madam – but that will not stop her knocking herself out on her behalf. The Friday before she had been to see her, had asked her, 'How would you like a new mummy, Rosie?' The child had expressed surprise. She had been satisfied with her old mummy and had not been aware that you had to change every few years; thought you got to stick with your original. She thinks she might have been consulted.

'How long before we expect a verdict in the mother's trial?' the chairwoman asks. 'I think we should keep her at Fairlawns until then. That may change everything.' These social workers, *Guardian*-readers to a woman, are among the few who do not see the verdict as a foregone conclusion.

'It's entering its second week,' Silvie tells her. 'Not long now.'

Nineteen

Steven Hale is on his feet as he speaks, opening the case for the Defence.

He explains courteously to the jury that his learned friend's interpretation of the facts is only one of many possible interpretations. The evidence against Maire O'Neill is circumstantial, relying on nothing more than her presence in the pub that night, the fact that she is Irish, and 'expert' witnesses whose 'facts' – as he will demonstrate – are no more than opinion. He puts the words Expert and Facts clearly in inverted commas for the jury. Juries do not like expert witnesses who baffle them with science and will rarely give a straight answer to a straight question. Except for Dr Kurowski, of course. He ends by telling the jurors that he relies on their innate intelligence and sense of justice to acquit.

He is calling two witnesses only: the defendant, Maire O'Neill, and Dr Mark Fletcher, formerly of the Home Office.

This is the moment everyone has been waiting for. The public gallery has been full for every day of the trial, but today the queues start at 5 a.m. The doors are opened early to allow every person in that queue to be body-searched. The Defence calls the accused to the witness stand to answer in person the charges against her. The public cranes forward as she passes the jury stand, covering the short distance from the dock.

They are disappointed by her ordinariness. She is such a small woman, thinner than ever after her months on remand. She wears a little powder on her pointed face. Her unruly hair has grown into a shoulder-length bob. She wears a straight grey skirt cut just to the knee, a matching single-breasted jacket and a pale blue blouse slightly open at the neck. She has tan tights and a pair of the sombre, low-heeled shoes known aptly as court shoes. Steven Hale himself chose all these for her, supplementing her prison clothing allowance. They are the best clothes she has ever owned.

She takes the oath. She is very composed, but throughout the hours that she speaks her Irish accent seems to grow more pronounced until the judge begins to ask – quite gratuitously, it seems to Hale – for her to repeat some of her answers.

Steven takes her gently through the evening of August 25th. She is unable to explain how she came to agree to the date with Brian Swinnerton, saying only that it was a 'grave mistake' which is not intended as a bad pun. She lives very quietly with her young daughter and has no men friends. This was the first date she had been on in six years.

'Did you notice the group of soldiers in the corner?'

'I did. They were talking a lot and laughing, you couldn't not notice them.'

'How far from you were they?'

'There was another table between theirs and mine.'

'From the time you arrived in the pub, until the time you left Mr Swinnerton, telling him that you were going to the Ladies, did you have occasion to pass their table?'

'I did not. It was in a corner. Mr Swinnerton went to the bar twice, once when we'd just arrived and once about half an hour later. I didn't leave my table at all until I left altogether.'

'There was a cigarette machine in that corner. Did you have occasion to use that?'

'No. I don't smoke.'

'So would it have been physically possible for you to plant the bag which contained the bomb under the bench at the corner table?'

'No.'

'You had a black bag with you that night?'

'I did.' She carries a small black clutch-bag now – a real leather one, also Steven's choice – and her fingers are stark white against it, so tightly is she clutching.

'And did you still have it when you left?'

'Of course. I had my purse in it. I had to open it to get out my bus fare.'

'What was that?' De Freitas asks. 'Could you repeat that remark.' She does so. 'Ah. Your *bus fare*. Continue, Mr Hale.'

'Have you ever knowingly handled explosives?' Steven asks.

'Never.'

'But you touched some of the furniture in the pub that night?'

'I did. The chair I sat on, the table.'

'The bar?'

'No.'

She answers each question after the smallest pause for consideration, wastes no words. Her voice sounds unemotional, detached. Several of the jurors think she should be more moved – that a woman who had been wrongly accused would be distraught. They judge her by their own standards, unaware of the reserves of self-control she has built up. She holds her head up. She is looking exclusively at, speaking exclusively to, Steven, like a public speaker who can cope with stage fright only by picking out one member of the audience to focus on. The jury concludes that she is afraid to face them, afraid to betray herself in her lies. There is little new in her evidence. She confirms the identity of the envelope man whom the police have been unable to trace. She repeats her ignorance of the IRA, of explosives; her innocence of the crime of which she is accused.

Barney Winch-Gore spends a long time on cross-examination. He cannot fluster her. If his questions come pouring over her too thick and fast, she floors him by asking politely, 'Which question do you want me to answer first, sir?'

'This black bag. It was a large shoulder-bag?'

'Yes.'

'Large enough to hold ten pounds of explosives and the detonators?'

'I wouldn't know.'

'Is it true that members of your family are rumoured to belong to the IRA?'

'Not so far as I am aware.'

'Do you know a Tommy Fagan?'

'I have an uncle of that name. My mother's brother.'

'A declared IRA supporter?'

Maire considers this a travesty of truth – Uncle Tommy is a naïve romantic and a singer of songs, no more – but replies simply, 'I am not aware of it. Besides, I have lost contact with my family.'

She pauses to compose herself – her estrangement from her own kin still has the power to pain her. 'I have not seen Uncle Tommy for six years.' A cold-hearted woman this, cutting herself off deliberately from her family.

She steps down from the stand finally after a total of six gruelling hours. She walks very slowly back to the dock, exhausted; her head is still high.

Twenty

Dr Fletcher is an untidy-looking man who has recently celebrated – or at least passed – his seventieth birthday and carries every year heavily. He declines to take the oath and when the judge asks his reasons replies: 'I am an old man and have no religious beliefs left to me.'

Steven puts his head in his hands. 'Now he tells me.'

Fletcher affirms and states his qualifications which are that he had worked for the Home Office as an explosives expert from 1952 until 1968, retiring with the rank of Chief Inspector. He keeps clearing his throat; it is still winter and he is an old man of a bronchitic tendency.

'Dr Fletcher,' Steven begins, 'are you familiar with the tests for explosives carried out by the Royal Armaments Research and Development Establishment? The Greiss test, thin-layer chromatography and gas chromatography?'

'Erm, yes. Quite familiar.'

'And do you agree with the conclusions of Dr Kurowski, which the jury has already heard, that nitroglycerine, and nitroglycerine only, could have produced those test results?'

'Erm. Well, of course, it's not possible to be *certain* of anything . . .' Steven wonders why Dr Kurowski could not have admitted publicly to that '. . . but, erm, it seems to me . . .' Fletcher pauses to take out a handkerchief and blow his nose '. . . that similar results could be obtained from nitrocellulose.' He stops and looks expectantly at Steven.

'Similar?' Steven queries.

'Erm, well, the same really.'

'Even at room temperature?'

'Erm. Yes. In my view, temperature does not make a significant difference.'

99

'And can you explain to the jury what nitrocellulose is and the uses to which it is put?'

'It's used in industrial-grade paint and varnish,' Fletcher says, becoming unexpectedly articulate. 'Such paints and varnishes are frequently used in public houses to protect the bar or furniture such as, erm, wooden chairs and tables.'

'And we have heard from Mr Giordano, the landlord, that the pub had recently been redecorated,' Steven reminds the jury. He returns to Fletcher. 'And traces of nitrocellulose can get on to people's hands if they touch the bar or furniture which has been so treated?'

'It's technically possible, yes. Particularly if it's, erm, mixed with alcohol.'

'Which would not be entirely unexpected in a public house?'

'Erm. No.'

Steven has no further questions. Winch-Gore rises. He does not attempt to demolish Fletcher's evidence since it is clear that the court is unimpressed by his performance. Instead he asks, 'Dr Fletcher, I won't detain you for long.' He wishes to underline the fact of Fletcher's age and – he thrusts – decrepitude. 'It is ten years, I believe, since you retired from your job at the Home Office.'

'Quite so. Quite so. A little over ten years, in fact. My wife's health . . .'

'How sad. It's very good of you to give up your time to be here today.' Winch-Gore raises his voice slightly, as if he thinks Fletcher may be a little deaf. 'But you were, in your working days, familiar with the work of RARDE?'

'Certainly.'

'What is your opinion of the professional competence of its officers?'

Steven Hale objects and the question is allowed.

'Erm. They are very competent, very competent indeed. Yes. Their work is equivalent to that being done in the science departments of our major universities.'

'And could you just tell me, Dr Fletcher, what is the extent of your *practical* experience in the sphere of forensic science?'

'It is not extensive.'

'Would it in fact be fair to say that you have never worked in a forensic science laboratory at all?'

Fletcher, hesitatingly, agrees that this is so then says with surprising spirit that he has never been to the sun but he still knows that it's hot.

'Thank you so much, Dr Fletcher,' Barney Winch-Gore says. 'I have no further questions, My Lord.'

Dr Fletcher is waiting outside when they adjourn for the day and approaches Steven and George French.

'I'm sorry,' he says. 'I haven't the experience in court. I was so nervous. All those people listening to me.'

French comforts him. 'You did what you could.'

'But I'm right,' the old man says. 'I know I am. And he's wrong, the other chap, for all his certainties. Can't I go back, explain again? I'll do better this time.'

Steven tells him that that is not quite how things work.

Twenty-One

Winch-Gore's speech is delivered elegantly and with confidence. He tells the jury that the evidence against the accused is overwhelming. Even if they have doubts about the more circumstantial facts, they have heard Dr Kurowski state categorically that the swabs taken from O'Neill's hands demonstrate that she had handled nitroglycerine.

Steven's speech is more leisurely; he is giving himself time for inspiration to strike. He reminds the jury that the police have been unable to prove the existence of the shadowy 'boyfriend' – Steven's voice sneers at this implausible notion – who is supposed to have given the explosive to Maire O'Neill. Corporal Carmichael has told them that he did not see Maire O'Neill approach his table at any time during the evening, so it seems that the planting of the bomb must have been physically impossible for her. She had not means, motive nor opportunity to commit this crime.

Most importantly, Dr Fletcher has cast serious doubt upon Dr Kurowski's certainties.

He reminds the jurors that it is not for Maire O'Neill to prove her innocence but for the Prosecution to prove her guilt. This they have failed to do, and it is the clear duty of the twelve jurors to return a not-guilty verdict.

De Freitas says that he will sum up tomorrow as it is getting late.

As Steven Hale sits down, French passes him another note. It says:

'You did your best.'

'Ladies and gentlemen of the jury, you have the grave responsibility of trying a very serious crime – a crime, I may say, among the worst it has been my misfortune to preside over in all my years at the Central Criminal Court. As Mr Hale told you yesterday, it is for Mr Winch-Gore to prove the guilt of the accused and unless you are satisfied, beyond a reasonable doubt, that Maire O'Neill is guilty of the crime with which she is charged, it is your duty to acquit her. A *reasonable* doubt, members of the jury . . .

'The case turns, it seems to me, on the testimony of our two expert witnesses – Dr Kurowski and Dr Fletcher. Dr Kurowski – a *practising* forensic scientist of no little renown – has told you that the substance found on the defendant's hands can only be nitroglycerine and can have been acquired only through direct contact with the explosive; he is quite certain of this. Dr Fletcher questions these conclusions but it is important to remember that Dr Fletcher's experience is more than ten years out of date and that he agrees that the staff at RARDE are highly competent forensic scientists . . .'

Steven grits his teeth. Why doesn't the old bastard come straight out and say that Fletcher is a doddering old fool who doesn't know a thin-layer chromatography test from a hole in the ground.

'You must decide for yourselves, members of the jury, which of these scientists you will believe . . .'

'Please do not think that I am seeking to pre-empt your decision on this important issue. You may take a different view of things to mine, but it seems to me that if Dr Fletcher is right, and the so-called Greiss test is of no value in isolating nitroglycerine, then Dr Kurowski has spent most of his professional life wasting his time . . .

'You must decide further what to make of the testimony of Maire O'Neill, a young woman, a single mother, struggling to make a life for herself in a foreign country. A self-contained young woman, she strikes me; you may think her hard . . .'

And so on, and so on.

Steven begins to consider his plea in mitigation, jotting a few notes: such a young, unworldly woman; misplaced ideals, misguided loyalty. No. Making a plea in mitigation would mean accepting a guilty verdict as a just one and they will, of course, appeal.

He looks across at Maire; she is looking his way and gives

him a sad, sweet smile. He tries to look hopeful for her sake. 'Remember,' he had told her that morning, their disagreements put aside, 'all my clients are innocent.'

Then he stiffens with anger and renewed aggression -- it is not in his nature to throw in the towel.

As the jury files out to consider its verdict, Maire asks one of the policewomen, quietly, if she can go for a pee. She has been crossing her legs for the last half-hour, not knowing what the etiquette is, not daring to interrupt the judge's summing up. What better proof of a guilty conscience than a tetchy bladder?

The two WPCs lead her from the dock, through a maze of underground passages, through a door marked 'Women'. They tell her not to lock the door of the cubicle. Maire doesn't mind; they all have to do it – the WPCs know what she is up to and it is better than a bucket under a washstand. One woman crouches slightly so she can see Maire's feet under the door at all times. They are nervy, ready to summon help with their radios at any second.

When Maire comes out, she obeys the bossy notice and now washes her hands, pushing the plunger on the soap dispenser, wincing at the too-hot water. The policewomen stand there, patient. Maire looks in the mirror and sees what they see: a wild girl, scarcely old enough to leave home – at first glance – but with an illegitimate kid and a deadly handbag.

Their eyes in the mirror are without sympathy or humanity, and Maire knows that she has already been judged.

There can have been little dissent in the jury room since the jurors return in less than two hours. They do not look at Maire, and Steven knows that it is over. The Guilty verdict is delivered many times. There is applause from the public gallery and the judge has to threaten to clear the court. But the court is already clearing itself: the gawpers have seen what they came to see; reporters are running for the telephone.

The *Evening News* that night carries the headline: 'Guilty as Charged – Life for IRA Death-Dealer'.

The judge is satisfied with the verdict and says so. There is only one sentence he can hand down – more's the pity, his manner implies; hanging would be too good for her. He recommends that Life in her case should mean at least twenty years and there is cheering from the remnants of the public.

Steven Hale is slumped in his chair, eyes fixed on the green leather inlay of his lectern, angry. He is not a good loser, has not had the practice. He has not taken an adverse verdict this hard in the whole of his career. This is not Justice, this is not even Law; this is a mindless lashing-out at the nearest ninepin.

Maire is standing in the dock, as she must, out of respect for the Crown.

Twenty-Two

Maire is taken back to Holloway until the end of the week. She is no longer on remand, no longer has privileges, even in theory. A new life is beginning for her, where each day is the same as the day before and these days are measured out in mealtimes, by plastic cutlery.

She refuses to allow French or Steven Hale to visit her, sees no point since she will not be asking for leave to appeal. The only visitor she will permit is Trish Murray, who is more overtly distressed by the verdict than her friend is. The two young women are left alone together for the last time; they stare at each other in despair.

'I want her adopted,' Maire says finally. 'She can't spend the rest of her childhood in a children's home.'

Trish demurs, says that Roisin can be fostered, still have a proper home with loving parents while remaining Maire's daughter. And what about the appeal, Trish asks?

'There will be no appeal.'

Trish misunderstands, draws back physically in her chair; an invisible barrier, like a glass wall, begins to materialise between the two women. Then she rallies, knows she is not that poor a judge of people.

'I must know, Maire. Tell me you didn't do it.'

'I didn't do it.' The glass barrier dematerialises.

'Then you have to appeal. Really. You must.'

Maire cannot explain her decision to Trish or to her lawyers, barely to herself. British Justice has had its chance to be honest and decent and true and has failed. She will not attempt that obstacle-course of appeals, of hope, only to be knocked down again. What matters now is Roisin's future. She must have a proper home, a real family.

'You're very brave,' Trish tells her. She stifles a sob, delves in that disorganised bag of hers for a tissue to hide behind. Maire looks away. She cannot allow herself to break down. If she starts to weep now, she will never stop.

'You could write her a letter,' Trish suggests, 'explaining . . . everything. I could see she gets it when she comes of age.'

Maire considers the idea – for it is tempting – then shakes her head. Better that she should forget and be happy.

Trish produces a recent photograph of Roisin, solemn in the gardens of the orphanage, then says goodbye. She wants to offer to write but knows that she is a poor correspondent – lost on paper for the words which come so easily to her mouth – and that it must end in disappointment.

Maire puts the picture away among her things where she will not happen on it at the wrong moment.

On Sunday afternoon she sets off for Durham maximum-security prison where she will start her sentence. The prison van is closed, of course, and she can see only out of the tiny shatterproof windows at the back as the grey suburbs of north London disappear behind her.

Nothing can be worse than Holloway, can it?

Part Two
Behind the Wire

One

Durham opens, like a whale's mouth, to swallow Maire O'Neill.

Think the unthinkable: that the surface of the planet has been torn apart by nuclear war or by some ecological catastrophe. Imagine the unimaginable: that survivors are all huddled into locked citadels deep inside the earth from which they may never emerge – never again to feel the sun on their faces or watch the moon rise. That is Durham H Wing: a prison within a prison. This is where women lifers start their sentence, especially those, such as convicted terrorists, who are considered a high security risk. It lies inside the men's prison – which is much larger – like the innermost babushka in a Russian doll. There are male as well as female warders here, men accompanied by savage, growling dogs, straining to get free.

Someone – some loud-mouth who has not read the details of Maire's case – demands in Parliament that she be allowed to serve her sentence at home in Northern Ireland. The Home Secretary, who has also, perhaps, not followed the case in detail, replies that it is not government policy. There is some desultory discussion of the point in the more serious papers. None of the people taking part in the debate has grasped the fact that she does not come from the North. Women's groups campaign for clemency, saying she is an innocent dupe.

The van passes through two sets of gates which take Maire into and through the men's prison. Then she arrives at another twenty-foot fence where she gets down from the van, escorted by two warders who press a button. No one else is in sight, but a man's voice barks to know who is there. The prison officers identify themselves and say they have a prisoner. Then they must all step back and face the camera before the gate opens.

She is led through a door, down steps; down and down. Still there are no people, only cameras and electronic voices. Soon there is a high door and another button and the same panto-mime is enacted. Although there is no daylight, everything is white, blazing, dazzlingly fluorescent. There are no seasons in Durham H Wing, no night or day.

She fills in her reception form after being strip-searched. This time, it doesn't seem quite so bad. It is starting to seem normal to her to stand naked in front of a group of sniggering women in uniform. One of them holds a recent copy of the *Daily Mirror* with Maire's photograph plastered over the front.

They are telling her: We know who you are, what you've done.

Name, age, sentence, distinguishing marks, religion? She has some difficulty in understanding their harsh north-eastern accents and is hated for it. She answers 'none' for the last two. They take her fingerprints once more.

She is to send a reception letter to let people know where she is. What people? Friends and family, of course. She declines the letter. The whole country knows where Maire O'Neill is: where she belongs.

A warder who identifies herself as Miss Shadwell leads her deeper into the bowels of the prison. She is a stocky, not unattractive, muscular woman in her late thirties, with one of those rictus smiles that contain no goodwill. She is ex-army and holds herself very erect – striding out as if on parade. Maire learns later that the prisoners refer to her as Miss Shagwell. Every corridor is alive with cameras. They climb to the second floor.

It is all single cells at Durham. There's a label on the door which says simply 'M. O'Neill – Life'. She has collected some bedding on the way and Miss Shadwell stands over her as she makes up the rudimentary iron bed. The bed stands some six inches from the wall at both head and side and Maire begins unthinkingly to push it against the wall, to Miss Shadwell's fury. Furniture may not be placed against the wall: the inmate could be using it as a cover to dig her way out through the brick with her fingernails.

She is locked in for the rest of that first day. The electronic door slides shut with a noiseless finality which is far more sinister than the clanging locks of Holloway; even then she hears the noise of bolts being drawn on the other side. She is fed in her cell that evening. She has a great deal of leisure to examine her new home.

The cell has one window set so high in the wall that you must – especially if you are as short as Maire is – stand on the bedstead to glimpse the sky. Standing on the bedstead is, she later discovers, a punishable offence. The window is made of unbreakable plastic, not glass which could become a weapon. Beyond the plastic are iron bars, then a metal grille, then mesh, then – six inches beyond that – barbed wire. She gets down again and draws the incongruous flowery curtain across to hide this caricature of a window.

The floor is rubber with a plastic mat. All the furniture – bed, wooden cupboard, small table, upright chair – stands awkwardly in the middle of the room as if it is waiting for something. There are the familiar plastic jugs for washing and drinking water. She has a chamber pot with a lid rather than the bucket she had in Holloway; she supposes that this is an improvement.

There is a small pinboard for personal photographs, postcards. It will stand naked for a long time. It will be many weeks before Maire digs out her snapshots of Roisin and uses it. They have taken away her sketchpad and her crayons – these are not allowed – so she cannot draw herself a picture. They have taken most of her books since no one can read more than one book at a time – it stands to reason. There is an emergency bell but Maire knows better now than to imagine pressing it. She would need to be dying.

She hears the rest of the prisoners being locked away for the night at about eight o'clock. She reads for a while then wonders how to switch off the light. After a search it dawns on her that the light is controlled from outside. She reads on until it snaps off suddenly at about ten. There will be nights when no one remembers to turn it off.

She sleeps fitfully to the regular clatter of warders' feet on the open-plan metal stairs as they make their frequent checks.

Where, she wonders, did it all start to go wrong?

*

It is early June 1972, a Saturday. They are celebrating her seventeenth birthday. Con has borrowed his father's old car and proposes to take her to the seaside. He has not passed his test but nobody cares much about that in this rural area; it is not so long since there was no driving test to worry about and people just picked the knack up from their fathers, as Con has done. Dervla is agitating to come with them. Con laughs and says she is just a kid and will be in the way. Her pretty face is ugly with envy.

'I'll tell,' she says. 'I'll tell.' She's childish although she will soon be sixteen.

'Tell what, goosey? My Da said I could.'

The car is a Ford van, about fifteen years old, but Con's father has looked after it and it will manage the few miles to the coast beyond Killybegs and back. If they do break down there will be someone who knows them, or someone who knows someone who knows them, who will help. They take parcels of food wrapped in clean clothes, and bottles of pop. There is an old horse blanket in the back of the van to sit on. Although these are the 1970s, this is rural Ireland, a developing country in the grip of an anti-sex priesthood, and the innocence of this expedition is timeless.

The sun is high behind them. As they drive through the treeless countryside, heading west, the corn is already tall enough to promise a record harvest by the standards of this poor soil. In two months, they will have no time to spare for jaunting; their help will be expected on the farms. Wild honeysuckle grows in the hedgerows and, after a few miles, the road signs turn into Gaelic. Here, beyond Killybegs, the Gaeltacht begins.

The beaches are empty, the sea bare except for a few returning fishing boats. The cove they have chosen has an over-hang of granite rock shielding them from the sight of passers-by on the cliffs. They walk and eat, run and shove. They have forgotten their swimming things, even their towels. They curse their stupidity. Then Con suggests that they bathe in the buff, dry out after in the horse blanket. Maire giggles, her hand covering her mouth.

Do they dare? Can he be serious?

Why not? There is no one to see. This cove is too shallow

*even for fishing boats and sheltered by rocks on either side.
Maire strips off her blouse without further argument, pulling
it over her head and flinging it on the nearest rock. A short
sleeve dips in the shallow pool. Con, startled, not expecting to
be taken seriously, stares at her small, pale breasts with their
flat brown nipples. He has not seen a woman's breasts before
except for his mother's when she was breast-feeding the
younger ones. These are nothing like his mother's which are
heavy and full with little silver stretch-marks zeroing in on her
pink teat. He feels his mouth go dry.*

*She has removed her jeans now and stands there in a pair of
white pants saying, 'What's keeping you? It was your idea. Not
got cold feet, have you?'*

*His revelations are less of a surprise. She has four brothers
and curiosity has led her early to spy on them at their bedtime.
What does surprise her is the great mat of hair on his chest
and belly – her father and brothers are smooth men. She stares
at that and he thinks she is frightened to look any lower.*

*'Come on, then.' Suddenly shy under her scrutiny, Con runs
down the beach and into the water, wincing as the cold makes
itself felt. 'It's, er, lovely in.'*

*She joins him, moving in a graceful breast stroke. They are
both strong swimmers. He ducks under water, watches her
naked body as it seeks to undulate in the motion of the sea.
Even in the cold of the water, his penis is stiffening and rising.
He feels humbled by the loveliness of her body, wonders what
a clumsy man can ever have to offer that will tempt a woman.
Yet they are tempted, all the time. They marry men, bear their
children, cook their meals, laugh at them behind their backs.*

*'Men are great when they're not on their knees,' his mother
and her friends would cackle to each other in the kitchen while
their husbands were down at O'Brien's, rounding off the day
with a pint or two. He had thought, as a child, that she meant
at prayer, and had puzzled long and hard over the remark.*

'Enough,' she says, after a while. 'I'm getting cold.'

*He runs out of the sea ahead of her so she will not see his
arousal, picks up the blanket and holds it against himself.*

*'Let me have a bit of that.' She joins him panting on the
shore. 'I'm dripping, you selfish bugger.' She makes a playful
grab at the blanket. Somehow it slips through his cold fingers*

and she snatches it clean away. She stares. This she has not seen.

'I'll share it with you.' He pulls the blanket round them both and they sit warming together on the deserted beach. His arm is round her, his thighs pressed up against hers, his penis still huge and erect like a totem between them. She begins to laugh.

'Does it often do that?'

'Often,' he admits. 'When I wake up in the morning. When I think of you. Or for no reason at all.'

'Can I touch it?' she asks, greatly daring.

'Please.'

Her fingers brush against the top. It twitches. She runs one index finger down the side, following a purple vein. 'It's not rough,' she says, 'not like you'd think. Almost like silk.'

'Damn!' he says, as a stream of white, opaque liquid spurts out and forms a congealing pool on the blanket. 'Damn!' A second spurt. 'Damn!'

She laughs. She knows that this was not meant to happen, that it was too soon, much too soon. The totem wilts, grows small and curls shyly into his thigh. But at Con's age, it will not be long before it rises again.

Two

The next morning, she is woken at seven and must give proof – verbal, or with the traditional shake of the leg – that she is still alive. The warder comes round again at half past and yells at her through the door to get out of bed although she is already up and dressed. Her cell is not unlocked until eight. She then has a few minutes to empty her potty in the open sluice on the landing and wash if she can. Hers is one of the last doors to be opened, so by the time she gets to the washroom, all the sinks are taken.

At eight-fifteen a loudspeaker crackles into life: 'Food's outside', and the gates are opened and the food brought in. The women pour downstairs to the ground-floor eating area and are ticked off on a list. Maire is told that the Chief Officer will see her straight after.

At breakfast she is given an egg-cup, three-quarters full of sugar. That is her ration for the day. Some days it will be full, some days half full; it depends who the officer in charge of breakfast is. It's Monday, so there's a strip of cold, reasty streaky as well as porridge.

Maire is at the back of the breakfast queue as she has not yet learnt to pummel and bicker her way to the front. There is one space left at a table near the door, and she slips silently into the chair, hoping that no one will notice her. Silence drops on the table like a snowfall. The other women stare at her without disguise – not friendly, not hostile. Newcomers are rare on this block.

One says, 'You'll need to keep a close eye on that,' nodding at the egg cup, 'or they'll have it off you.' She clears her tray away and leaves.

Someone is shouting, 'Line up for work.'

Soon only Maire and a tall, heavy black woman remain at the table. The woman is older than most of the others – perhaps forty. She wears her hair long in a disorderly tangle round her face. There is a faint silvery scar on one of her cheeks, running down almost into the corner of her mouth. Her eyes are wide and black, her pupils a pinprick as she watches Maire in the glaring neon of the dining area. She is dressed all in denim: jeans, shirt, jacket. The jacket has had its studs pulled off; they are not allowed.

Maire eats her food as fast as she can, hardly pausing to chew, just wanting to get the ordeal over. There is an unpleasant smell in the room, like open latrines, and she almost gags once as she shovels food in too quickly. The porridge is lukewarm but she has tasted worse. The tea is adequate.

The black woman is smoking and drinking strong sweet tea and still watching. Maire looks up and gives her a faint smile. She goes to clear her tray away but the woman reaches across the table and takes her wrist.

'You don't use any of your sugar.' Her voice is slightly husky and she has a Caribbean accent with Birmingham overtones.

'I don't take it in tea,' Maire answers.

'You a skinny little thing,' the woman says, 'why don't you give me your sugar ration. Then we be friends and I take care of you. Otherwise . . .' She gives Maire's wrist a little twist which ought to be painful, but Maire used to play at burning-bracelets with her brothers and she doesn't flinch '. . . if you don't have someone take care of you, people pick on you.'

Maire shrugs, sliding her small hand deftly free from the other woman's ham fist. 'Have it. I don't want it.' She pushes the egg cup across the table.

The woman looks at her with something like irritation. 'You new to all this, honey?' Maire nods. 'What you in for?' Maire tells her as briefly as possible and the woman gives a low whistle.

'Hard case. Still, we all hard cases here. We mostly lifers here in Durham. Me, I kill me old man. You know? With a knife.' She begins to laugh very quietly so the warders won't hear her; it's not wise to let them think you're enjoying yourself. 'Got off with manslaughter, though. Good brief. Pretty lucky, huh? You think so? They give me life sentence all the same.

They send me to H Wing all the same. They say I hard to control. You see,' she adds simply, her voice giving the word a capital letter, 'I get these Rages.'

Maire can think of no answer to this, since condolences do not seem to be required, and just waits.

'You don't know you born, or what?' the big woman goes on. 'It no fun bullying someone, won't play ball. You don't just give me your sugar like that. You don't want it, you swop it for two, maybe three, roll-ups.'

Maire looks puzzled and the woman gives an exclamation of disgust. 'Cigarettes, greenhorn. Home-made ciggies.'

'I don't smoke either.' And there is nothing else she wants; or nothing she can get in exchange for a few spoonfuls of sugar.

'You know something?' the black woman says. 'You really do need someone take care of you. You talk funny. You foreign? Lots of foreigners here. Don't speak English, half of them. Where you from?'

'Donegal.' The woman screws up her face, has evidently never heard of it. 'Ireland.'

'What your name, honey?'

Maire tells her. She repeats it uncertainly, drawing out the word into a Caribbean phrase. 'More-Ra? What the hell sort of name is that?' She doesn't wait for an answer. 'I think I like you, More-Ra. You can call me Billy.'

Another woman comes unsteadily to the table to join them although she has no food and does not sit down. She is a pretty, though faded, blonde in her late thirties, dressed in a very feminine way with a frilly blouse, high-heeled shoes and lots of blue eye shadow. She looks at Maire with hostility.

'I thought you going to report sick, Gloria,' Billy says.

'Oh, I'm sorry,' Maire says. 'Are you ill?'

'She always ill.' Billy speaks roughly. 'Half the women here ill every day. You be ill soon. This sick place. This is Gloria. Gloria, this is . . . Irish. New kid.'

'Hello, Iris,' Gloria says grudgingly. Maire does not bother to correct her; she has lost her identity.

'You too late for breakfast, Gloria.'

Gloria shudders and asks how she can eat when she's ill and with that bloody awful smell everywhere. Maire ventures to ask what the smell is and is told that the punishment cell is right next to the dining area and that inmates shut in there for days frequently soil the walls with their own shit. She wishes she hadn't asked.

'Gloria just doing bed and breakfast here,' Billy says.

'What?' Maire doesn't understand.

'She means I'm only doing three years,' Gloria translates, 'for arson. Weren't much. I just like lighting fires.'

'Like I say, bed and breakfast.'

Maire wonders if Gloria has Rages too but Billy says, 'They send her here 'cause she like to cut up – draw attention to herself.'

There is another yell of 'Line up for work', followed swiftly by an 'Are you fucking deaf, Gibson', directed straight at Billy who replies, 'What you say, Miss?' cupping her hand to her ear, but gets up, taking Maire's sugar with her.

'We talk later. By the way, honey . . .' She pauses and points at Maire's empty plate. 'I wouldn't eat that stuff if I was you. Don't you hear that yell, "Grub's up"? The men, they make the food. They piss in it, spit in it. Jerk off in it. Tell them you vegetarian, gotta have boiled eggs; they can't mess with those. Come on, Gloria.'

Maire stares at her empty plate in horror, then shrugs it off. It tasted all right. Billy is just trying to frighten her.

Someone is bellowing her name – just her surname – which echoes up the full four floors of the prison and back down again. She jumps to her feet and tries to find the source of the shout.

The Chief Officer rules H Wing and even the Governor doesn't interfere with her decisions. Strangely, she is not especially rough with Maire that first morning. She knows who the new prisoner is and what she has done, but O'Neill stands before her meek, defeated, vulnerable – no threat to the system in the eyes of a woman who has grappled with the likes of Myra Hindley. She has met many new lifers, sees that O'Neill is still in shock. She will come to terms with things; eventually, after a few months, when she realises how slowly time is passing, how many years there are left to do, there will be a crisis.

'You've got to get your mind into H Wing,' she tells Maire,

'learn to adjust. This is a Category-A prison and we're a lot tougher here than they are at Holloway. There's an easy way and there's a hard way, so take my advice and just do your sentence and don't give any trouble. In a way, it's up to you how long you spend here before you get moved on.'

She asks if Maire has any questions or anything she wants to say. Maire says nervously that she is a vegetarian and gets a wry, 'What? Another one? I'll make a note of it.'

Maire has been classed Labour 1 – fit for any work. The Chief Officer tells her that she can wash up the breakfast things this morning after which she will be on cleaning work for the first few weeks. Then she will probably be moved to the workroom making overalls for soldiers. Education must be done in her own time unless she is illiterate. She refused her reception letter; is she illiterate? She need not be ashamed to admit it.

Maire is not illiterate and the interview ends. As she leaves the Chief Officer adds, 'A friendly warning, O'Neill. Be careful who you associate with. Billy Gibson and her girlfriend are trouble.'

In fact the breakfast things have already been washed and Maire spends the rest of the morning on her hands and knees scrubbing the floor of the wing with a green pot-scourer and a bar of soap to the tinny jangle of Radio 2.

Later that morning, Miss Shadwell distributes the post. Maire, to her astonishment, is handed three letters forwarded from Holloway. The envelopes have been torn open and the contents read.

'What are these?' she asks stupidly.

'Proposals of marriage.' Miss Shadwell hoots with laughter. 'Or something along those lines. One from a man who seems to be more or less illiterate, one written in crayon and one from a clerical assistant in the DTI living in Camberwell. He's the most explicit. Your sort always get them.'

For a moment Maire thinks this is some sort of sick joke then it dawns on her that the warder is serious. She really is receiving letters from men sexually excited by the newspaper reports of her crimes.

'Aren't you going to read them?' Miss Shadwell asks. 'The

clerical assistant has quite a vivid imagination. Got me quite hot.'

Maire tears the envelopes, with their letters still inside, into small pieces. Her hands are dirty; she goes to wash them.

Then there is exercise – one hour in the concrete yard without grass or trees, which is the only daylight Maire will see for the next two years. Male officers with guard dogs patrol beyond the fence and the ever-present cameras watch and watch.

There are two benches only and there is a scramble for them; Maire does not attempt to sit but sees that Billy is holding court on one with Gloria – who has apparently decided against reporting sick – nuzzled up to her. It is a damp March day although not actually raining and a cold wind is blowing from the North Sea, so Maire prefers to keep on the move. No one speaks to her and she speaks to no one.

After about ten minutes, she is startled by a sudden outburst of shouting from windows in the surrounding buildings. She has not yet got her bearings but realises at last that the yard is overlooked by a men's wing.

'Bitches!' yells a Glaswegian roar.

'Whores! Lezzies!' Other voices join the chorus.

'Murdering cunts!'

This, she will learn, is the tune to which they must take their daily dose of fresh air – weather permitting. The midday meal is next, then back to work. She is told to scrub the same bit of floor again, which she does without comment.

After dinner there is association, just as at Holloway, for an hour or two. She has noticed now that very little food is actually consumed at mealtimes and that most of the women are nibbling biscuits, crispbreads and jam bought from the canteen with their wages. She has no wages yet and no one shares in prison.

H wing holds thirty-six women currently and they split up into natural tribes. There are about a dozen women who don't speak much English and they form small, mutually incomprehensible cliques or sit alone if they are the sole representative of their linguistic group. Others read or chat. Nearly all of them are puffing at home-made cigarettes and the smoke stays on the still air.

Billy and her entourage are playing cards, childish games like

Snap and Happy Families, and Maire goes and sits on the edge of this circle. Billy is losing and the game soon breaks up as a result.

She begins to introduce people – Cilla and Pam and Kate and Jill and Lizzie and Brenda. Gloria sits by her, less hostile now, but probing. She asks who is waiting for Iris outside: husband, boyfriend, children, parents? Maire skirts the question but Gloria doesn't notice and begins to talk about her two young sons who live with her mother in Uxbridge.

'Oh!' Maire says. 'I thought . . .'

Gloria, it turns out, had been living with a man until her last conviction. She is a 'kickster' – a woman who turns lesbian only when she is in prison and there is no alternative. She tells Maire simply that she needs someone to love and looks at her hard and Maire gets the message that she is being given an unnecessary warning to keep off the grass.

'He buggered off when I got sent here,' Gloria continues. 'Left the kids with our Mum. Lucky she thinks the world of them.'

'Do you . . . are you allowed to see them?' Maire asks. Gloria says that they come twice a year – it's all the DHSS will pay for. Mum writes, sends pictures. It isn't easy.

A television plays in the corner but only the non-English-speakers, who cannot understand, are huddled in front of it, watching the pictures. There are the remnants of three tabloid newspapers on the table.

The women are subdued on Mondays – it is a long time until visiting day. To Maire, who expects no visitors, it makes no difference. She is relieved when the time comes to collect her water for the night and be locked in her cell, achieving privacy, if not peace.

Three

Six, eight, ten weeks pass; then fifteen, then twenty. If the judge's recommendation is to be followed, Maire will serve over 1000 weeks, but she does not let herself think about that; she tries to survive one day at a time. She is kept locked in her cell for twelve hours overnight. She still has the radio which Trish brought her at Holloway. She plays it all night, very quietly so that no one else can eavesdrop on her listening. Late, when Radio 4 closes down for the night, she returns to the World Service. Reception is poor but she takes comfort from knowing that she is sharing these broadcasts with people thousands of miles from this place. The early-morning news in French and German reminds her that there is a world outside these walls.

Her days are spent stitching in the workroom where she makes dungarees, hats, bags, belts for NATO and American soldiers. It is piecework and if she is to earn her paltry £2.50 wages a week, there can be no slacking. She prefers it to scrubbing at first, but soon finds her hands turn blue from the dye of the coarse denim material instead of red from constant immersion. Even so, there is an element of camaraderie in the sewing room and talking is tolerated so long as the buzz does not rise above a certain level.

In a way, it is a new education for her. She had been aware, vaguely, of how sheltered her upbringing in Donegal had been. The family had been large and averagely poor and the children left to scramble themselves up as best they could, but there had always been enough love to go round and twice as many hugs as slaps round the legs. Then, during the years in High Wycombe, she had closed herself off from the world, closeted herself away with Roisin. Now her eyes and ears are opened to new ways of life.

She listens with shocked incredulity as Pam talks matter-of-factly of being raped by her father when she was six. Pam is serving a life sentence for abetting the murder of her own toddler at the hands of a paedophile. At her last prison she had been on Rule 43 – the regime designed to protect sex offenders from the retribution of their peers. Since coming to Durham, where surveillance is constant, she has ventured out – been, to some extent, accepted. She indulges often in these attempts to – if not justify – explain. The others have heard it all before.

She is a short woman and almost as wide as she is tall, constantly bloated with severe water retention which no one will diagnose or treat. She is uneducated, even a little simple-minded. Her words are distorted, slurred partly by heavy medication and partly by a full set of false teeth which she has had since she was fourteen and which do not fit properly and probably never did.

Maire wonders at times during the course of her narration if she is hearing correctly.

'I thought it might not be right,' she is saying in her even, unexcitable Scottish voice. 'Something inside me said that a little babby's body wasn't made to be used that way by men. But how could I be sure? It was the way I was used myself since the earliest I can remember. I told myself: perhaps all babbies get used that way and it's only that folk don't talk about it.'

The story unfolds in its monotonous horror; Maire listens as though hypnotised. She feels sick, angry and sick. Her anger is not directed at Pam but at Pam's father, her brothers who helped, her mother who stood by and watched. Kate, a forthright Barbadian, tells Pam brusquely to put a sock in it as she's making them all want to puke. Maire literally wants to puke. She gets up and begins to move in the direction of the lavatory.

'And where do you think you're going, O'Neill?' Miss Shadwell is on her feet at once.

Maire mumbles, 'Toilet, miss.'

'Ryman is in there. Sit down. I'll put your name on my list.'

For, although there are three lavatories in the block, only

one woman may go at a time and she must put her hand up like a kid in school and get permission.

'But, miss . . .' Maire puts her hand to her mouth. She had been so hungry at lunchtime that she had eaten some soup; there had been tough, gristly strands of meat in it like thread-worms. She can taste it coming back again.

'Sit. Down.'

Miss Shadwell's voice is getting dangerous and Maire is receiving warning looks from several sources. It is disobey or be sick on the floor. She flees from the room, retching, and reaches an empty cubicle just in time.

'Here . . .' Cilla looks over the door. Every cubicle has a half-door only and no real privacy is possible. 'I was on the list, Iris.'

'Ryman!' Miss Shadwell is at the door.

'I was on the list, miss,' Cilla protests. 'I never told her to come in here with me.'

'Get back to your work since you've obviously finished.' Cilla obeys, relieved to escape punishment. 'O'Neill!'

Maire comes out of the cubicle, wiping her mouth, breathing hard. She takes a long draft of water from the nearest tap to clear the taste of the vomit, gargles and spits it out again, splashes some water on her hot cheeks.

'I ate something which upset me, miss,' she explains meekly. 'I didn't want to be sick in the workroom.'

'Rest in cell,' the officer says. Maire's heart sinks. She knows this means she will be locked up until tomorrow morning at the earliest and will lose a whole day's pay.

'I feel better now, miss.'

'See the Chief Officer in the morning,' Miss Shadwell continues.

She marches Maire back to her cell, posts up a card marked 'RIC' on the door, and locks her in.

They drive home late in Con's father's van, feeling the chill now. The blanket has been 'lost' in a cleft of rock and will be missed. There will be a row but damning evidence must be concealed.

Maire sits in silence in the passenger seat. There is a soreness between her legs as if something has been torn – as, of course, it has. There was, luckily, no blood. She is disappointed and senses that he is too. So that was it, the thing that she and Caitlin had discussed and conjectured about through so many giggling hours. She had never imagined that she would beat Caitlin to it. How is she to tell her what a let-down it was? Best to keep silent.

It had started off well, with him stroking her, kissing her, nibbling her ears – all the things he had done so many times. Nuzzling her breasts, which was a new but pleasant sensation. Then, too precipitately, the pushing apart of her legs, his stifling weight on her, 'Please, Maire! Please let me!' That rug of chest hair almost choking her, the reality of that tearing feeling which made her clench her teeth in pain, a moment of panic, and then it was all over again with another 'Damn!' He had apologised: she was too lovely, he was too inexperienced, he would last longer next time. But she had been secretly thankful.

He mumbles something she can't hear and she asks him to repeat it. He will borrow the van again next weekend, he says, nip over the border into the North, find the nearest chemist's, buy something. Until then, they must just be careful. He adds that he loves her. He fumbles, removes from the little finger of his left hand a narrow silver ring and gives it to her as a token. It is slightly too big even for the middle finger of her right hand and she can twist it freely.

She realises that she is committed now. That this thing, once started, must be done again and again. She supposes she will get used to it. She has heard old matrons tell new brides, 'Stop belly-aching, girl, you'll get used to it. We had to.'

Besides, she loves him. She felt a great tenderness for him, holding him in her arms on the beach, sensing him half proud of his conquest, half vulnerable in his ineptitude. When he asked if she had enjoyed it she had, of course, reassured him. There are plenty of places they can go to be alone and she will soon get used to it. They will be careful.

Not careful enough.

Maire sees the Chief Officer the next morning and is fined an additional day's pay and put back to scrubbing floors for two weeks.

*

The weather turns bad at the end of March: late snow falls and the winds are cruel. Exercise is cancelled almost every day and the hour allotted for it is spent locked up. Maire's normally pale skin begins to take on a greyish, almost transparent cast; but at least she is spared the verbal abuse from the men's wing.

Like the other women, she eats little of the food provided – mainly things that cannot be tampered with such as eggs and sticky slices of white bread which she toasts herself. She has risked nothing cooked since the disaster with the soup. Mostly she survives on crispbreads, bought from the canteen with her wages, which she covers with peanut butter rather than the more popular jam, since she knows this is healthier. This extra food and the precious batteries for her radio take up all her money. She has no one outside, as most of the others do, to send her extra.

Quarrels break out occasionally: petty jealousies are common. But since they are watched continuously, sudden out-bursts of temper – hair-pulling, scratching – are swiftly and harshly dealt with.

Maire resists all overtures of particular friendship from other women, preferring to stick with Billy who is already 'married' to Gloria and who has shown no sign yet of one of her Rages. She does not object to lesbian affairs by other women, although she had barely known such things existed before being sent to prison, but the thought of anyone trying to embrace her own skinny body sends shudders through her. Unlike Gloria, the last thing she wants is someone to love; she has learnt that those you love are always taken from you.

In fact physical contact, other than a little kissing and strok-ing, is rare. Lesbianism is not illegal; it is not even against prison regulations, it is just not allowed. Inmates may not be in each other's cells except with the door wide open. Further-more the women are lethargic, many of them heavily drugged with tranquillisers by day and sleeping-pills by night. The cold of the wing dampens their spirits.

She has learnt to swear, a little. There are times, mostly lying in bed on sleepless nights, with nothing but sport or business news on the World Service, when it is a necessary outlet. She has learnt too the importance of not appearing weak: it is not only the other prisoners who would despise her for it, but the warders too.

Boredom, as usual, is the main enemy, boredom and futility. At weekends the women do not go to the workroom but extra cleaning is done and the same floors scrubbed that have been scrubbed from Monday to Friday. Each Saturday a small proportion of the women are allowed visits. On Sunday, they sometimes get a film show, but the films are passed on from the men's wings, chosen by the men, and are pornographic or violent or both.

The prison officers are also bored. They too spend a large part of their lives in this submarine-like atmosphere and are fond of saying that they are serving a sentence just as much as the inmates and with less justification. To relieve the monotony they carry out a full cell and body search every ten days or so. Miss Shadwell is the most zealous over these. She loves to read the women's personal letters even though they have already been censored on arrival, pass rude comments about the people in their photographs.

Maire is surprised the first time she is taken away from her work for one of these. She has had no opportunity to obtain anything illicit to secrete in her cell or on her person. She cannot see the point. The other women groan: this means they won't be able to fulfil their quota in the workroom today and will lose pay. She is locked in her cell like all the other women and left to wait her turn. She can hear Miss Shadwell's voice two cells away along the corridor.

'Is that your husband, Brody? What an ugly git. A jailbird if ever I saw one. Runs in the family, doesn't it? Out at the moment, isn't he? That won't last long. I notice he never comes to see you when he's out, got another little bird keeping his bed warm, I'll bet.

'Are these your kids, Greenbaum? Which one's the mongol? They all look thick to me.'

The butts of her ill-humour are frequently reduced to tears, which is the object of the exercise.

Then it is Maire's turn and she is told to strip. Her pockets are checked and even the seams and linings of the garments are tugged and rubbed before she is allowed to dress again. Miss Shadwell eyes her empty pinboard with disappointment, nor are there any letters on the table for her to read aloud, mocking the poor spelling and handwriting. Later, when Maire can bear to put up her pictures of Roisin, she always takes them down again when a search is due.

Everything is tipped from her furniture: clothes are examined and cast to the floor; books are bent back until the spines crack and shaken until at least one page comes loose and floats across the room. The bed is stripped even to the mattress cover and pillow case.

'All right,' Miss Shadwell says, when she has left the room looking like a jumble sale after all the good stuff has been bought. Maire starts to pick her things up from the floor but is shouted at.

'You do that in your own time, O'Neill, not ours. Get back to work.'

'That Shagwell,' Billy mutters to Maire as they file back to work, 'she tear my good blouse right down the back seam — like it wide enough to hide anything!'

Four

Maire understands soon that she was born to this — that it is her destiny. To survive in prison you have either to be one of the mob or entirely other: she is both. The middle one of seven children, she learnt early how not to stick out in the crowd and how to retire inside when she must. Of small stature, she learnt to wound, when she had to, with her tongue.

The middle one, she is used to a hierarchy, a pecking-order. She knows how to protect the weak, how to mollify the strong. She learnt how to make her eldest brother Matthew laugh so he would take her with him on his boy's games into the hills and birds' nests and fishing streams of Donegal. She was the sherpa, carried the bags with the soda bread and the strong cheese and the pickle, and the lemonade which dribbled into her pockets.

Matthew and Connor were best friends and Matthew was the first person apart from Con that she told about the baby. Matthew didn't say a word but went straight off and beat Con up. Neither of them ever spoke of it but Con, who was by far the larger man, appeared next day with a cut lip and a broken finger. That was an end of it and their friendship survived.

Matthew gave her twenty pounds he'd saved up towards a new shotgun and that helped pay her fare to Liverpool two months later, before their mother noticed the absence of used sanitary towels, before Dervla started her chant of 'I'll tell, I'll tell'.

She had not suggested that Con come with her. His palpable fear when she had first told him the news had separated them more surely than any departure of hers.

None of her family had made contact at the time of her trial.

Not content with disgracing them in the traditional way, she had thought up new ways to shame them. They believed, as they always had, what they read in the papers, what they heard on the RTE news. Her mother crossed herself, Dervla was glad, Matthew doubted but was silent; the younger ones had all but forgotten her in the excitement of their own burgeoning lives. Her father would not let the matter be mentioned in his hearing and sorrowed in O'Brien's bar.

Connor did not write.

To be fair to Connor, he had not heard of her arrest until the case came to trial in the February of 1979; he had missed the original newspaper reports, being on holiday in Ibiza that August. By that time he had been married for two years with a child and another on the way and a wife who had always been jealous of Maire O'Neill – could it be? Yes, it is, Caitlin Sweeney of the deranged discus – and who watches his every move.

Not to act, as ever, was the easier and safer way.

She had learnt how to concentrate on her homework at the kitchen table while the baby screamed and Dervla – The Pretty One – clashed the last of the dishes in resentment that Maire – The Brainy One – wasn't made to help. She had memorised French irregular verbs and the principal battles of the American Civil War while Michael and Sean watched *The Virginian* on TV, firing off imaginary six-guns at them all and blowing into their smoking fingers. It had been hard, especially, to ignore Dervla, who was what was known in the local parlance as a 'Notice Box', someone constantly drawing attention to themselves.

So Maire's training has been thorough and now she reads during the brief periods of association as the other women play at cards or dominoes or arguing. If she has made a friend it is, against the Chief Officer's advice, Billy.

Maire is a good listener – another legacy of a large family who all talk at once – and often Billy will not let her read but chooses her as her confidante. If Gloria is being tiresome and neurotic, whining in her little-girl voice, Billy prefers more sensible conversation. Sometimes when Gloria is like this she hits her to shut her up, shrugging off her punishment.

Maire puts her book away readily enough and listens

to Billy's lullaby voice. As the weeks pass, she hears all her story.

Billy's life sentence for manslaughter is only the latest in a string of sentences dating back to youth custody at fourteen.

'Okay, I used to push drugs,' she tells Maire. 'I take them myself – fifteen, twenty years back.' She laughs her rich, throaty laugh and a warder frowns in their direction. 'I come to prison them days to get clean. Like six months at a health farm only it don't cost you nothing. See?'

Some health farm, Maire thinks, as Billy lets out a bronchitic wheeze. Where's the swimming-pool, the sauna, the beautiful acres of garden, the hot, clean towels?

'Get knocked up every time I come out. Three kids by the time I twenty. Have to keep them somehow, right?'

'What about your husband?' Maire asks. She has heard the story many times before but she knows when to feed in the right questions and Billy gives another happy, rumbling laugh at her naïvety.

'Where I come from, what they call my culture . . .' she strings the word out – kullchewer '. . . women do work and men do lay home all day and drink beer and rum, and smoke.' She shrugs, unresentful. 'Besides, the first two kids not even his.

'Then I get bored with all that,' she goes on, 'try to keep out of trouble. Got the kids out of care, did a bit of work even, legit: working the petrol pumps, pubs. Cash in hand, of course, how I afford to pay them taxes?'

At some time in the evening, she will always revert to the fatal stab to her drunken husband.

'He come home, in mean mood. Very mean. He very big man. Start hitting me about till I think I better say goodbye to sweet life. We in the kitchen. I grab at drawer, get knife, slash out with it. Next thing I know, he stone dead.'

'And they gave you life for that?' Maire asks. 'For killing him in self-defence?'

'You right, Irish,' she tells her, 'that was a bad idea. I knew that bastard find a way of ruining my life one day. I out for six years before that happen, clean as whistle.'

She has been in Durham since the wing was opened four

years earlier. She says it's the worst prison in the whole system and most women stay here only two years, three at most, but they make her stay because she gets into trouble periodically.

'Baaaaad trouble.' She rolls her eyes. 'Can't help it. Something go snap inside me and I have one of my Rages. You be good, More-Ra honey. Don't get no Rages. Get out of this place fast as you can. Styal better, even Holloway better. Hell better, most like.' She giggles. 'That there Mr Devil: he frightened of Miss Shagwell.'

'Still, though . . .' She looks at Maire thoughtfully. 'You don't must be too meek – too much "Yes, miss; no, miss" – that way they think they won. One day you gotta turn round and say, "Fuck you, miss".'

'Oh, I couldn't.'

'Gotta do it. One day. Or you go under.'

After a few weeks, Maire plucks up the courage to ask timidly if Billy has ever sought treatment for her Rages.

'Sure,' she says cheerfully. 'They promise me last time that I go to Rampton next time.'

Billy is forty-three, Maire learns, and a grandmother five times over. She is almost illiterate, and Maire reads and writes her letters for her – is glad to, having none of her own.

'That Gloria,' she says, 'she write my letters before you come but she don't spell good, don't explain things good. I can tell. Don't ask me how I know, I can tell. You, you been to school, done good. You can spell, I can tell, and see how neat you write like a little fairy flying across the paper.'

For weeks Maire avoids questions about her own life and for weeks Billy is content to hold the stage herself. But finally Billy begins to delve and probe and quickly winkles out the truth. Then, once the floodgates are opened, lets her talk for hours about her child. It is for her that Maire fetches out the photographs, long tucked away in the bottom of her bag.

'Luvverley girl,' Billy says. 'Handful, I bet?' Maire nods. 'Look just like you – like she not have a father. Want to tell me about her father?'

'No.'

'Later maybe?'

'Maybe.'

She starts to remember. She has been shutting Roisin out of

her mind and heart for the sake of her sanity, and it has been killing her slowly. Now she starts to open her heart again.

'Every year I tried to save a little bit, to take her on holiday, to take her to Ireland; not home to Donegal but somewhere else on the west coast: Galway, perhaps, or Connemara. But every year the prices went up: food, her clothes, the rent, and I could never quite manage it. We never had that holiday together and now we never will.'

Maire finds she can bear to look at the pictures now, even smile at the child's happy, cheeky face, and puts them up on her noticeboard.

That night, for the first time, she switches off her radio, allows herself to be alone with her memories, cries herself to sleep. In the morning, she feels less like a zombie – less like a dead woman – than she has at any time since her arrest.

Sometimes they just sit in silence and Billy strokes Maire's hand or her hair and Maire feels oddly comforted by the platonic contact. Gloria glares at these moments but, since she knows the relationship is not carnal, confines herself to the odd jealous scene which will either amuse Billy or make her angry – there's no telling which and Gloria does not much mind so long as she gets her lover's attention.

'It been quiet here late, Irish,' Billy ruminates one evening in late June. 'Too quiet. Trouble coming.'

Five

She is right: there is a row the next day – the first in a series of rows escalating to tragedy.

Gloria is wearing perfume at breakfast. It is cheap floral stuff but unmistakably perfume. Perfume is not allowed. As it happens, Maire can see the logic of this: with three dozen women all wearing a different scent, the stale air would be more unbearable than it is. Mostly the women smell faintly of sweat – with baths available only weekly and just three sets of clothes per woman, an odour of unwashed bodies is inevitable.

Today, everybody is sniffing the air and asking what it is that smells like the worst kind of air-freshener.

Gloria is hauled before the Chief Officer and, crumpling at once under pressure, admits that the perfume is a gift from Billy. Her room is searched and the bottle confiscated and smashed into the sluice. She gets five days' loss of remission and a fine and leaves the office in tears.

Billy is next in.

'All right, Gibson, where did the perfume come from?'

'I dunno, miss. I never see it before.'

'Don't play dumb with me. You must have had it brought in on your last visit.'

'I searched after, miss, like always.'

'Not thoroughly enough apparently. Let me see . . .' she consults her records '. . . last Saturday – that was your daughter, Corinne.'

'Corinne good girl, miss, don't smuggle nothing. Keep out of trouble.' Billy adopts her bovine look, which can always be relied upon to infuriate the Chief Officer.

'Very well,' she snaps, 'no visits for a month, since you can't be trusted . . .'

'Not in here to be trusted, miss.'

'Don't interrupt me! I'm revoking your visiting privileges for one month and fining you a week's wages.'

'Miss. Thank you, miss.'

'Now get back to work.'

Billy marches out of the office, straight into the workroom.

'You're late, Gibson,' Miss Shadwell says, 'take your seat and get on with . . .'

Billy ignores her and walks straight past her own seat to where Gloria is sitting near the back of the room, intent on a blue peaked cap she is making. She doesn't look up but cowers in her seat like a dog about to be whipped. Maire half rises to her feet, then realises the futility of it and sinks down again. Billy will not be deterred from self-destruction.

She clips Gloria hard across the face with the back of her hand, leaving a white oval mark on her heavy blusher. Gloria begins to whimper. Miss Shadwell and the other prison officer restrain Billy with difficulty and only after they have summoned a male warder to their aid.

'What good it do you to get me punished too?' Billy yells at Gloria as they bundle her out. 'Another time you keep your ugly mouth shut, say you don't know where it come from. And what you want to wear it in public for, anyway, stupid slag?'

The workroom is left momentarily unsupervised and work ceases at once and heated conversation flares up instead, until Miss Shadwell returns and extinguishes it. She forbids all talking for the rest of the day. The women are on edge now, excited.

Billy spends the next five days in the punishment cell where she shouts a great deal in the night and sings lewd songs. Gloria is distraught.

'I wore it for her,' she whimpers to Maire. 'To smell nice for her, Iris, since she gave it to me.'

Maire has never been in the punishment cell. Gloria explains that there is nothing there but a mattress, which is taken out during the day, and a cardboard potty. Billy's clothes are taken from her and she wears nothing but a strip dress – made of a virtually untearable fabric – instead.

When Billy gets out there is a noisy reconciliation.

'You going the right way about giving me one of my Rages, though,' Billy tells her.

The descent into Rage is gradual, the individual stages barely discernible.

Billy never quite reverts to her pre-perfume placidity. She still sits with Maire in the evenings, tells her the same stories, but her voice has lost its soporific lilt and become hard and emphatic. Maire tries to distract her with tales of growing up in rural Ireland, with legends and fairy stories, but she will be pacified for no more than a few minutes at a time.

'Nice,' she says when Maire is halfway through her tale. 'You tell stories nice,' and pats her hand to stop her.

She complains, as do all the older inmates, about the noise as the younger girls – little more than puppies, some of them – take out their frustrations in a constant diet of pop music and loud, mindless bickering.

'Shut the fuck up!' Billy screeches at them, time and again. 'Turn that music down. I don't hear myself think.' Then the cacophony subsides for a few minutes.

The acoustics of H Wing take sound and magnify it, repeat it, reverberate it.

'There a man once,' she tells Maire one night, 'say stone walls and bars not make a prison.'

'Richard Lovelace,' Maire replies. '"Stone walls do not a prison make, nor iron bars a cage".'

Her deep voice fills the mean room. 'He lie.'

Her affair with Gloria is becoming more physical – both in caresses and blows. Maire refuses to keep guard on Billy's cell door while they are inside together and earns her contempt for several days as a result. The mood swings follow no pattern. Today, Maire is the only friend she has left; tomorrow, even she is her enemy.

Next she has one of her wild days when she gets it into her head to tattoo Gloria with some broken glass she has secreted and some blue ink. She goes to Gloria's room during association, dragging Maire with her, and produces these spoils from her capacious pockets.

Gloria rolls up her left sleeve as instructed, her arm trembling slightly, and submits herself. Billy tells her it is a test of love. She starts to scratch a heart on her upper arm, enclosing her vaccination scar, all red and raw and ugly.

Maire watches, fascinated and appalled – grinding her teeth together in empathic pain.

Billy offers to tattoo Maire as well, and Maire is tempted to accept. This desecration of her body – the pain, the risk of disease – will show the authorities, perhaps, in a way that words cannot, how much she cares.

Gloria is whimpering now as the blood runs and the ink mingles with it and gets into the wound and stings. She begins to cry and moan and Billy gives an exclamation of disgust and walks abruptly away, losing interest. A few minutes later, Gloria runs whining to a warder, wanting first aid. The wound turns septic.

This is Maire's first experience of a full wing-search. It takes the whole day. She is locked in her cell while men with dogs search the toilets, showers, landings. Then she and everything – even the furniture, except for the bed which would have to be dismantled to fit through the door – are bundled out on to the landing and the dogs invade the cells. Maire is not afraid of dogs, having grown up in farming country, but she is afraid of these dogs.

The cells are turned upside down until the glass and ink are found in Brenda's closet. Brenda – despite her plausible protestations of ignorance – is punished.

Billy spends a week in the punishment cell this time. The Chief Officer is grim and determined. Things have been quiet for several months and Gibson is not going to cause trouble. She will nip this madness in the bud. If it comes to a trial of strength between herself and Gibson, she will crush Billy like a beetle.

The day after she gets out, Gloria – now recovered from her septicaemia and with only a scar and a tender patch on her arm to remind her – appears at breakfast with a swollen face and bleeding mouth. She cannot eat all that day and says she fell out of bed.

'She don't mind,' Billy tells Maire when she remonstrates with her. 'I tell you, she always cutting up. Likes it.'

*

She does all the right things in Liverpool: registers with a doctor for ante-natal care, finds a cheap, but clean, bedsit. The nurses call her Mrs O'Neill, although the sexual revolution is in full swing in England and she is by no means the only single mother at the clinic, not even the youngest. It irritates her slightly that they are determined not to recognise her manless status.

She finds work as a waitress in a greasy-spoon café, even though she has morning sickness for the first two months she is there and the smell of frying often makes her heave. When the sickness begins to abate she starts to show, and the manageress sacks her. Pregnant women are not good for business. She signs on the dole.

She spends the next four months walking the streets of the city by day to occupy and stimulate herself. It is still a time of full employment and hopes for the future and the squares and byways are bustling.

Occasionally she treats herself to a ride on the Birkenhead ferry, but mostly she stays away from the docks in case she sees anyone she knows stepping off the Dublin boat – perhaps her father or Matthew or even Con come to search for her and bring her back. But if any of them come looking, she never hears of it.

She may save to buy a seat at the very back of the Playhouse or the Everyman. She spends hours at the Walker Art Gallery. She buys loose clothes from Oxfam as her old ones cease to button over her swelling front.

She misses the meals at the café; lardy though they were, they were filling and, best of all, free. She goes there once or twice on a Thursday, which is the manageress's day off, and the other waitresses feed her for nothing. She does not go more often, is afraid to impose on their goodwill or risk them their jobs.

Roisin is punctual. One of the neighbours runs out to the nearest telephone kiosk to summon an ambulance. It occurs to Maire that she may die, that women still do, very rarely, die in childbirth. If she does they will not know what to do with her; she has claimed no next of kin, she will have a pauper's grave. But these morbid thoughts are soon subsumed in the sheer, undreamt-of pain. Her labour is long: her hips are narrow and, although the baby is small and the right way up, it's a struggle to get her out.

She emerges finally in the small hours when everyone concerned is exhausted, and is taken away at once to be put in an incubator as she weighs less than five pounds. Maire is distraught. A new doctor comes on duty in the morning and gives her back her baby, pointing out to the clucking nurses that such a tiny mother would be expected to have a tiny child and that both are perfectly healthy and that rules are made to be broken. It is he – this kindly, reasonable man – who takes the photo of the baby for her to send to Con.

Four days later she is discharged, goes back to her bedsit for a few days to rest, then packs up her things and heads south. There are no docks in the Thames Valley; she need never know that no one has come looking for her.

She will not allow her memories to pass this point, does not want to recall the next five years as she watches Roisin grow from a tiny screaming bundle into a real little person with a very decided personality of her own. The struggling years, the long wait for the council flat; life seemed hard back then. Her own childhood, the few happy months loving Con: these are safer places to go in her journeys of the imagination.

Six

*E*ven after the incident with the tattoo, things seem to be calming down, but Miss Shadwell chooses this time to get bored and start one of her whispering campaigns. Gossiping with one inmate about another, stirring up ill-feeling between women who have formed tentative friendships; this is how she takes her pleasure.

She knows that the relationship between Maire and Gloria is an uneasy one – that Gloria is jealous of the confidences Billy shares with Maire and fears to lose Billy to her. So one Sunday, as she opens the door of Gloria's cell just after eight o'clock, she comes into the room, pushing the door to behind her, and stands over Gloria who is still in bed.

'I'm just getting up,' Gloria says groggily. She has bought an extra sleeping-pill from Pam with two roll-ups and taken a double dose. She is still a little dazed.

'You weren't at association last night.' Miss Shadwell bends down towards Gloria's face on the pillow as if she will give her a good-morning kiss. Gloria has forgotten to remove yesterday's make-up and there is a smear of face powder on the pillow case. She is grubby and a little unsavoury.

'Sleepy,' Gloria murmurs. 'Locked in early. Bad period pains.'

'Well, well.' Miss Shadwell smiles her spasm smile. 'When the cat's away, eh?'

'What?' Gloria attempts to sit up but sinks down again with a moan. She is not wearing a nightdress and the sheet slips away, exposing her flaccid breasts.

'Just thinking how generous it was of you to leave the field clear for O'Neill.'

'Iris? What?'

'The two of them – your Billy and O'Neill – curled up together last night like two little kittens. Well, one little kitten and one big, fat, black cat.'

'No.' Gloria shakes her head. 'Not right.'

'Well, it's lasted quite long, as these things go. I mean to say, O'Neill's a lot younger than you are, a lot . . .' she pinches the nearest piece of sagging flesh '. . . firmer. And there are plenty of other fish in the sea, eh? There's always Brenda, for example. She's lonely now Jean's been sent back to Holloway.'

'Euh.' Gloria is still trying to wake up, still trying to unjumble what this insidious voice is whispering in her ear about cats, kittens, fish. Has the fat, black cat eaten the fish? Billy is queen of H Wing and Gloria wants to be the queen's consort. Besides, she loves Billy. Doesn't she?

'I think you've had a rough time, Latinski,' Miss Shadwell tells her kindly. 'Gloria. Here.' She carefully places two ciga-rettes – real ones, out of a packet, with filters – on the pillow and leaves.

Gloria stares blearily after her. She shakes her head hard, she thinks she is still asleep. She hides the cigarettes under her pillow, handling them with love like a favourite child.

Like Maire, she is on Two's Landing, and when she has finally got up and dressed, she slips along the corridor to Maire's room, finding it empty. Maire has already slopped out and gone down to breakfast.

It is a bell, bar and bolts day; the warders are going round from cell to cell checking that the emergency bell is in working order, that the women have not been gnawing their way through the window bars with their teeth and that the bolts on the outside of each door are intact and oiled. They take the opportunity at the same time to nag prisoners about cleanliness or pester them about tidiness, writing down any infringements of these two household gods in a little book.

Halfway through the morning, Maire is pouring disinfectant down each of the three lavatories off the workroom. The disin-fectant is diluted in case any of the inmates should suddenly decide to swallow some and she is sniffing doubtfully, uncon-vinced that hygiene is being served, when she hears her name called.

'O'Neill!' If the warders want a particular inmate, they bawl her name in their broad Geordie accents, and the walls bounce it, distorted, to every part of the prison.

'O'Neill, to her room. Now!'

Maire hurries to see what is wrong, delayed only by other women she meets on the way who tell her she is wanted. Although she is at the other end of the wing, she knows she will be expected to manifest herself outside her cell in no time at all. She runs up the two flights of stairs to Two's Landing and comes to a halt, panting, at the door of her cell. Mrs Parsons, one of the kindlier warders, stands there tapping her foot, waiting.

'This won't do, O'Neill.'

'Sorry, miss,' Maire begins automatically, 'I was in the . . .' then comes to a halt; she stands staring through the door into the wreckage of her room. It looks worse than when Miss Shadwell has been doing a cell search. All her belongings are scattered on the floor, along with the mattress and her bedding. The contents of someone's chamber pot have been deposited in the centre of the room.

'Oh my God!'

Mrs Parsons is gentle, takes her into the cell and pushes the door to, lowering her voice. 'I know there are times when something just seems to snap, dear, but really it's no good taking it out like this. You harm no one but yourself.'

'But I didn't. I don't know . . .' Maire tails off. What is the point? She will most probably not be believed and if she is believed, investigations will be made and that will make her a grass.

'You're lucky it was me and not Miss Shadwell,' Mrs Parsons goes on. 'Just hurry up and get everything cleared up and put away and we'll say no more about it – this time.'

Maire says, 'Thank you, miss,' in a dazed voice. Mrs Parsons says she will come back in about forty minutes when she has done the other landings and will not write anything in her book until then.

Maire heaps her clothes higgledy-piggledy back into the wardrobe to be sorted later. She remakes her bed as fast as she can. In a moment of inspiration, she fetches her mop and bucket and the bottle of disinfectant from the workroom lavatories and clears up the mess on the floor and wipes it over with the contents of the bottle. It is stronger than she had thought; she sleeps with the stench of disinfectant in her nostrils for the next two nights.

As she works, she puzzles over this attack. What little privacy the inmates have is mutually respected and an unwritten law says that a woman does not enter another's room without invitation. Is it a personal assault on her, Maire, the High Wycombe bomber, or just some inadequate, Pam perhaps, having a brainstorm?

She decides not to mention it to any of the others.

Gloria jostles Maire as she leaves the breakfast queue the following morning and sends her tray crashing to the floor. Maire, as a lifer, is allowed one cup of her own and the white china mug with blue forget-me-nots – one of the few reminders of home – smashes into shards on the concrete floor.

'Oops,' Gloria simpers. 'Butterfingers.'

The warder on duty, one of the more motherly of the officers, a dispenser of full sugar rations, has heard only the crash and comes across.

'Sorry, miss.' Maire begins to pile the pieces of china on to her tray. 'I was clumsy.'

'Get it picked up,' the woman says, 'and mop up that spillage. It's almost time to line up for work.'

By the time Maire has fetched a cloth and soaked up the tea it is too late for her to get another mugful. Her throat is dry all morning and she is puzzled and resentful. Gloria sits at her sewing machine with a smirk of triumph on her face. At the end of the morning's work, as they are being marched out to exercise, Maire dodges up the line to catch Gloria and tackles her.

'Why did you do that?'

'Do what?' Gloria's demeanour is a mixture of hurt innocence and defiance.

'Deliberately spill my breakfast.'

'Don't be silly. I was nowhere near you.'

'Was it you wrecked my room yesterday morning?'

'I don't know what you're talking about. You're getting . . . what's that word?' Gloria frowns. 'Oh yes. Par-a-noid.'

They reach the exercise yard and Gloria moves quickly off, leaving Maire staring after her. She spends the hour making up to Billy, gives her one of the real cigarettes.

'Where you get that?' Billy asks sharply.

'It was a present.' Gloria pouts; it has just dawned on her that she may be able to keep Billy's love by making her jealous.

'Child-killers!'

The tedious litany from the men's wing starts up. Pam begins to cry quietly. She is sure that it is her they are attacking.

'Unnatural bitches! Murderers!'

'Hang them! String the whores up!'

'I'm not a murderer,' Gloria yells back at the unseen taunters. 'Her.' She points at Maire. 'She's a murderer. Not me. Her.'

'God sake, Gloria,' Billy says. 'Shut up. What get into you today?'

Miss Shadwell watches from the sidelines, smiles her aching smile.

The next day, when Gloria comes to her after the afternoon session in the workroom to ask for a fresh sanitary towel, she gives her a little more encouragement. She has just seen Maire and Billy going into Billy's cell. She knows that Billy has had a letter that day, censored it herself that morning, and that she has just asked Maire to come and read it to her.

'All over, then?' she says.

'What?'

'You and Gibson. I see O'Neill's with Gibson in her cell. All water under the bridge, eh?'

Gloria almost runs from the room, her sanitary towel incongruously clutched in her hand. She bursts into Billy's cell where Maire and Billy are sitting side by side on the bed, their heads bent together over a sheet of cheap lined paper; they are laughing.

'Hello, Gloria,' Billy says. 'You wanna hear what my Corinne . . .'

Gloria seizes Maire by the hair and pulls upwards. Her grip is unexpectedly strong and Maire rises to her feet, following the hand up, fearing that a hank of hair is about to be torn out by the roots. Billy, recovering from her initial surprise, tries to get in between them, snaps at Gloria who for once will not listen to her or obey her.

'It was you who messed up my room.' Maire is gasping with the pain. 'I knew it was.'

'And I'll do it again,' Gloria shrieks. 'Whore! Bitch!' She sounds oddly like one of the men. 'Oh!' She is running out of insults. '. . . Home wrecker!'

Billy grabs a lock of Gloria's hair in her turn but Gloria, in her jealous fury, seems beyond pain. The three women struggle in the tiny cell and a chair goes flying. As they stumble about the confined area in a parody of a dance, the small wardrobe is the next thing to go, toppling sideways with an almighty crash.

Then the room is even fuller as Miss Shadwell and her deputy intervene; shouting, issuing direct orders which are not heard, let alone obeyed. Billy kicks Gloria on the shin and, when that has no effect, punches her straight in the face. Gloria screams and lets go of Maire's hair. Maire lurches backwards and cannons into Miss Shadwell who takes the opportunity to administer a sharp slap of her own.

Gloria stands in the centre of the room screaming; her hands are pumping up and down for all the world like a small child having a tantrum. Since she holds a white oblong of cotton wool and gauze in one hand and a few strands of Maire's thick black hair in the other she looks ridiculous and Billy begins to laugh helplessly.

Two male warders arrive, one with a dog. One of them says, 'Just a bloody cat fight,' in disgust. Billy sits down on the bed, grasping her sides, shouting with laughter. The dog begins to growl uneasily, then to bark.

'Take that one . . .' Miss Shadwell points at Billy '. . . down to the punishment cell. Lock the other two in their rooms. O'Neill and Latinski, confined to cell until further notice. On report in the morning.'

'You done this.' Billy stops laughing now, like a tap being shut off. She jabs her finger in Miss Shadwell's face as she is taken out. 'I dunno why, but you behind all this. I know you, seen you do it before. Shit stirring.' She spits at her. 'Screw you, screw.'

'Get her out of here,' Miss Shadwell yells. 'All right, the rest of you . . .' half the wing is now standing outside Billy's cell, attracted by the noise '. . . the show's over. Get back to your own rooms, or I shall put everyone in confinement.' The corridor empties as if by magic.

'As for you, Gloria,' Billy calls from halfway down the stairs, 'we finished, over, done with. Hear me?'

'Well,' Miss Shadwell says to her deputy as they go to make themselves some well-earned coffee, 'that passed the time, didn't it?'

The other woman says, 'Yes, Angela,' sycophantically, and smirks.

She had not dared hope for such a quick and satisfying end to her campaign. Latinski, her little puppet, has dangled perfectly on her string. She rubs her hands together in a washing gesture.

'Dirty black dyke.'

Seven

She strips her bed then remakes it neatly but leaving one sheet off. From the spyhole the bed now looks normal.

She begins to tear the one sheet into thin strips.

She does it slowly so that there will be no ripping noise even though no one is likely to hear through the electronic door.

She soon has a dozen strips about an inch wide.

She plaits three of them, then tugs the resulting braid between her hands. It holds.

She plaits three more, joins the second braid to the first.

She now has a thin rope about five feet long.

She plaits another three strips and adds them to the rope.

She puts one end of the rope under her feet and tugs at the other end. One of the knots gives way.

She reknots and tries again. This time the rope holds.

She looks at her watch. It is nearly ten.

She puts the rope under the mattress and slips into bed with her clothes on.

She hears somebody fumbling at the spyhole five minutes later and feigns sleep. The light snaps off. She will not be checked again for at least an hour.

She gets out of bed and gropes her way in the dark, feeling for the rope under the mattress.

She is calm, calmer than she has ever been in her life.

She clambers up on the bed-head and opens the plastic window. An adventurous breeze braves the endless barriers to whisper against her face.

She passes one end of the rope round two iron bars, tugs again. It holds.

She makes it fast with a knot dredged up from her memory from Brownie days.

She fashions the other end into a noose and passes it over her head and tightens it.

She teeters on the iron bedstead, almost loses her balance. Not yet, not yet.

She should write a note, get down and write a note to Billy. But Billy cannot read, so what's the point? O'Neill would have to read it to her.

She should write a note for her boys, tell them she is sorry.

She is not sorry. Billy, Billy will be sorry — sorry for what she said, for speaking to her that way.

She is looking forward to seeing Billy's face when she hears.

She wonders: are her clothes right? Should she change?

She wants to die in her good clothes, wants to look her best when they take her down and carry her out, in case Billy sees her.

She is wearing Billy's favourite outfit — a baby-blue dress with a lace collar. There is no need to change.

She is ready.

She lets her feet walk off the slippery iron rail.

She dangles from the rope. It holds.

She twitches for a few minutes, is surprised that it is not quicker, had dimly thought that her neck would break, that it would be instantaneous.

She strangles slowly, loses consciousness. Death takes longer. The baby-blue dress is soiled at the end.

And so the Rage begins.

Eight

Billy is allowed out of the punishment cell the next morning. She emerges blinking, unsure why she is being let out so soon. She stands barefoot in her strip dress which is too small for her. The wing is unnaturally quiet for this time of day. The women are still locked in their cells; besides, they are in shock.

'Make way for the grieving widow,' Miss Shadwell says. Her plan has been a little too successful, even for her liking, and she is taking refuge in *braggadocio* although she knows the tragedy cannot be brought home to her. She has agreed, however, to break the news.

They are not good at breaking bad news. When Cilla's mother died unexpectedly just after Easter, she had been summoned to the Chief Officer and told, 'Oh, by the way, your mother just died.'

'Where is everyone?' Billy asks. 'Mass break-out? They all escape while I in punishment cell? Just my luck.'

'Latinski hanged herself last night,' Miss Shadwell tells her without preparation, without asking Billy to sit down and expect a shock. 'With a rope made out of sheets, from the bars of the window.'

For a moment Billy does not react. She turns very slowly towards Miss Shadwell, peers at her, then closes her eyes, then reopens them.

'Gloria?'

'Yes.'

'Gloria did hang herself?'

'Yes.'

'Last night?'

'That's right.'

155

'Aaarrggghh.' With a great roar, Billy launches herself at Miss Shadwell's head.

'You do this. You do this. You Shagwell bitch. You drive her to it. Whisper lies in her ear. You think I don't know. Gloria dead. Now you die too.'

Mrs Parsons screams and runs for help. On the landing above, the doors are finally being unlocked and a group of tousled, muted women file out on to the landings and look over, through the suicide netting, to see what is happening on the Flat.

'Billy! Billy! Stop it. Stop.' Maire comes clattering down the stairs. Billy does not listen, does not even hear, and Maire's tugs at her arm are like a flea trying to restrain an elephant. Miss Shadwell is on the ground now with almost two hundred pounds of Billy on top of her. Billy is holding her by the back of the neck with both hands, head-butting her again and again. The warder's face is streaming with blood and her nose is obviously broken.

'Billy,' Maire begs. 'Billy. Listen to me.'

'I kill her.' Billy is dimly aware now of an audience. 'I in such a Rage. Gloria dead.'

'I know. I know. But Billy . . .'

'She does it.' Billy continues her assault between phrases. 'She whisper, stir trouble . . . All the time . . . Always get away with it before . . . Not get away with it this time . . . They not do nothing to her . . . Me, I do something . . . For Gloria . . . Owe it to Gloria.'

Two more female warders have joined the small group but neither dares tangle with this mad woman who is now apparently trying to wrench Miss Shadwell's head off. She is kicking, biting, tearing with her strong, sinewy fingers. She has her hands round Miss Shadwell's throat now.

Mrs Parsons reappears with four male warders. It takes all seven of them to overpower Billy and pull her away from the pitiful remains of Angela Shadwell. Maire sinks to the ground and sits with her unconscious head cradled in her lap, blood seeping over her jeans from the battered face.

'Get a doctor,' she calls, although she doesn't know to whom. 'Get an ambulance.' She does not much care what happens to Miss Shadwell but the worse she is, the worse it will be for

Billy. She tries to stem the flow of blood with a handkerchief but it is soon sopping. There is blood all over the floor. Searching for its source, she sees that Billy has bitten off the little finger of Miss Shadwell's right hand.

'Oh God!' she murmurs. 'Oh God!'

The seven warders are still struggling with Billy, trying to get her back into the strip cell. No one has answered Maire's plea for help. The other women are just watching, transfixed from their landings; they have forgotten how to take responsibility. She lays Miss Shadwell carefully down on the floor and runs to the office to telephone for an ambulance. When she returns, Billy has just torn herself free from her captors and lurches towards Maire. A man shouts 'Look out!' Billy wraps her up in her powerful arms and kisses her hard and full on the mouth.

'Goodbye, More-Ra honey,' she says as they drag her off again. 'We not meet again.'

As they throw her into the cell, Maire carefully wipes her mouth on the back of her hand.

In the strip cell Billy begins to scream and they hear the noise of her head being banged against the wall.

Maire becomes aware of shouting and hooting from every landing. The women, roused from their usual torpor, are shaking their fists, stamping their feet.

'Bil-ly! Bil-ly! Bil-ly!'

The chanting begins quietly, builds up to a crescendo, then stops as abruptly as it had begun. An ominous silence follows, then a new, sinister song to the same music:

'Shag-well! Shag-well! Shag-well!'

Maire cowers against the wall out of sight of the chanters; she is afraid. Mrs Parsons is also afraid, dreading a riot, women barricading themselves in their cells, setting fire to bedding and clothing. She has witnessed one such uprising and never wants to see another. She has minutes, perhaps seconds, to regain authority. She stiffens her back and takes a deep breath.

'Back to your rooms, girls.' She marches up the stairs, keys rattling. 'Before I get the dogs out.' The women recede before her, melt back into their cells. The fight is gone from them: they are outweaponed and used to obedience.

Mrs Parsons, trembling slightly with relief, begins to lock them back in.

'You too, O'Neill,' she calls back down the stairs.

Maire stares briefly into the punishment cell, then at Miss Shadwell who is regaining consciousness and starting to moan.

'Is she going to be all right?' she asks. No one answers.

'O'Neill!' Mrs Parsons calls down. 'That was a direct order.'

'I'm coming.'

Maire spends the rest of the day lying on her back on the bed staring at the ceiling. She hears the siren of an ambulance both coming and going. She hears the noise of Gloria's body being removed from the cell a few doors from her own with a man grumbling, 'God, she isn't half a dead weight.' She hears Billy shouting, screaming, banging for the rest of the morning and half the afternoon. Then there is silence. No work is done that day, no exercise, no association, and the women are fed in their cells.

By the next morning, the punishment cell is empty.

Nine

Maire asks to see the Chief Officer first thing after breakfast and is refused. She asks after morning work and is refused. She asks after exercise and after afternoon work and is finally told she will be given a few minutes.

'Well?' the Chief Officer asks coldly. She is holding Gloria's file in her hand. It has a large letter F inside a circle stamped in red in one corner; that means that Gloria is considered a suicide risk and must be checked frequently, but Maire does not know this.

'I want to know what's happened to Billy Gibson.'

'That is not your concern.'

'Yes it is. She was my friend.'

'I warned you.' The Chief Officer gets up from her chair, unsmiling. 'I warned you about her. Very well, O'Neill. I suppose there's no reason you shouldn't know. Gibson has been transferred to Rampton.'

'But that's for the criminally insane,' Maire protests.

'Gibson has been certified,' the officer says, 'and not a moment too soon in my view.'

'It's this place,' Maire says, 'it's enough to send anyone mad. She should never have been here. She's a victim. She killed only in self-defence . . .'

'Is that what she told you?' She makes an angry clicking noise with her tongue. 'Billy Gibson and her lover killed her husband – hacked him to death – while he was asleep.'

'I . . . I don't believe it.'

'Oh, she's very convincing, I know. Sometimes I think she believes that wronged-innocent, self-defence story herself, she's told it so many times.'

'Hacked to death . . .' Maire, dazed, cannot envisage it.

'Then they tried to dispose of the body by cutting it into little pieces and burning it. She tried to plead insanity at the trial but the jury weren't buying it and found her guilty of murder. Now she's where she should have been all along.

'And I must say, O'Neill,' she goes on, 'that I don't hold you entirely blameless in this fiasco. She needs someone to feed her fantasies and that's exactly what you did.'

Maire is speechless. There was nothing she could have done, no way in which she could have acted differently in the days leading up to the 'fiasco'. Her attempts to reason with Billy, to give first aid to Miss Shadwell, to fetch an ambulance; do they count for nothing?

To the Chief Officer it is an administrative inconvenience. There will have to be an internal enquiry, they will have to keep it out of the newspapers if they can. She has lost one of her best and most experienced officers since, although she is recovering in hospital, Miss Shadwell will not be returning to H Wing. Her power – her authority – has been destroyed.

To Maire it is not a fiasco nor an inconvenience, but a tragedy. She says so and is sneered at.

'For someone who blew, what was it, five people, six? to smithereens, you're very po-faced all of a sudden about Latinski's death.'

'I never killed anyone,' Maire says, with dignity.

'Of course not! You're an innocent victim, aren't you? . . . Just like Gibson.'

Then she remembers something that Billy said to her a few weeks ago. Now is the right time. She speaks loudly and clearly.

'Fuck you, miss. Just fuck you.'

She leaves the room without waiting to be dismissed, leaving the Chief Officer staring after her.

She has come to terms at last with the limitless future stretching before her. She understands now that she was in danger of going under, of turning into the meek zombie these officers want to make of all their charges. That way, she will end up a drugged doll like Pam or with Gloria's fragile hold on reality which could end only as it did. Billy has shown her that some fight is essential to survival; but Billy's way will not be her way.

She has regained herself, and the next woman to address her as Iris is blasted halfway across the workroom.

She demands to see the rule book, learns the rules by heart. For the rest of her two years at Durham, Maire O'Neill is known as a champion of the underdog – a barrack-room lawyer speaking up for women who are too ignorant or too frightened to defend themselves. She listens to their stories, works patiently through their Open University courses with them, helps write their parole pleas. She never calls a prison officer 'Miss' again.

She is a thorn in the Chief Officer's flesh: O'Neill has come back to life, and live women are so much harder to handle.

Ten

Maire is being moved at short notice. For some reason
– be it policy or simple inefficiency – moves are
usually at short notice. Sometimes visitors arrive in
Yorkshire on Saturday to the news that their wife, daughter,
mother was transferred to Bristol on Thursday. Too bad. There
is rarely any mention of why you are being moved: because
you have been a good girl or a bad girl, whether what you are
going to is punishment or reward.

Maire has been in Durham for just over two years and she
is going to another closed prison at Styal in Cheshire. She has
twenty-four hours to say goodbye to such friends as she may
have made. This she does; there are many tears at her departure, but none of them are hers.

She has been allowed her sketchpad and crayons at some
point during her confinement, ostensibly for good behaviour,
and she spends her last evening doing swift cartoons of some
of the women and warders, unerringly picking out what makes
them unique. She gives one to Mrs Parsons – the matronly
bosom; the eyes benevolent, a little sad – and the warder
accepts it with a smile and tells her to take care and, whatever
she does, not to come back.

Brenda bets her a bottle of hand-cream that she will not give
the Chief Officer her portrait. Maire takes up the challenge,
draws, tears up, draws again, knocks on the office door. The
sketch – a woman in uniform: very erect, unbending, sharp-
mouthed – is taken without comment and Brenda pays up.

Five women climb into the back of a closed van the next morning, clutching their meagre belongings in plastic bags. Maire
has the regulation three sets of clothes bought with her annual

allowance, her books, the same hairbrush she took into Holloway with her on her arrest, a few toiletries including the precious hand-cream.

Three of them are going to Styal; two are going to Risley remand and allocation centre pending yet another move in a week or two. They have three warders with them – two female and one male.

Maire heaves herself up with difficulty; her stomach is bloated and sore. She is constipated, like most of the women, almost all the time. She has eaten little in the way of fresh fruit or vegetables at Durham, and she will not use the chamber pot in her cell at night for the taint it leaves on the air. After two years of this denial, her bowels no longer function naturally.

One warder climbs in with them and the van is locked from outside. Maire asks for a seat at the back, by the windows, and the others gladly move up for her. She wants to see the picturesque town of Durham recede behind her for ever.

They are told they will be stopping for lunch in Bradford. Cilla says she could fancy a Chinese with a nice bottle of something and is told to shut up. They have forgotten to give Pam her Triptazol this morning in the rush and she is alternately boisterous and tearful.

The van pulls up at a police station on the outskirts of Bradford and the women are hurried inside and shut in a cell where there is not enough room for them all to sit, so they have to take it in turns. There is a toilet in the cell. It has no door.

A plate of sandwiches is brought to them – corned beef, which Maire loathes – and a jug of water. The sandwiches are made with flaccid white bread which seems to cling to the teeth. Maire is hungry because her stomach was churning too much in fear of this move to allow her to swallow much over the last twenty-four hours. She bites into a sandwich and tries to think of something else as she gulps it down with the minimum of chewing and swills some flat water after it.

They are kept locked in for an hour and a half while the warders relax in the canteen, eat pie and chips, drink hot coffee and swop horror stories with the beat constables.

Eleven

As she waits in the reception area at Styal with its relentless blasts of Radio 1, Maire looks out of the window and can see women prisoners walking around in well-kept gardens, their faces open to the sun and air. A warder, seeing her looking, tells her quickly that she mustn't get the idea she can walk around freely; you need a reason for going from A to B, or else. Maire just smiles.

But first Pam and Cilla and Maire must be strip-searched. They were strip-searched on leaving Durham, of course, and have been locked up for the entire journey, but it is part of the ritual of humiliation and control, to get the new inmates off on the right foot. Once naked, they are made to jump up and down in case they have secreted drugs in their vaginas.

She fills in another reception form, declines again a reception letter, explains once more that, no, she is not illiterate and doesn't want to join the Adult Literacy Scheme. She refuses, again, a Volunteer Associate to visit her in default of real friends. She does not want to see the RC chaplain.

At Styal the women live in houses, averaging twenty inmates per house. Each house appoints its own cook and the food is better – and hotter – than at Durham as a result. Maire and Cilla are sent initially to Martin House. Pam goes to Howard which is, they later discover, the 'Muppet House' – a dumping-ground for disturbed women.

The women in Martin are friendly enough in the usual wary way. Most of them are young and serving short sentences for possession of drugs or petty theft. Maire will be assessed over the first month and then allocated suitable work, possibly gardening. She flexes her fingers in pleasure at the prospect of feeling the cool, moist soil running through her hands and sticking under her nails.

The house has a common-room where the women spend their non-work time; there is no 'association' as there was at Durham – a miserable hour or so a day in which you had someone to talk to. You do not spend your free time locked up.

No one asks that night what the newcomers are in for, nor for how long; prisoners are an incurious lot. Or perhaps it's that they have so little privacy that they've learnt to value it highly. If people want to talk about what they've done and why they're here, well and good; if not, leave them be.

Maire feels less tense, is able to laugh at a silly joke that first evening with real joy. Styal is a holiday camp after Durham. Her young companions, girls who have not tasted life in Durham or Holloway, complain about it; but to those who have, this is almost a taste of freedom. Even the prospect of sleeping in a dormitory cannot dampen her spirits; for that night she sees the moon rise.

The next day she is walking across to work; she has been put in the workroom for the time being, sewing yet more uniforms for soldiers. She is being shown the way by another inmate of Martin House, Marge, who strikes her as being not far short of simple-minded. As they walk the gravel pathways, taking care not to step on the grass, Marge nudges her and mutters, 'Don't look now but . . .' and lowers her voice so far that Maire can't hear her.

'What?' she asks.

The girl speaks a little louder. 'That's Maxine Harris, over there, going into the Centre.'

'Where?' Maire has only the vaguest notion who Maxine Harris is but she looks anyway as Marge seems to expect it.

'She's gone now.' Marge loses interest; her attention span is, Maire discovers, infuriatingly short.

Maire had initially expected to be picked on in prison as a callous, indiscriminate murderer, but she has found that the other inmates reserve their venom for women who have killed children. In Holloway and Durham she has heard many times the cooing chant of 'Suffer little children to come unto me';

followed by the savage hiss of 'Nonce', growing and echoing until the woman concerned retreats into the lonely safety of Rule 43. There had been no children in the Hope and Anchor that night. Maxine Harris, she recalls now, is a child-killer.

They have stopped to watch this nondescript woman open a door and walk through it. A warder shouts, 'No dawdling in the avenue!' at them and they scurry on.

'She's in the lifers' house,' Marge says. 'You're a lifer, aren't you?' Maire agrees that she is. 'I expect you'll be sent there soon. You get your own room there.' She speaks enviously as if it might be better to be doing life so you could have your own room. She pauses for what passes for thought then says, 'She's all right, Maxine. All right. Live and let live, that's what I always say.'

Twelve

Marge is right and Maire, after a brief period of assessment, is sent to the lifers' house where there are only eight other women and she has her own room. She is able to shut herself away there at night with her books or her sketchpad when the blare of TV sitcoms and soap operas downstairs becomes too much.

The rooms are not locked – indeed, there are no warders in the house overnight – and she has access to a lavatory, so her bowels return, very gradually, to normal. Her health improves generally now that she has better food and some fresh air and a view of trees and birds; her skin grows less sickly grey with every day.

She is not let loose on the garden after all but is put on a work party to do repairs and decorating on the prison buildings, which is, in its way, even better. She learns to plaster and to glaze and to hang wallpaper and to point brick under the supervision of fat, bald, middle-aged Trevor who lives in the neighbouring village. All the workmen are middle-aged and unattractive in case they prove tempting to these cloistered women.

The work is physically hard and that tires her and helps send her to sleep at night. She is searched after every morning and afternoon stint in case she has hidden a hammer or a screwdriver about her and plans to use it, but she is accustomed to that and the perfunctory rub-down affects her no more than a ladybird walking up her arm. There are frequent arguments between the work parties and the gardeners as to who gets priority with the baths but these are minor irritations compared with the gains.

Trev, like the rest, is curiously uncurious about the inmates and talks to Maire quite naturally, as if she were just a woman he had met at the bus stop and passed the time of day with. He shares his Thermos flask and sandwiches with her at tea break. As they sit and munch, he comments on last night's telly or complains about the government or the Common Market. He gives her glimpses of normal life.

After a fortnight he tells her sweetly, paternally, that it does his heart good to see her looking daily so much bonnier, by which he means healthier, less skinny. Two weeks later he asks out of the blue, 'Irish, are you?'

'Why, yes.' Maire laughs because she knows that her accent is still as Irish as whiskey.

'Thought so.'

If her name rings any bells with him, he is not letting on.

The chances are that she will stay at Styal until the time comes for her to move to an open prison, but she cannot be sure. She could equally well be bussed off to Cookham Wood or back to Holloway tomorrow.

She is not happy, how could she be? But she does not know here the despair she sometimes felt in H Wing. It is much pettier than Durham, with warders enforcing discipline in a manner that often seems arbitrary. Women are harshly punished for stepping on the grass or smoking in the wrong place or talking in the medicine queue.

There are days when this pettiness and unfairness grind her down, but now she has an outlet for her frustrations. She relieves her feelings by slapping paint furiously on a wall or skirting-board, yelling 'Shit, Bugger, Fuck' at the inoffensive plasterwork. There is no one but Trev to hear her and he either smiles, saying that if she was his daughter, he'd put her over his knee and smack her bottom for her; or says, 'Atta girl! Don't let the bastards get you down,' depending on his mood.

So Maire must be left in Cheshire, two years into her sentence, for she still has a long way to go. Nothing much new will happen to her until the spring of 1991, another ten years from now.

Part Three
Rosemary Mason

One

She has always known, of course, that Robert and Elizabeth Mason – Bob and Betty – are not her real parents. She remembers the children's home – Fairlawns, they called it. She had to share a room there, something which seemed alien to her and wrong. She remembers it all as crowds and factions, as the noise of quarrelling and the silence of sulking.

Bob and Betty married late and, having given up hope of a baby of their own, were told that they were too old, at thirty-nine and thirty-six respectively, to be considered for a healthy, white baby. They could have a handicapped child, it seemed, or a black one – that was before it became politically incorrect to place a black baby with a white family – or they could be considered for an older child: one who might be 'difficult', who might have been rescued from a background of physical or even sexual abuse, who might not know how to respond to their overtures of love.

They chose the last option and they chose Rosie. They went to see her at Fairlawns, taking her out for picnics and cinemas. Later she was invited home with her little suitcase for the weekend. She was quiet and biddable and responded gladly to their affection since that was the very thing she had been missing at the home – the hugging, the reassuring arms of someone who would be always on her side. For it seemed to her that there had been such a someone once but that they were lost now.

After they had fostered her for a few months, she moved in with them for good and papers were signed; she had a new birth certificate and became Rosemary Mason. She had another name before but she no longer remembered what it was. At Fairlawns they had called her Rosie, and that had seemed all right. She was five at the time and everything before that was a blank. She had her own room now. She was to be their only child and she was glad of it.

She was chosen. She was special.

The Masons moved house a year after the adoption, went to a new part of the country where no one knew them, because they were tired of people saying: 'But it's not the same as if it was your own, is it? I mean, it can't be.'

They knew that it was.

Bob Mason was the manager of a supermarket – part of a big national chain – and he applied for a transfer and the family moved to Nottingham.

No one – no stranger – has ever been told since then that Bob and Betty aren't Rosemary's blood parents, as if they can't guess. They are both plump and fair: she blonde, now white; he red-haired, now as bald as the dome of St Paul's. Tiny and dark, Rosie is as obviously not their natural child as if she were indeed black.

In Nottingham Rosie flourishes, grows up healthy and strong, happy and bright.

Mr Graham takes her for A-level English. On the day that she wins the school essay prize, he ruffles her black hair with pride and pleasure and calls her a clever little colleen. She isn't sure what he means and looks it up in the dictionary which says it is Irish for 'girl'. Simon whispers jealously that Graham fancies her but she knows that it is just their shared love of words which gives him joy.

So by the spring of 1991 her life, her future, is mapped out. A-levels in June, university in the autumn to read English – at Oxford, if all goes well. She has everything: loving parents, Simon, many friends, academic success.

It is about three weeks before her eighteenth birthday – the middle of March – when things begin to change. There seems nothing unusual about that Thursday evening at the time, but she sees later that that was the evening of the newscast and the evening she and Simon decided to put their relationship on a different footing, and that those things combined together to change the future she had planned for herself.

Two

She and Simon usually stop off at his house on the way home from school. His mother is a widow and doesn't get home from work until about six-thirty. It had been a large family – Simon has two sisters and two brothers – but they are all much older than he and have long since moved out, so they have the place to themselves for a couple of hours each evening. The house is much smaller and shabbier than the Masons' and the furniture isn't so good nor so new, but it's always cosy once they get the gas fire going.

That day they settle at the Formica-topped table in the kitchen and Simon starts peeling potatoes and chopping broccoli for the evening meal. He is very domesticated and he and his mother are very close. He is her baby – her Little Afterthought, as she calls him. Rosie makes coffee for them both and they talk about their French homework, an essay on *L'Ecole des Femmes*, which is one of their set books.

'It isn't really a triumph of Romantic Love,' she points out. 'Things only work out for the young people because Agnès's father had intended her to marry Horace all along.' Simon frowns, says he takes her point, and pitches another potato into the saucepan. 'Simon,' she says, 'you're doing enough potatoes to feed an army.'

'Aren't you staying?' he asks in surprise.

'I didn't tell them I would.'

'Give them a ring now. You know Mum won't mind.'

Rosie knows she won't. She likes Mrs Lawrence, who has had a hard life – still does have come to that – but is always cheerful and, above all, generous. She rings home but her mother says she has already started supper and Rosie promises to be back by six-thirty.

'I can have the extra ones fried up for breakfast,' Simon says, putting the pan on to boil. 'Let's go and catch the news.'

They curl up together on the sofa next door and switch on the six o'clock news on the BBC with Anna Ford. The main story is of the release of the Birmingham Six – a group of men imprisoned since the mid-seventies on terrorist charges whose convictions have finally been quashed on appeal. They can't help smiling at these harsh alien accents – at the stertorous Ulster tones not one whit diminished by fifteen years in an English prison.

'Hon-doo-ted-ly,' Simon says, mimicking a television political correspondent who comes from the same part of the world.

The newscast shows photos of them taken at the time of their arrest: they look older now, of course, greyer, but also smaller and thinner as if time and sorrow have worn them away. They have grandchildren they have never met. Rosie gazes at the screen as though mesmerised, wondering if they will be able to go on and make something of the rest of their lives, or whether their experience has left them too bitter.

'Imagine, though,' she murmurs. 'Imagine . . .'

'What?'

'All those years in jail, for something you didn't do. It's almost worse than murder, it's stealing part of their lives. We can pay them compensation, and all that rubbish, but we can't give them back more than fifteen years of youth and health.'

They are both silent for a moment. Rosie tries vainly to imagine what prison would be like if, via some unimaginable course of events, she were to find herself in one. Documentaries on television always seemed to be about men's prisons and never speak about the things that linger in the backs of everyone's minds: homosexual rape, drugs, AIDS.

One of the Six speaks directly to the camera through a microphone set up on the pavement outside the Old Bailey. He calls for a review of all prisoners serving sentences for alleged terrorist offences and for justice for some people called the Maguire Seven.

The newscast ends and Simon goes over to switch the set off. At home Rosie has a remote-control unit and watching him get up to click a switch is as old-fashioned as if he'd suddenly broken into a foxtrot.

'Have you thought any more?' he asks, sitting back down beside her and putting his arm round her.

Rosie has known Simon since the fourth year; they had been part of the same group of friends for a couple of years and started going around as a couple the previous summer. They have discussed sleeping together but have as yet reached no conclusion. They are both virgins. Anyone reading the tabloid newspapers might be led to think that there is something bizarre about a seventeen-year-old virgin – that it is a species on the point of extinction. Simon and Rosie are by no means unusual. They want to be sure that they are ready, they want it to feel right.

Lately they have grown closer, come to trust each other completely; to feel comfortably domestic, closeted together in the kitchen, preparing the evening meal and mulling over the events of the day. Simon had declared at the weekend that he feels they are ready now but that she is, of course, under no pressure.

She leans closer to him and her hand slides inside his white shirt and on to his well-fleshed ribs. He is a tall, well-built man and he makes her feel very frail.

'We have to decide first about precautions,' she says. He draws her to him and kisses her more passionately than he ever has before, and there is a strange heavy feeling in her pelvic area, behind the pubic bone – strange but pleasant.

'Condoms?' he asks when the kiss ends.

'I think so, don't you?'

'I'll get some before Saturday.'

His mother works on Saturdays too and they can be alone for hours in the smaller bedroom – the teenage boy's bedroom with the football posters, the swimming certificates proudly framed on the wall.

Rosie realises that they might sound ridiculously cautious to any eavesdropper, unreasonably sensible for two such young people. Simon's sister Jenny had an unplanned pregnancy at the age of eighteen. She had wanted to be a singer, had a strong untrained soprano voice. After much family discussion – Simon had been too young to be consulted but had huddled halfway up the stairs listening to the raised voices and to Jenny's sobbing, not half understanding – she had decided to have the child and had hurriedly married the father, a twenty-year-old bank clerk called Colin. They appear in the wedding photos with forced smiles and Colin doesn't look old enough to shave.

Ten years on, Colin is an assistant manager in Worcester, they have a comfortable house and the usual hopes and ambitions, and seem as happy as most married couples. But there is an emptiness about Jenny which frightens Rosie – as if somewhere behind the neat clothes and the well-brushed hair, the Ford Fiesta and the new three-piece suite, some part of her has died. She never sings now.

Bob Mason laughs at his daughter sometimes and tells her she was born middle-aged and that one of the reasons they fell in love with her at Fairlawns was that she was such a solemn little thing and that it took them months to coax the first real laugh out of her. It took a chimpanzee's tea party at the zoo to do it. Bob pretended to be a chimpanzee and Rosie had been first astonished and then amused at this big man, this kind stranger, capering about, displaying, unafraid to make a fool of himself to cheer up a tiny girl. Since then, they have laughed together a lot.

They hear Simon's mother's key in the lock at that moment and draw back apart as she comes into the room and flops down in the armchair on the other side of the gas logs – her coat still on.

'What a day! Hello, Rosie. How are you, love?'

'Terrific, Mrs L.' She looks at her watch in horror. 'Oh God! I've got to run.'

'Not staying for supper?' she asks, easing her feet out of a pair of black court shoes and flexing her toes with a small wince.

'Not tonight, thanks very much. Mum's expecting me.'

'Give her my regards.'

Simon sees her to the door and calls, 'See you tomorrow,' up the street after her.

She runs the half-mile home with her satchel flapping against her legs and is sitting down to her lamb chop ten minutes later.

Three

Rosie has a free period after lunch the next day, the Friday, so she gets the bus down into town at the end of morning school to try on some jeans she had seen in the Broad Marsh shopping centre the previous weekend. Simon, though blessed with many qualities, is inclined to be forgetful, so when she calls in at Boots to buy some Lemsip for her mum, who has a bit of a sore throat, and the contraceptive display happens to catch her eye on the pharmacy counter, it seems like a good idea to buy a packet of condoms in case it slips his mind.

She puzzles over them for a while. There are a lot of different types although they all seem to be the same size. She concludes that there would be no market for a 'small' size. They have to be sold like packets of soap powder: large, extra large and elephantine, although perhaps not 'family-sized'.

She picks up a packet more or less at random and hands it to the assistant. She is annoyed with herself for blushing. The girl, unimpressed, takes her money, puts both packets in a small paper bag with the receipt, and Rosie sticks them in the front compartment of her satchel.

That small packet is another crucial part of that eventful week. Simon has remembered, of course, and she needn't have bothered and then her dad wouldn't have found them and they wouldn't have had the row and he wouldn't have said what he did. But that was later that day.

It seems strange to her, looking back, that she didn't ask Bob and Betty Mason about the first five years of her life. She had supposed either that they knew nothing about it or that they did and had chosen not to pass the information on to her; she trusted their judgment.

If she thought about it at all, she had assumed that she was one of those neglected or ill-treated children who turn up in the papers so regularly. She assumed that she had blotted out the memories, for her sanity and protection, the conscious mind suppressing the unthinkable. Yet she detected nothing in her subconscious either, no nightmares or irrational fears.

Her school reports describe her from the earliest as happy, co-operative, bright, well-adjusted, if strong-minded to the point of stubbornness.

Four

She goes straight home on Fridays as it's late-night closing at the supermarket and her mum likes a bit of company while her dad is working late. She can see at once that her mother is feeling worse – her nose is raw red where she has been blowing and wiping it all day and her eyes are puffy.

She puts her arm round her and kisses her cheek and her mother pushes her half-heartedly away, saying that she mustn't catch her cold. She looks old and a little faded. There are glamorous film stars who are older than she, but she spends no time or money on her appearance and her hair is grey and her face lined. She is wearing an old blue woollen dress and an apron and her slippers and looks like somebody's old mum, which is what she is.

'You should be in bed,' Rosie tells her, and she says that she has been spring-cleaning the sitting room as if that couldn't have waited. Rosie shrugs off her duffle coat and hangs it at the foot of the stairs with her satchel.

She puts the kettle on and mixes up the last of the old supply of Lemsip with a spoonful of honey and makes her mother go and lie down for a bit with a fresh box of tissues while she gets supper. She goes quietly and Rosie knows she must be feeling even iller than she looks to desert her post without protest.

They are having fish. It's funny, she thinks, how traditional it seems to be to have fish on a Friday, even when you're not Roman Catholic. The fish is to be grilled and won't take long, so she leaves that until Dad gets home and prepares some early new potatoes for boiling and makes a salad. She puts the radio on at low volume and listens to the news and picks at some cheese since she is hungry.

The Masons have a breakfast bar in the kitchen which is up against the radiator and is one of her favourite spots in the house on a cold day. She often sits there for hours, leafing through the papers, drinking coffee. She settles there now; it feels like the heart of the house.

She feeds Mr Sourpuss, a truculent ginger tom who had adopted them about seven years earlier. He has to have his meat cut up small as he's lost most of his teeth. He eats about half of it then waddles out through the cat flap and clambers laboriously over the fence. It is nearly spring, though cold still, and the garden is gradually coming into flower. Rosie is glad to see the end of winter, which has always struck her as the saddest season, when everything is dead and cold.

The house seems strangely quiet and peaceful and Rosie has that happy Friday-evening feeling. She fetches her homework from her bag, deciding to get it done tonight instead of leaving it until last thing on Sunday as is her habit. This seems such a good idea that she wonders why she doesn't always do it this way instead of having it nagging at her all weekend. She skims through it in no time and feels a great sense of release.

She slips upstairs at about seven to see if Mum needs anything but the sound of quiet breathing tells her she is asleep.

Dad gets in just before eight-thirty and calls out 'Anybody home?' He has done that every night of his married life, knowing perfectly well that the only times Mum hasn't been home to greet him was the time she had been in hospital having a lump – which turned out to be benign – removed from her breast, and the time of Grandma Collingwood's last illness when she was away in Basingstoke for nearly a week, saying goodbye and then sorting out about the funeral. Rosie shushes him and explains about Mum.

'I'll go and see if she wants anything.'

He takes off his coat and the flat cap he always wears to cover his bald head, drops them on the hall stand and starts up the stairs.

Rosie lights the grill for the haddock.

'She doesn't want any supper but she says she could use another of those lemony things,' he says, coming down again, puffing slightly. 'Her throat's parched like someone's sand-papering it.' He pulls open the drawer where they keep the aspirins and the crêpe bandages and the Elastoplast and begins to rummage in it without method or order. 'Good day at school, love?'

'There aren't any more in there,' she calls over to him, laying two pieces of fish on the grill pan and putting the third aside, intending to put it back in the fridge later. 'There's a new packet in my school bag, in the hall. In the Boots wrapping.'

He goes out obediently to look for it.

There can't be a father in the world – not a normal, healthy father, anyway – who isn't heartbroken at the discovery that his little girl is becoming sexually active. It's part of his job, in a sense, programmed into him since caveman days, to protect her from predatory males. His reaction is unlikely to be rational, especially when he has just worked a twelve-hour day and his wife is tired and ill in bed. He doesn't stop to reason that the presence of a packet of condoms in her satchel means that his daughter is being sensible and responsible, not the reverse.

Rosie will never blame him for his outburst that evening. Indeed, she supposes she should be grateful: if he hadn't found them, she might never have known the truth about her past, might never have so much as heard the name of Maire O'Neill.

But she scarcely recognises him when he comes walking back into the kitchen, walking slowly as if a great burden has just been laid upon his shoulders. She looks away from the grill, where the haddock is now sizzling nicely, to say something to him – something jocular about it being impossible to tear Mum away from her spring cleaning, short of death's door – and the words catch in her mouth.

This is not the kindly foster parent who had imitated a chimpanzee to make a sad orphan laugh, the father who had let himself be buried up to his neck in the sand at Bournemouth without complaint, who had bandaged hurt knees and kissed them better; this is a cold-eyed stranger, looking at her now with something like hatred. She has never seen him really angry – this mild, docile man – but it is obvious now that he is struggling to control his temper. His bald head is a fierce red and his fists are clenching and unclenching on a small blue and white paper bag.

Then she remembers.

'Dad . . .' She steps towards him, holding out her hand in truce and supplication, but he backs away from her.

'Don't you "Dad" me,' he says after a pause.

'Dad!' she repeats, feeling a pain more severe than any she has ever felt. She thinks for a moment that he might strike her. She is out of her depth. They don't do this, not in her family. She has been at friends' houses when they have embarrassing rows with their parents about their hair or their clothes or the time they come in at night. Even those trivial disagreements make her cringe. This is real.

'After all we've done for you,' he says, 'taking you in, trying to bring you up decently, give you an education, love you. We couldn't have loved you better if you'd been our own.'

'It's not so bad as you think . . .' she begins.

His anger is feeding upon itself; he picks up the word.

'Bad. Bad blood,' he says with an effort. 'Betty said it was environment that counted, not heredity, but I was never so sure. Besides, she brought you up for five years; that's long enough.'

'What are you talking about? I don't understand. Who brought me up? What do you mean, bad blood?'

'Your mother was a murderer, a *mass*-murderer . . .'

She puts her hands over her ears, willing herself not to hear, but his voice, though not particularly loud, pierces through her armour and she can hear him clearly.

'An IRA bomber, a terrorist. No more than a girl, barely older than you are now. All little and skinny and innocent-looking just like you pretend to be. Maire O'Neill. She killed half a dozen people . . .'

'No!'

'With a bomb. In her handbag . . .'

'No!'

In a pub. In High Wycombe . . .'

'Stop it!' she screams. 'Stop it.'

'Twelve, thirteen years ago.'

'I don't believe you! You're making it up!'

'Would you like to see the cuttings? The newspaper cuttings. They're in the attic. I thought one day you might need to know, that it might be only right to tell you. Betty said not, but everyone has a right to know their roots.'

Out of the corner of her eye she sees Mr Sourpuss jump on the worktop, taking advantage of the commotion to seize Mum's portion of haddock in his few remaining teeth and retire with it, a cunning look on his face. Smoke is coming out of the grill and the potatoes are boiling over and making the gas hiss. The scene is taking on a nightmarish quality of chaos, as her father talks on and on as if in a trance.

'I didn't think it would be this soon, you so sweet and good and clever with your ten GCSEs and butter-wouldn't-melt-in-your-mouth.'

'Liar! Bloody bloody liar!'

She runs past him. He tries to stop her but she is too quick and too small and too desperate and ducks under his arm. She grabs her coat and her purse. She knows she will be sick if she doesn't get some air. She grabs her keys and then throws them down again. The house smells of charring fish. She will never be able to smell fish cooking again without gagging. She hears her mother stirring upstairs, coming painfully out on to the landing.

'Rosie? Lovie? Are you hurt? I can smell burning.'

She wrenches open the door and his voice joins in the calling: 'Rosie!'

The anger is gone in an instant. In the dim light of the porch, she sees a look of horror on his face. He has come to his senses all in a moment and cannot believe what he has done, can hardly face explaining it to his wife.

She slams the door behind her and runs down the path, struggling into her coat as she goes. It is a cloudy, moonless night but she runs in the damp darkness, wanting to put as much distance as possible between herself and the Masons' house. She runs as far as King Edward park where she stops and fills her aching lungs before walking on.

Mrs Lawrence takes her in and puts her straight to bed in the boxroom. She asks no questions and will not let Simon ask any either, not that night. Rosie begs her to say that she is not there if anyone asks and she gives her her promise. Rosie would stake her life on Mrs Lawrence's promise.

Five

Simon, who is calm and logical, says that it doesn't matter: that she is Rosemary Mason, the daughter of Bob and Betty Mason who have brought her up and not Thing-ummy O'Neill. She is the same Rosie Mason she was yesterday, the Rosie Mason he loves. She wants to believe him but logic, for once, is not enough. She has to know the truth about Maire O'Neill. Mrs Lawrence, who has hurried home at lunchtime to hear all about it, backs her up.

Rosie did not wake until almost noon this Saturday, as her body recovers its strength. Now she sits at the kitchen table, rocking slightly back and forth on her chair as she always does when something upsets her, and tells them the whole story over beans on toast and coffee. Simon interrupts continually, asks questions, but Mrs Lawrence listens in silence.

'I remember the case vaguely,' she says when Rosie has finished, and adds apologetically, 'There have been so many.'

Simon turns his frown upon her, wanting her support, but she shakes her head at him.

'She needs to know, Simon. It's all very well for you to say that it doesn't matter. You know who you are; you know your mother, remember your father and grandparents. You have brothers and sisters.' She turns back to Rosie.

'It was an unusual case, now I come to think of it. Such a young girl, standing so erect and proud in court. That was one of the things that counted against her: that she seemed to show no emotion, no remorse.'

Something she said a few minutes earlier registers in Rosie's brain: There have been so many.

Like the Birmingham Six? The Guildford Four?

'Perhaps she didn't need to show remorse,' she says slowly.

187

'You don't feel remorse for something you haven't done.'

Simon swears softly. He gets up and walks over to the window. 'I won't let you do this,' he says in a tight voice. 'I won't let you work up a fantasy about a wronged woman, an innocent victim. It could ruin your life. She was tried and found guilty. She's been in prison all these years, presumably. She's a hardened criminal now, if she wasn't then.'

'Simon has a point,' Mrs Lawrence says. 'I can see that you have to know about your early life, your infancy, but don't go running away with a mad notion of miscarriages of justice.'

'If you're not with me, then you're against me,' is Rosie's only reply. Her lip curls in a familiar gesture of defiance.

Simon and his mother look at each other for a moment, then he says, 'What can we do to help?'

'Nothing at the moment. Just be here for moral support. I have business in town.'

She had imagined a room full of yellowing newspapers, dating back who knew how many decades. Instead the librarian shows her to a terminal and opens a filing cabinet full of little boxes.

'What date was it you said you wanted?'

'1978,' she says. 'I'm not sure of the actual date. Late summer or early autumn, I think.'

She extracts a little cardboard box marked July 1978 and shows Rosie how to thread the microfiche on to the reader and how to move it backwards and forwards and how to zero in on a particular spot.

'I'll just be over at the desk if you have any problems or if you want to photocopy anything,' she says, leaving her to it.

She begins to page through July. At first she is just looking for the appropriate headline, but she soon becomes absorbed in this alien world – the pre-Thatcher era which she barely remembers. There is no Channel 4, she quickly notices; the clothes are drab, the faces glum, houses absurdly cheap. Air-traffic controllers are on strike and Jeremy Thorpe, whom she read about two years ago for her GCSE history project, is on trial for conspiracy to murder.

July does not throw up the story she is looking for and she rewinds it and moves on to August, threading it wrongly to start with so that the stories appear in mirror writing. She runs the fiche forward at, as it were, walking pace so that she can catch the headlines as they stroll past. There is more misery for air travellers. The Prime Minister, James Callaghan, is being urged to call an autumn election.

There is something strange in reading these daily papers, knowing already what the future holds for the characters in this soap opera. Knowing – as the people quoted do not – that there will be no autumn election, that there will be a Winter of Discontent leading to a rout of the Labour party in May the following year. It is all so long ago – pre-Falklands, pre-AIDS – in her lifetime but also in her history books.

'OUTRAGE!'

She stops the fiche at the front page of Saturday, August 26th and magnifies the top half of the page.

'Six dead: dozens injured,' proclaims the smaller headline underneath. 'IRA pub bombers claim more lives.'

She reads slowly, carefully, absorbing each word. A bomb had exploded in the Hope and Anchor public house in High Wycombe at eleven o'clock the previous night, just as it was at its most crowded, just as they were calling last orders. The pub had been a favourite drinking place for off-duty soldiers from the local barracks; four soldiers had been killed outright and a fifth had died at Wycombe General Hospital during the night. A barmaid was also among the dead.

There is a photograph of her. She is about twenty-five, an ordinary-looking sort of girl with brown hair and a comfortable face; not brassy in the traditional barmaid way. She is smiling in the photo. The text says that she had been helping out in the pub to earn a little extra money before her wedding the following Easter. Her distraught fiancé is being comforted by friends.

Turn to page three for more pictures; editorial comment, page fifteen.

Page three shows the debris, like pictures of the war. Safe as houses, they say; buildings – bricks and mortar – are a metaphor for security and protection. What a delusion – see how easily they crumble and break.

The editorial on page fifteen calls for increased police powers under the Prevention of Terrorism Act – extra powers to detain without charge, to deport, to search. A continuation on the back page says that no one has, as yet, claimed responsibility but that the soldiers concerned had recently returned from a tour of duty in Northern Ireland and the explosive used, nitro-glycerine-based, is typical of the IRA 'bomb factories'.

Rosie pages on. The fiche does not include the Sunday papers and she goes on to Monday where a small paragraph at the bottom of page three tells her that a woman is helping police with their enquiries.

On Wednesday she catches a glimpse of her face at last, on page two, under a picture of stubble burning. A woman being held in connection with Friday night's bombing has appeared before magistrates in High Wycombe and been remanded in custody. She is climbing out of a police van, shielded by a bulky man in a suit and two younger men in uniform. Some sort of missile is striking the van behind her. There had almost been a riot.

She cannot make out the features, but on Thursday the police release a photograph of the woman who has been charged with the murders. Rosie magnifies it until it is just grainy black and grey dots, then draws back again. She sees a small woman, thin, looking much younger than her stated age of twenty-three. Her hair is black and ruffled like Rosie's, her eyes cold with anger. She recognises the pain in those dark eyes, understanding by instinct this woman who could not erupt in the heat of anger but only bury it in ice, deep within herself.

'Face of Evil,' says the headline, and it is Rosie's face.

Maire O'Neill: she reads the name below the picture, the name which would have meant nothing to her two days ago. So who is she, Rosie? There is no mention of a child.

She pages back and stares for a few minutes at the death and destruction, haunted by the waste of it all. She has no doubt that this woman is her mother, no doubt that she is incapable of this appalling crime.

These are the first rumblings of memories she has buried deep within her psyche, memories to which her conscious mind has no access – yet.

The next question is what is she going to do about it?

Six

She has been taught to do her research properly. The evidence so far is hearsay – her father – or circumstantial: a blurred face in a black and white photograph. After she leaves the library, she goes straight to the Citizens' Advice Bureau. She knows, dimly, that there is some provision for adopted children to find out who their real parents are. She has never bothered to look into it before; she has not until now been interested in the past – except academically – only in the present and the future.

A motherly woman interviews her in a cluttered office. Rosie puts her question to her.

'You can indeed have access to your original birth certificate,' she tells her, 'but not until you reach the age of majority which in your case . . .'

'. . . is in two weeks' time,' Rosie finishes for her. The woman looks startled but accepts her word.

'In that case, you can apply then. Take along your adoptive certificate which will, of course, confirm your birth date, and they'll let you have a copy of your first one.'

She hesitates then says kindly, 'It may not tell you very much, my dear. Just your mother's name, quite probably not your father's, and the chances are that your mother will long since have left the address given, have moved away, married, changed her name . . . She may not even want to be found.'

'I think I know who my mother was . . . is,' Rosie says, 'and exactly where she is to be found now. All I want is the confirmation of her name.'

The woman smiles at her uncertainly, wondering perhaps if she is a bit dotty, if she thinks she is Princess Anne's love-child or something like that. She wouldn't be the first. All children go through a phase of believing that their parents are not their real parents, that they were switched by the fairies or that there was a mistake at the hospital; that they are really royal, special. Adoptive children especially are prone to this.

The problem of how and where she is going to live vexes her on the bus home but she has reckoned without Mrs Lawrence – or Barbara, as she now insists Rosie call her – who will not hear of her leaving. No one else needs her boxroom and three cost very little more to feed than two.

They all sit that evening, after supper, looking through the photocopies Rosie made at the library. Simon, having accepted that she is going to do this and that there is no way of dissuading her, is brimming with practical suggestions, and she loves him for it.

He says that she should look up the recent reports of the appeals of the Birmingham and Guildford cases, see if she can find mention of a lawyer who specialises in this sort of thing, who might be persuaded to take an interest in her case.

He also volunteers to visit the university library where a friend of his works and look up the weekly news magazines for 1978 and 1979, dig out any more in-depth analyses of the O'Neill trial. Rosie is bursting with gratitude to them both.

After a silent consultation between mother and son, in which only the eyes speak, Simon tells her that her mother has rung twice that afternoon and her father once, looking for her. They are, naturally, frantic with worry, but the Lawrences have not admitted to her being there.

'I didn't actually lie,' Barbara points out. 'You weren't here when they rang. But they're talking of going to the police, Rosie, you must get in touch.'

'Tomorrow,' she mutters, 'or Monday.' She wants them to hurt for a while, to suffer a little as she is suffering.

'You're seventeen,' Barbara says, 'they can't make you come home if you don't want to, but have a little pity on them, Rosie, please.'

It seems strange later when she remembers that today was the day that she and Simon had earmarked for their first sexual experiments, which decision has caused a chain reaction that has exploded her life.

Now he sees her to the door of the boxroom and drops a chaste kiss on her forehead, wishing her a good night. They both know that there will be no space for their personal life until she has seen this unfinished business of hers through to a resolution, one way or another.

Seven

She had apparently taken no personal effects with her to the children's home. She surfaced into life as a five-year-old with three sets of clothes – all quite old but neatly mended, clean and pressed – and that was all. There had been no books or toys, no family photographs, no memories. It seemed that she had left home in a hurry, which ties in with what she is now being told.

Had she had a father – a blood father, Maire O'Neill's husband? Had he been implicated in the bombing? There is no mention of him in the newspaper reports; she is forced to conclude that he does not exist. That is not a new sorrow: children given up for adoption are usually reconciled to being fatherless.

When she started at the new school, in the autumn of 1978, she could already read and write. She remembers that. She must have taught her, the woman with her face, have cared enough to do so.

There had been stories too: strange tales about kings and queens and sorcerers who had been dead a thousand years, of swans who were enchanted people and people who were bewitched gods. Her classmates did not know them, thought them bizarre, but told other stories outside her knowledge: about Cinderella and Snow White and Little Red Riding Hood.

One of the first gifts Bob Mason had given her, before he was officially her dad, was a box of crayons – a dozen different colours – and a pad of thick, stiff paper to draw on. He could not have made a better choice. The first thing she drew was him, very big and solid and real.

Simon and Barbara have a long-standing arrangement to go for Sunday lunch today with Simon's eldest brother, Andy, and his family in Mansfield. They try to persuade her to go too, but she doesn't want to intrude on a family party and, besides, she has a lot of thinking to do. They leave at about half past eleven and she makes herself a sandwich and some coffee an hour later.

It is clear that she is going to have to go home at some stage to get a change of clothes; she had run out in what she stood up in – her usual schoolwear of jeans, shirt and sweatshirt – and she hasn't even got a clean pair of knickers. Perhaps Simon will go for her. Or perhaps she can go one day when there will be no one there, when her dad is at work and Mum at the shops. Her parents are creatures of habit, of routine, and Mum always does a big food shop on Tuesday morning. She can last out until then. She feels rather low suddenly; yesterday it had been a big adventure, but today she feels very young and too small and helpless to be running away from home.

It is barely three weeks since the last of the snow. The little house is cold and she doesn't like to turn up the heating because she knows that Barbara has to be careful with her money. She borrows an Aran pullover of Simon's and drapes it across her shoulders – it is, of course, far too big for her.

She doesn't know what to do, can't settle anywhere on the unfamiliar furniture, leafs aimlessly through some of Simon's books, longs for the warmth of her breakfast bar at home where she would now be finishing her Sunday dinner and proposing to drag her father out for a brisk walk.

At three o'clock the front doorbell rings and her first instinct is not to answer it. But it keeps on and on ringing, interspersed with bangs on the knocker, and she has left the light on in the front room so it's obvious that someone is at home. Finally she decides to answer it.

She can see who it is as soon as she gets out into the hall. The top half of the door is frosted glass and she can make out the bulky silhouette of her father, pressing his nose against the glass in an attempt to see through the opaque clusters. She takes a deep breath and pulls the door open.

He recoils slightly as the door swings away from him; he has not really expected an answer after all this time. He takes his cap off when he sees her standing there and twists it in his fingers. He's wearing his Sunday clothes – an old pair of corduroy trousers and a baggy jumper, a tweed jacket, his gardening boots. His bald head is ivory today. He hasn't shaved. For a time, neither of them speaks.

'I didn't go into work yesterday,' he says at length. 'I rang in sick.' This might strike a stranger as an odd opening remark but Rosie knows that he means it to show how upset he has been. He has not had a day's sick leave since she was seven and they both succumbed to German measles. He prides himself on his ability to soldier on.

'Come in,' she says, backing away before him. 'Don't let all that cold air into the house.'

He follows her in, pushing the door to behind him, wiping his boots elaborately on the doormat, and they both stand there in the hall. Rosie feels a little shy. On Friday she saw him stripped of the carapace of civilisation, while he had swallowed the bitter pill of knowing that she is no longer a virgin – or so he thinks. They need to establish a new relationship; the old one will no longer do.

'How's Mum?' she asks.

'Her sore throat's nearly better,' he says, grateful for the opening. 'She would have come with me but I made her stay indoors in the warm.' He looks around him. 'Isn't Mrs Lawrence here?' She explains. He looks relieved. They are best without an audience, at least until they've rehearsed some more. 'She said on the phone that you weren't here, but I didn't know where else you would go if not here.'

'She just said what I asked her to. Anyway, I wasn't here when you phoned.'

He clears his throat.

'I'm sorry, Rosie. I'm that sorry, love. I can't begin to tell you how sorry I am.'

She begins to cry and all at once she is in his arms and he is smoothing her hair and petting her shoulder and going 'There, there', just the way he did when she fell and hurt herself as a child or when she didn't get the part of the Virgin Mary in the play at primary school which she wanted so badly, and she knows that the old relationship will do them very well still.

'I've got the car outside,' he says. 'There's some ginger cake for tea. Get your things, love.' She makes a gesture with her hands because she has no things, just what she stands up in. 'We'll go home and forget all about it. Eh?'

'I'll come home,' she says, putting on her coat, 'but I can't forget what you told me, Dad. I can't just forget it.'

He makes no comment, almost as if he's truly forgotten the earth-shattering news he had broken to her. She leaves a note for Simon saying she will see him at school on Monday and they drive slowly home, with him remarking only that the clutch is slipping.

'Which reminds me,' he says, 'why don't I buy you a course of driving lessons for your birthday? Then you could use the car in the evenings this summer, and when you're home from university for your holidays.'

She recognises vaguely that this is a bribe, since he has been opposed to the idea of her driving his precious car until now.

'I have to know all you know about her,' she says, as they pull into their street. 'Maire O'Neill.'

He swings the car into the side of the road and stops the engine. They are a long way from their house. He sits staring moodily out of the window.

'I'll never forgive myself for telling you. She's nothing to do with you. Forget you ever heard her name.'

'I can't. You must see that. What about those press cuttings you mentioned?'

'There aren't any press cuttings.' He won't look at her. 'I made that up. I was just hitting out blindly. I'm a liar, like you said.'

She explains that she has been to the library, that she's verified the few facts he has told her about the bombing, the arrest.

'It's only what they told us at the Social Services,' he insists. 'It might not be true. They might have . . . I dunno, got you mixed up with some other kid at the home.'

'It's not very likely, Dad,' she says gently, and he shakes his head since he agrees with her.

'Oh, my love,' he says. He restarts the engine.

'The whole truth is the only birthday present I want,' she tells him.

'We'll see,' is all he says as he pulls neatly into their driveway. 'We'll have to see.'

Eight

Simon is sad. He loves Rosemary Mason but fears he cannot compete with this glamorous new mother, this martyred soul. He loves her with a love mature beyond his years. She is not pretty but there is an elfin quality about her which has enslaved him. Two things make Rosie special: he can be completely himself with her and she never bores him.

He is afraid of the white-faced woman in the old newspapers, wishes – almost – that they had hanged her twelve years ago so that the matter might now be beyond earthly appeal. He hates himself for wishing this. He can only wait and give what help he can.

He comes back from the university library Tuesday lunchtime and Rosie knows at once that he has something for her but doesn't want to give it to her. He avoids her eye all afternoon and shuffles about in the corridors between lessons with his hands in his pockets and his shoulders hunched. He has Spanish last period and she has History so she waits outside the school gates until she sees him come hurrying out with the Spanish teacher, jabbering nineteen to the dozen about Borges.

The Spanish teacher calls out a goodbye, diving into his Seat car, and Simon falls into step beside her on the pavement.

'Well?' she says. 'What have you found?'

'It's nothing really,' he says reluctantly. 'Just an article about children and prison. I mean about what happens to children when their mothers are sent to prison for any length of time. Very young babies can be kept with their mothers in special mother-and-baby units but . . .'

'It mentioned my mother?' She cuts across his irrelevances.

'It mentioned the O'Neill case,' he replies carefully.

'Was there a child?' A thought strikes her. 'Or children?'

This is a new and alien idea: that she might have brothers and sisters somewhere in the world. She doesn't like it. It doesn't fit with the person she feels herself to be.

'One child.' She feels relief. 'A girl. She was five at the time of the arrest. Her name was . . . I don't know how you pronounce it.' He spells it out. 'R.O.I.S.I.N.'

'Rho-Sheen,' she answers automatically. She stops walking. Somewhere inside her head she can hear a voice calling that name . . .

'Roisin. Roisin.'

It is familiar to her, this – literally – outlandish name.

She is happy to hear the calling. It is a low, tuneful voice and commands respect and love. She obeys its summons joyfully. She is a slight but sturdy child, not a toddler; older, four or five. She is playing on a patch of grass outside a block of council flats – not an unpleasant tower block but a three-storey building with a green door and bright curtains at the windows and the occasional window box. There are trees and a small garden and a car park. She is playing by herself but she is absorbed in her solitude, watching butterflies circle each other in the late afternoon sun. She is wearing a pink and white gingham dress and has got soil and grass stains down the front, but she knows that no one will mind about little things like that.

'Roisin. Tea's ready.'

The voice is calling from an open window and she cannot yet see the face behind it clearly.

She jumps to her feet, dusts herself down and skips into the block of flats, up one flight of stairs, in at an open door where there is a smell of fruit scones just cooling from the oven . . .

'Rosie! Rosie!' Simon waves his hand in front of her face with a forcedly comical expression. 'Anyone at home? Look, let's nip round to my place and you can have a glance at the article and we'll talk over that English essay.'

'I shan't be doing my A-levels this summer,' she says. 'Not this year. I have things to do – things that won't keep.'

'Wait until your birthday,' Simon says, taking her hand in his. 'Wait until you've seen that birth certificate, until you're quite sure.'

'I am sure. I am Roisin O'Neill.'

Nine

Rosie sat down to read the magazine article Simon had brought her.

The Forgotten Victims
– punishing the children of women offenders –
by Anne-Marie Doyle

I'd like to introduce you to Mandy who is eighteen. She's a very ordinary-looking girl, similar to the daughter of one of your neighbours, with a round, childish face, red cheeks, the remains of her teenage spots, brown hair cut spikily short. She is expecting her first baby any day now and she is afraid; she doesn't know what to expect and there is no one to reassure her.

She has long since lost contact with the baby's father who, in any case, would not be allowed to be with her at this crucial time. She is permitted to see her mother and older sister for two hours once a fortnight, but they cannot always afford the train fare.

Mandy has not been able to see her own GP. She has not been offered a scan. She has little opportunity for exercise, has had only cursory ante-natal advice and has been offered no books on pregnancy or childcare, nor can she afford to buy them.

Mandy is an inmate of Styal prison in Cheshire. Over a year ago she was charged with shoplifting – the result of a 'dare' gone badly wrong – and assault – she hit the store detective in her panic. She was remanded on bail for five months awaiting trial; the police did not oppose bail, no one expected that her trial would result in a prison sentence.

She realised during this time that she was pregnant – the result of a brief and unsatisfactory relationship with a boy she had met in a pub. She did not consider an abortion, having an inarticulate conviction that it was 'wrong'.

As a first offender, she would have got off with a fine on the shoplifting charge alone, but the magistrates sent the assault charge up to the Crown Court where the judge took a serious view of it and sentenced her to nine months' imprisonment. No thought seems to have been given to non-custodial alternatives such as community work.

Styal is not considered an appropriate prison for young offenders like Mandy – it's a closed prison designed for long-term adult prisoners – but it has a mother and baby unit. It is also at the other end of the country from her home town of Maidstone, hence the difficulties her family have in coming to visit her as often as they would like.

So Mandy is in Mellanby House, along with ten other pregnant women, most of whom are serving sentences for drug offences or violent crime. Many of them are, themselves, drug addicts, many will give birth to addicted babies; many are able, against all the odds, to obtain drugs still.

Ironically, it is these women who have given Mandy such information as she has about pregnancy and have attempted to quell her terror of childbirth. Ironically, too, it was the governor of Styal, James Anderson, who was forced to resign in 1986 as being 'too soft' after he had stated publicly that pregnant women should be paroled before confinement – a practice widespread in the judicial systems of other 'civilised' countries.

Mandy is kept at work all through her pregnancy: hard, physical work which includes scrubbing floors. She is told that this is good for her. The prison medical service is quite separate from the NHS and operates under its own rules; a convicted prisoner has no right to a second opinion.

A nurse sleeps in Mellanby House at night in case any of the women go into labour in the small hours, but she resents being disturbed. When Mandy's contractions start at 1 a.m. one cold December night, two weeks before the baby is officially scheduled, the nurse denies that she is in labour and tells her to stop disturbing the house with her shouting.

Mandy is cowed but the other women kick up a fuss until an ambulance is sent for. Mandy is by now in the last stages of labour and her baby daughter is born an hour after her admission to hospital.

She is left unguarded at the hospital for the rest of the day, but her outdoor clothes are removed. She is in a ward on her own with no one to talk to although the nurses know she is from Styal and she has some curiosity value for them.

The following morning two warders arrive to move her back to Mellanby House, but she is bleeding slightly and the doctor will not let her leave. There is an argument but the doctor prevails and she stays in hospital for four days. She is allowed ten days' bed rest when she gets back to Styal. Post-natal depression will not be tolerated.

Mandy is breastfeeding. Short-term prisoners are not allowed up in their dormitories during the day except by special permission which is rarely granted, so she feeds baby Dawn in the common-room. Male warders often wander in and out as she does so.

She is allowed to see Dawn only at certain times of the day and she must be put down to sleep at a fixed hour and not picked up again – however much she cries. Taking the baby into her bed to feed or comfort her is a punishable offence. Prison notions of childcare are ante-deluvian, or at least ante-bellum – fixed four-hourly feeds, strict discipline; too much cuddling makes the child 'soft'. Prison warders are very down on anyone who is 'soft'.

But Mandy is, in a sense, one of the lucky ones. When Dawn is two months old they both leave Styal on parole and Mum is waiting to take them in back home in Maidstone. Longer-term offenders may keep their babies with them until they are nine months old; then alternative arrangements must be made. If the father is unable or unwilling, if there is no mother, sister, aunt who will take the child, then the only alternative is 'Care', which means either a children's home or fostering. The child, thrust into the hurly-burly of a council home with its noise and lack of privacy, might as well be in prison itself although it has committed no crime, been convicted by no jury and sentenced by no judge.

Older children are allowed to visit their mothers in theory. In practice a social worker or probation officer must be found to accompany them and the money for the journey is often not *available. If the mother is serving a longish sentence, say more than two years, the breakdown in the family bond is almost complete. The child will be settled with the relative or the foster family who took it in and the mother will probably have no home to offer it on first being released.*

Chris is serving a ten-year sentence for manslaughter, also at Styal. She has three children, ranging in age from twelve to four. Her boyfriend, Errol, who is the father of the youngest child but not of the two eldest, cares for all the children and has had to give up his job in order to do so. They live in the London Docklands, in a council flat – these are original docklanders, not incomers from the City.

The Social Services should, in theory, pay for them all to visit Chris at least once a month, but they say the fares are too steep. Instead Chris saves up her visit entitlement and, once every six months, she is transferred to Holloway for five days where her children and Errol can come and use up half a year's visit in less than a week.

Sometimes the transfer to Holloway will be called off at the last minute under the pretext that there are not enough officers available to act as escort. Errol is no longer on the phone, could not afford to pay the bills, so a complicated system of messages with neighbours has to be employed to save him and the children a wasted journey.

Often, the warders at Holloway will insist that Chris is entitled to only one visit during her stay and she must demand to see the governor before her rights are admitted.

The youngest child, Becky, is always over-excited on seeing her mother and tearful to the point of hysteria at the end of the week's visiting. Chris searches her conscience to ask if it would not be kinder to stop the visits altogether. Her greatest fear is that Errol will get tired of waiting for her, meet someone else, and that all the children will be taken into Care.

But these problems are as nothing to those faced by the children of a 'Lifer'. There are few women who fall into this category in Britain – perhaps fifty in the whole country. They may serve as little as seven or eight years, they may serve twenty or more; there is no way of knowing. In such circumstances, there may be no alternative to giving the child up for adoption. The mother is often, understandably, reluctant to do this and in extreme cases the court may order an adoption. The child and the mother are thus lost to each other for ever.

A case which springs to mind is that of the IRA bomber, Maire O'Neill, convicted of murder in 1979 and recommended to serve at least twenty years. A young woman of twenty-three with an illegitimate five-year-old daughter and no other family, she gave young Roisin up freely for adoption. Other women, perhaps mothers themselves, can only try to imagine her agony, and praise her courage in putting her child's best interests first.

Anne-Marie Doyle is a solicitor specialising in family law. Born in Belfast of Protestant stock, she has long been settled in England and now lives and works in Oxford. She is a legal consultant for the Prison Reform Trust.

Rosie realises then that she has been blaming her mother for putting her up for adoption, when really she had been thinking only of her future.

There is a small photograph of Anne-Marie Doyle which has cut the top of her head off. It shows a woman in her late forties or early fifties, serious-looking, unglamorous in her specs and a crisp white blouse. Almost severe.

She is the one whose help Rosie wants. Simon is patient. She is a specialist in family law, he points out, not criminal law. She is a Belfast Protestant and will have scant sympathy with a convicted IRA terrorist.

'She's the one who can help me,' Rosie persists. 'See how she praises Maire's courage. She'll understand.'

Simon sighs and changes the subject and two days later he brings her Anne-Marie Doyle's address and telephone number. She still lives and works in Oxford. Rosie sits down to write to her. She takes her time over the letter. There is still almost a week to go to her birthday.

Ten

On Monday, April 8th she holds her original birth certificate in her hand. It holds no surprises. She is Roisin Cathleen O'Neill, born at Liverpool Royal Hospital on April 2nd, 1973 to Maire Deirdre O'Neill of 14 Dorset Street; father unnamed.

Anne-Marie Doyle has not answered her letter. Term is just starting at school but she will not be going back. On the 9th she buys a day return to Oxford and goes to find Anne-Marie. She doesn't tell anyone where she is going.

The journey takes a long time. The train is late leaving Nottingham and she almost misses her connection at Coventry; but four hours after she set out from home, she finds herself at last on Oxford station.

Anne-Marie's address is in an area called Jericho – a quarter of artisans' cottages which she thinks she recognises from her reading of *Jude the Obscure*. She buys a map of the city at the station and finds that the street is within walking distance.

She crosses a river she assumes to be the Thames and begins walking north along Walton Street. She has been to Oxford only once before, for her interview at Worcester College where she had hoped to be going to read English and History that autumn if her grades were good enough. She passes the college now without a second glance. All that belongs to another part of her life; no, to another life.

She doesn't know why she has come. It is half past eleven in the morning. It's obvious that Anne-Marie Doyle will not be at her home address, that she will be at work. Rosie doesn't know where she works but perhaps one of the neighbours will be able to tell her. It's a long way to come on a wild-goose chase, and she has always seen herself as such a logical person.

It must be that Irish blood, she thinks, allowing herself a little joke to raise her spirits. She shakes her head to upbraid herself but plods on.

She stops outside the house, which is in a narrow road leading down towards the canal. It's a two-up-two-down cottage with a shiny red front door and red window frames. She can see no doorbell, only a brass knocker. There is no garden – the cottage fronting straight on to the street – but there is a window box full of daffodils and a hanging basket of trailing greenery.

There is no net at the window and she finds herself looking straight into a through sitting room – rather sparse with a polished wood floor and just a couple of sofas. A desk stands in front of the window and she is disconcerted when a figure rears up from it to stare back out at her. She backs away in alarm, then takes her courage in her hands and bangs the knocker.

Eleven

She opens the door and says, 'Can I help you?' rather coolly, as anyone might to a street urchin peering in at their private window. She is older than in the magazine photo, naturally enough since it is three or four years since that article appeared. She is not 'well-preserved' but looks what she is: a tired, overly thin woman in her middle fifties. She is wearing the sort of clothes you wear to lounge around in at home when you're certain no one will come to disturb you: a black jersey skirt and a black and yellow sweatshirt; bare legs and feet, no make-up. Her straight dark hair has a wide stripe of white across the left side. Her glasses slip down her nose and she peers over them as she waits for her visitor to speak.

'My name's Rosemary Mason,' she blurts out. 'I wrote to you . . .' It seems so hopeless all of a sudden, and she wonders what has possessed her to come all this way without so much as an appointment. Does she really think that a teenage girl and a cross-looking middle-aged woman are going to take on the whole of the legal establishment – judges, juries, police, the Home Office – and win? But she has Anne-Marie's interest now and she says, 'You'd better come in.'

Rosie follows her into the austere room she glimpsed through the window. The desk is littered with papers and open reference books, and more books and papers stand around on the floor on either side and on the coffee table.

'I work at home most days,' she says, gesturing at the mess. 'I do know where everything is.' She begins to move the pile of debris on the coffee table, then changes her mind. 'We'll be better off in the kitchen.'

She turns and Rosie follows her to the back of the house where she sits at a scrubbed deal table while Anne-Marie makes instant coffee. The room has been extended into a sort of conservatory at the back and is very warm where the spring sunshine shines through the expanse of glass. There are ferns and herbs; cork boards sprout clusters of bills and photographs.

'I'm sorry I haven't got round to answering your letter,' she says. 'I can't imagine why you picked on me, to be frank. I specialise in family law although I have done the odd bit of juvenile crime. You want someone like Gareth Peirce.'

Rosie begins to explain again about the magazine article but she waves her silent.

'I remember that article. I've rehashed it a few times since. It's a sort of hobby horse of mine – the punishment meted out to the families of offenders who're made to suffer although they're innocent of any crime, the children especially.'

'You have children of your own?' There are several photos of children on the pin boards. A blond boy of about six beams out, his red football shirt wet with fresh mud, his cheeks flushed with cold and pleasure.

'No.' She follows Rosie's gaze. 'None of my own. Those are nephews, nieces; the mud wrestler's my godson, Teddy.'

She takes the last cigarette from a packet of Silk Cut and ignites the gas ring to light it, holding her hair back out of the way as she stoops to the flame. She sits down opposite Rosie. She inhales then blows the smoke up high at the ceiling so it won't go in her visitor's eyes. Then she looks at her hard for a moment and says, 'I remember the O'Neill case vividly. In fact I was in court on some of the days. You had to get there early, there was quite a queue for seats. It was a sell-out.'

'It wasn't a circus,' Rosie says in disgust.

'But justice must be seen to be done,' she says. 'There were a lot of IRA bombings in the seventies. Feeling was running high.'

'I don't know why I came.' Rosie stares out of the window into the tiny garden. 'You're from Northern Ireland yourself, aren't you? You must hate the IRA.' She gets up clumsily, jogging the table. She fears she is going to cry.

'You just sit down,' Anne-Marie says, 'you've come a long way and you haven't even drunk your coffee.' Rosie obeys her: it seems the right thing to do. The tears recede. 'You're here because you think your mother was innocent. Isn't that right?

So what I think about the IRA is neither here nor there since, according to you, she's not one of them and never was.'

She has one of the soft Ulster accents which can sound so tuneful in a woman's mouth, and it seems to grow more noticeable as she speaks. She also has an eloquence, a fluency, which Rosie has noticed before in Irish people.

'And if you want to know,' she continues, 'what it is that I hate – it's not the IRA nor the UDA but the everyday bigotry and prejudice that was part of my girlhood: all the unthinking talk of "Prods" and "Tegs" and do you come from the Shankill Road or the Falls? And me stuck in the middle with my Catholic-sounding name, being treated like a spy by both sides. And that was before the Troubles began, mind; well, the latest wave of them, anyway. All clear?'

'Clear,' Rosie mutters. The older woman's severe mouth relaxes into a half smile and Rosie smiles back and drinks some coffee.

'Feeling was running high,' she says again, 'which is why I'm prepared to believe that your mother may, just possibly, not have got a fair trial.'

'Then you'll help me?'

'Perhaps. My first instinct on getting your letter was to write an anodyne reply saying I couldn't help, was too busy, that it wasn't my field. Then I thought back a bit, remembered her standing there in the dock like a royal princess, so calm and contained.'

'Was she?' Rosie feels a lump form in her throat and, in embarrassment, takes a long swig of coffee.

'That very composure told against her with the jury, you see. Do you remember the Lindy Chamberlain case, in Australia; the dingo baby case, a few years ago?'

'Vaguely.'

'She had the same problem. The jury couldn't believe that anyone who was innocent could stand there calmly and unemotionally in the face of such terrible accusations. They thought that anyone who was innocent would shout that innocence from the rooftops.'

'That's what I would do,' Rosie agrees.

'The papers branded Maire the Cold Calculating Killer. The judge, in sentencing her, called her a Heartless Fanatic. She impressed me. I can still see her clearly after twelve years. When the jury returned their verdict, she closed her eyes for a second. That was the only sign she gave of the pain and fear she must have been in. It was as if, whatever happened, she wasn't going to let them see that they'd beaten her.'

Anne-Marie drags on her cigarette with venom. 'That's all you hear nowadays: that you've got to get "in touch with your feelings". It doesn't seem to occur to people that you can be in touch with your feelings without hurling them in people's faces like custard pies.' Her mouth twists in distaste or distress. 'Sorry. I don't know what brought that on.'

She gets up and stubs her cigarette end out in the sink. Her unthinking sluttishness appeals to Rosie who sees a woman who has been alone too much and for too long.

'You are so like her,' she says, sitting down again and brushing a few crumbs off the table on to the floor.

'Didn't she appeal?' Rosie asks.

'I doubt if it would have done any good. There were no grounds – no fresh evidence, no misdirection of the jury by the judge – but she didn't even try. Plenty of people took that as an admission of guilt. They locked her away and quietly forgot about her because that was what it suited them to do.'

'You believe in her innocence, don't you?' Rosie leans forward eagerly, lays a hand on her arm. She flinches slightly as if she is not used to being touched but, with a visible effort of will, does not draw her arm away.

'Do you?' she says.

'Yes!'

'Why? Do you remember her? You can't have been more than four or five. Have you kept in touch?'

Roisin explains how she had discovered the truth of her past less than a month earlier. 'But I know she didn't do it,' she says, 'and I won't let you help me unless you know it too.'

Anne-Marie begins to laugh. 'You come here begging for my help and now you tell me you won't accept it unless I can pass certain tests. I recognise Maire O'Neill's daughter, all right.'

Rosie apologises quickly and touches down to earth for the first time that day.

'I've no money.'

'Don't worry. It'll all come out of legal aid, assuming we can make some sort of case and get it to the Court of Appeal.'

'You'll take the case, then.'

'It looks like it, doesn't it.' She shakes her head slowly. 'I never intended this. It'll be a long, hard slog. The government's been embarrassed enough by the Birmingham and Guildford cases. They'll block us every step of the way. I must be mad. On the other hand, I'll be retiring soon. It would be quite nice to go out in a blaze of . . . publicity, if not glory.'

It will give her something to care about again.

'You have my services full time as a researcher, stamp-licker, general gopher,' Rosie says.

She raises her eyebrows. 'Haven't you got school?'

'This is more important.'

'Then I shall make you some lunch before we go any further. That's the least I can do for my unpaid assistant.'

Twelve

They eat a bachelor girl's meal of tinned spaghetti and sliced white bread followed by ice-cream and fill in the gaps.

'As it happens,' Anne-Marie says, 'I looked up the details of the case after I got your letter, to refresh my memory. She didn't make a confession, the way a lot of the others did.'

'Why does anyone confess to something they didn't do?' Rosie asks.

'To make the police stop. They just go on and on at you for hours – the same questions, the same accusations. In the end it seems easier to confess, anything to make them stop badgering you, take it back the next day. Except that by then it's too late.'

Rosie is silent, being unable to imagine herself into such a situation of fear.

'On the other hand,' Anne-Marie goes on, 'Gerry Conlon, of the Guildford Four, was made to confess with the threat that his mother or one of his sisters back in Belfast would meet with an "accident" – a sniper's bullet, say – if he didn't.'

Rosie is shell-shocked. 'I don't believe it!'

'That's not how we do things in this country, you mean? I don't *want* to believe it either.'

'But . . .' Rosie recovers herself '. . . if she didn't confess . . .'

'Her conviction was on purely circumstantial evidence and some forensic,' Anne-Marie goes on. She explains that they found traces of nitroglycerine on her mother's hands the day after the bombing.

'That's the key to our appeal. Other than that they have nothing but the fact that she was there at the pub that night, that she was seen running away – running for a bus, she says

– a few minutes before the bomb went off and that the government desperately needed a conviction to prove to the public that they were containing these outrages.'

'It all sounds so paltry,' Rosie says, 'to put a person in prison for years and years on nothing more substantial than that.'

'Indeed. I'm a little surprised the case wasn't reopened later, after the dust had settled. In fact, I wondered at first if she was still alive . . .' The young girl lets out a gasp of horror; that possibility has not occurred to her. Anne-Marie is quick to reassure her. Since receiving Rosie's letter, she has done her homework thoroughly.

'She's alive and even well. She spent two years in Durham H Wing, ten in Styal, in Cheshire, and she's recently been moved to Askham Grange in Yorkshire. Now Askham is an open prison which means she's sane and not considered a danger to the public.'

'Sane!' Rosie echoes.

'A lot of long-term prisoners have psychiatric problems. How would you feel being locked up in a cell for hours every day for years on end?' Rosie shudders. 'A lot of prisons have psychiatric units which can also serve as punishment blocks. That's the worst threat they can make to an unruly prisoner: that they'll be sent to Rampton or Broadmoor.'

'An open prison?' The idea is new. She has thought inevitably in terms of bars on windows and barbed-wire fences over impossibly high walls; of watch towers and dogs.

'The fact that she's been moved there indicates that the end of her sentence may be in sight. They may give her a release date soon. Alternatively they may keep her in there for another ten years; the judge recommended she serve at least twenty, you know.'

'What will it have done to her?' she asks slowly.

Anne-Marie answers her without equivocation. 'Some get bullied, beaten up, put through a living hell. Some become the bullies: get hardened so they'll never love or trust anyone again. She may have been institutionalised, may have lost the will, the ability, to think for herself, to survive in the outside world.'

'She's only young still,' Rosie protests. 'She's barely thirty-five.'

'Even so. Some survive surprisingly well, though: often the dreamers, the ones who have a rich inner life, a private world into which they can retreat and where no one can get at them. But sometimes that world becomes too real and they can't get back out of it again and then . . .'

'Broadmoor? Rampton?'

'Yes.'

'Thank you for being so honest with me.'

Anne-Marie looks her up and down, her glasses sliding down her nose again. 'I'm not sure you're not making me feel guilty. You look so young. You're at the age when you should be out enjoying life with boyfriends, looking forward to university, not embarking on an almost hopeless quest. Maybe I shouldn't be encouraging you.'

'Plenty of people have tried to put me off already.'

'I bet they have.'

'It did no good.'

'I bet it didn't. You understand that Maire O'Neill may be a bitter, destroyed woman, that she may not want to know you, that *you* may not want to know *her* in the event. But you won't let it stop you, will you?' Rosie just smiles. 'What shall I call you?' she asks. 'Rosemary or Roisin?'

'Rosie is what people call me and will do for both.'

'Well, Rosie, the next thing for me to do is to write to your mother at Askham and ask her to let me have a visiting order. You realise that we can't do anything without her consent? But once I tell her who my client is . . .'

Rosie is frightened suddenly that this great wheel she has set in motion may lurch out of control and run her down. She has a mother, and a father; a home and a life. She interrupts. 'I would like to remain anonymous for the time being.'

Anne-Marie stares, then shrugs. 'It might be an awful shock for her to know you were there, in the wings, after all these years. Okay; if she'll see me, well and good, but if she won't answer my letter or won't let me visit, you may have to be my trump card. Fair enough?'

'Fair enough.'

Anne-Marie Doyle — middle-aged, divorced, childless — wonders if righting this miscarriage of justice is what she has been put on earth to do.

'We'll need the best barrister we can get,' she muses, 'and I think I know where to find him. Ever hear of a man called Steven Hale?'

Thirteen

Maire turns the letter over several times without comprehension. No one has ever written to her before, not in all these years. And yet it is for her: a white oblong with a neat inscription – Miss M. O'Neill, HMP Askham Grange. A first-class stamp, an expensive stamp, a 22p stamp. Surely it can't cost 22p to send a letter!

She pulls the gummed flap open clumsily since she no longer knows how to open a letter. It is typewritten and that reassures her in an odd way – it is business, then, not personal; nothing personal, how could it be?

She looks first at the signature. She can't make it out – a great looming A at the start, then something which might be an M – but the name is typed underneath: Anne-Marie Doyle. It means nothing to her. What does this Anne-Marie Doyle want with her?

She puts it in the back pocket of her jeans and goes off to open the library. She will think about it later, decide what to do.

Roisin's mother sends a visiting order about a week after receiving Anne-Marie's letter. Nothing else – no note, no word of comment. The visit is for two weeks' time, and Anne-Marie promises to look in on Rosie on her drive north since Nottingham is, by great good fortune, on the way from Oxford to York.

Her mother – this is getting confusing; she means Betty Mason now – has gone very quiet. She is hurt and disapproving and Rosie does all she can to convince her that this desire to help her birth mother is not at her expense.

Her father, after his one big explosion, is more supportive

but perhaps he has less to lose – there being no sign of a birth father wanting to take his place. He is sad that she has dropped out of school so close to her goals, but says pragmatically that she can take her A-levels with the resits in the autumn or next summer, and probably do even better with the extra tuition.

Since her sixteenth birthday, her parents have paid her a monthly allowance so that she can learn to handle money responsibly. This now stands at fifty pounds a month, which is adequate for her day-to-day needs and a few items of clothing but will not cover endless train fares to Oxford, London or York with overnight stops. However, she has a little money in a savings account and her father wordlessly presses a cheque for £200 into her hand for her birthday, saying, 'For expenses.' She thinks she can manage. If necessary, she can always get a part-time job.

Meanwhile she is reading everything she can lay her hands on about the High Wycombe bombing, from the first ugly pictures to the trial itself. She reads up about the successful appeals of the Birmingham Six and the Guildford Four. She is making lists of people involved: the judge, the prosecuting counsel, the forensic experts – looking them up in *Who's Who* to make sure they are still alive and find out where they can be contacted. Only the judge has not survived. She is drafting letters to her MP, to the Home Secretary, to Ludovic Kennedy.

She is surprised to find that the Steven Hale Anne-Marie mentioned had been her mother's defence counsel at her trial. He has tried once and failed; she is not inclined to give him a second chance.

'He'll have all the more reason to try harder this time,' Anne-Marie says on the telephone that night, 'and he'll do it on legal aid as he did before.' Rosie still demurs. 'He knows the case inside out. I've spoken to him since I saw you and he believes in Maire's innocence; he always has. You must at least meet him, talk to him. Trust me, Rosie.'

She trusts her.

Fourteen

The day of the prison visit arrives and Anne-Marie pulls her little Fiat to a halt in the Masons' driveway shortly after eleven. It is only the second time Rosie has seen her, but she is already an old friend and they embrace on the doorstep, much to the surprise of her mother. Anne-Marie is still a little stiff in her arms. She makes the introductions and her mother nods cautiously. She takes Anne-Marie up to her bedroom where they can talk privately.

'What message shall I give your mother from you?' Anne-Marie asks slyly.

'None,' she answers.

She raises her unkempt eyebrows. 'Not changed your mind? I thought you might have.'

'It's been a long time. She . . . she may have forgotten me.'

Anne-Marie smiles gently and shakes her head. She hesitates, then, making up her mind, speaks.

'Let me tell you something – something I haven't talked to anyone about for more than twenty years. When I was seventeen I had a baby, an illegitimate baby. I was just the same age as your mother must have been when she had you.'

'I thought you said you didn't have any children,' Rosie blurts out.

'I haven't. We're talking about 1954, Rosie. It was still a terrible disgrace then to have a baby if you weren't married. I was at school, doing my exams, planning to read Law at Queen's. My parents wanted to make me marry the man. He agreed reluctantly; I was the one who refused. I had realised that I didn't love him, you see.'

'That was very brave of you,' she murmurs.

'I like to think so. I tell myself he would have made me

221

miserable, that I would have made him miserable, that it wouldn't have lasted. But, because I wouldn't agree to a botched-up shotgun wedding, I was persuaded instead to give my child up for adoption as soon as it was born. There really didn't seem to be any alternative.

'I hid the pregnancy with loose clothes and jokes about eating too much until I was about six months, and then I was sent away to an aunt in Edinburgh to have the baby in a hospital there. I didn't even miss school – it was the summer holidays and I explained missing the start of the next school year with a bout of glandular fever.'

'What happened?'

'The baby was born. I'd already signed the adoption papers before I went into labour. They were supposed to take the baby away as soon as I'd had it but the young nurse with me hadn't been told and she gave it to me to hold as soon as it was washed and dry and snug in a honeycomb blanket.

'It looked like a little bald pixie and it grizzled away all the time as if it knew that life was a terrible thing to wish on it. I suppose it was already crying out for food but my milk hadn't come and anyway there could be no question of my nursing it.

'Then the sister came in, ticked the nurse off good and proper and snatched the baby away from me.'

'How cruel. How needlessly cruel.'

'I suppose they would have said they were being cruel to be kind, not letting me get attached to a baby that no one was going to let me keep. Anyway, the nurse went into a sulk, blaming me for her scolding. I couldn't get out of that ward fast enough, I can tell you.

'I went home, back to school, passed my exams, top of the class. I went away to university in London instead of staying locally as I'd planned. My parents were glad to see the back of me. I had never been able to regain their love and trust. They're dead now.'

'And you never saw her again?' Rosie asks.

'Who?' Anne-Marie looks momentarily puzzled. 'Oh, I see. Sorry. It was a boy – a Him not a Her. No I've never seen him but I've never forgotten him either, although he was so wrinkled and ugly and he lay in my arms for less than five minutes. So your mother, who kept you against all the odds, who loved you and had the care of you for five years and gave you up only when there was no hope left – do you honestly think she will have forgotten you?'

'I forgot her,' she says guiltily.

'It's not the same thing, believe me. What you did was to blot it out. It's quite normal, honestly. Just in the way people blot out terrible memories – like sexual abuse – you blotted out the happiness once it was lost to you because, as Dante says: There is no greater sorrow than to recall a time of happiness in misery.'

'How can you know we were so happy?'

'The tabloids did a hatchet job on Maire O'Neill but even they couldn't find anyone to say she was anything but an exemplary mother. Trust me: she remembers.'

'Never wavering,' Roisin says.

'What's that?'

'. . . I don't know. Something which popped into my mind just then, a song or a story, something about people who went on loving each other for years, against hopeless odds, never wavering.' She gives herself a little shake. 'Sorry. Bit like that feeling they call someone walking over your grave. But we were talking about you. Do you wonder about him?'

'You know, about fifteen years ago, they passed that law giving adoptive children the right to have access to their original birth certificates when they came of age, so they could seek out their birth mothers if they wished. He would already have been of age by then. I waited, hoped; it was at about that time that my marriage broke up and it seemed that I had nothing left: Every time the phone rang I knew it was him, except that it never was. He felt no need to know who he truly was or where he came from. I suppose a girl might have done. Men are different – they don't set so much store by these things. I should have had a Her, not a Him.'

Rosie is not so sure. She had had no thought of tracing her birth mother until her father's outburst had thrust the truth into her lap like a struggling rabbit.

'And you weren't able to have other children?' she asks diffidently, grateful for Anne-Marie's confidence but not wanting to pry, to risk hurting her. 'Later, when you were married?'

'I hadn't the courage. I was afraid that if I had another child,

I might lose that too, that it might be taken away from me somehow. Isn't that pitiful? And it's too late now.'

She stares at the wall, at the ballet posters, anything. Rosie stands up and goes to her and puts her arms round her. They hug and this time there is no awkwardness on Anne-Marie's side. By the time they release each other, both their shoulders are a little wet.

'To tell you the truth,' she goes on, 'my marriage didn't last long. Oh, I suppose there were about four years between our eyes meeting across a crowded room and the decree nisi, but we actually lived together for little more than a year. It was one of those things which was destined to be a mad affair, not a life-long commitment; only, it just happened, unfortunately, that we were both free to marry at the time, so we did. Hardly thought twice about it, we were so sure. It would have been much better if he'd been a married man and I'd been the much-put-upon other woman.' She sniffles a little. 'Let's talk about something else. Anyway, I must get off in a minute.'

She peers in the dressing-table mirror. 'Do I look all right, not as if I've been crying?' She doesn't care much either way and is just asking because it's the sort of thing women ask their girlfriends. She doesn't wait for an answer but sets off down the stairs.

'I would still rather remain anonymous at first,' Rosie says as she sees her to her car. 'It might be a terrible shock to her – Maire, Mother.'

What had she called her: Mother, Mum, Mummy, Ma? Or had she called her by her strange but pretty name – Maire – like the two good girlfriends that they were?

Fifteen

Anne-Marie has no special status as a visitor. She has been sent an ordinary visiting order and must queue to be searched with the sisters and mothers and daughters who wait with an acquired and seething patience for this ritual which eats into their visiting time.

When it is her turn she meekly opens her bag and turns out her pockets. See: no weapons, no drugs, no forbidden nail scissors or tweezers. She passes through into a sort of hall, perhaps a gymnasium, where rows of tables are set out, a chair on either side.

She recognises Maire O'Neill without difficulty, sitting silent and motionless, looking out of place in this bustling hall. She has scarcely changed. She is thirty-five now but looks more like twenty-five. Her hair is still thick and black and tufty. She is still as slender – and as upright – as a wand. It is as though time has not moved for her in all these years.

Anne-Marie gives herself a mental shake; she knows that prison is not the rest-cure of popular mythology – freedom from responsibility and unlimited porridge and TV.

She introduces herself and Maire shakes her hand like someone who has forgotten how, and they both sit. Anne-Marie is unaccountably nervous; even afraid. Her fear is for Roisin, for her ultimate disappointment, since it seems to her that somewhere inside this calm, self-possessed young woman, something has died.

Then, without warning, a curtain billows and a shaft of sunlight illuminates the dingy room, transfixing a tiny spider on the table between them. Maire turns her head slightly to one side and smiles at Anne-Marie a smile of complicity. She holds out a finger and the terrified spider scuttles over it and to safety down the table leg. Then Maire is speaking in her tuneful Irish voice.

'I'm not sure who you are or why you are here. Who sent you?' She speaks quite slowly as if she has lost the habit of serious conversation.

'I sent myself.' Anne-Marie tells the small white lie and keeps her promise to Rosie.

She talks and Maire listens very gravely, not taking her eyes from Anne-Marie's face. She explains about the Guildford Four and the Birmingham Six. Maire understands the significance, remembers the brusque forensic expert with his cruel mouth explaining to the jury how there was no possible way she could have got nitroglycerine on her hands without handling explosives.

The Home Office cannot possibly refuse her leave to appeal under the circumstances, Anne-Marie says. Steven Hale is anxious to do better this time. Will Maire trust her and appoint her as her legal representative? Will she trust Steven and let him try again?

Maire looks away; trust is a luxury little seen in prison; she must not waste her paltry reserves. She will think about it. It's a big step to take. She has spent more than a third of her life in prison. She cannot think, now, what her life would otherwise have been.

Anne-Marie considers playing the Roisin card, but she had sworn that it would be her last trump. She gives Maire her home telephone number and they shake hands again, very formally, and Anne-Marie leaves to await her decision.

After weeks of brooding, Betty Mason takes the bull by the horns.

'What's going to happen, Rosie, when, if, your . . . other mother comes out of prison?'

'I don't know, Mum. I just don't know.'

'Where will she live? What will she do?'

'I haven't been able to think that far ahead.'

Betty's pent-up misery bursts out in recrimination. 'That's your trouble, isn't it? Head full of grand schemes and no common sense. Never a thought, either, for how they affect other people. Are you even doing her a favour? Have you asked yourself that? Taking her away from the only home she's known in over a decade.'

She is chopping carrots for stew, topping and tailing them with a savage blade. Rosie stares at her placid, fixed mother in amazement.

'I suppose I was going to lose you anyway,' she goes on, 'even if this hadn't happened. You would have gone off to university in the autumn and I would have lost you that way. I suppose it doesn't make any difference in the end. You always lose your children, have to let them grow up.'

She begins to cry; she has had her daughter for so few years, feels short-changed.

'You haven't lost me.' Rosemary puts her arms round her. 'You'll never lose me. You're my mum, and I love you.'

But Betty breaks free of her embrace, thrusts her away. 'You've got a funny way of showing it.' She puts her foot on the pedal and tips the carefully scraped and sliced carrots into the bin, into the mess of used tea leaves and eggshells. 'You've got one mother; that would be enough for most girls.' She flings the knife into the sink, where it resounds against the aluminium, and almost runs from the room. That night they eat take-away pizza.

Sixteen

The next day Maire receives another visitor. She is on her way back to work after lunch, leaving the canteen with some of the other women, when one of the warders – a decent but no-nonsense woman named Bridges – calls her back and tells her that there is someone to see her. Maire stares at her, puzzled; it isn't visiting day and she can think of no one who would be coming to see her if it was.

'You're sure they said me?' she queries.

'Pick your feet up, O'Neill,' Miss Bridges says impatiently. 'Don't keep an important visitor waiting.'

Maire follows her along the corridor without another word. They pass the hall where visits normally take place but do not pause there. Instead Miss Bridges opens the door of another room next to it, a room where Maire has never been, and motions her to precede.

She enters the room which is like somebody's office: box-like, carpeted, with a weary spider plant on the window sill and a desk in the middle. Miss Bridges follows her in, shuts and locks the door behind her and stands at attention against it, hearing no evil, seeing no evil.

The man at the desk stands up as they enter, then sits hastily down again as if it has dawned on him that she is a criminal and not entitled to common courtesy.

'Miss O'Neill?' She nods. 'My name is Robinson, John Robinson. I'm from the Home Office.' He stands up again and stretches a hand out across the desk. She holds her own out and shakes his feebly.

'Do sit down,' he says, doing so himself. She draws up the chair on her side of the desk and waits. 'This interview is quite

off the record. You might almost say that it never took place.'
She says nothing. He clears his throat a little and shuffles some
papers on the desk in front of him.

'Her Majesty's Government,' he begins, rather pompously,
'is concerned about an attempt to reopen your case in the light
of recent appeals where convictions similar to your own have
been deemed . . . unsatisfactory.'

'That's right,' she says, 'especially the Birmingham Six where
the forensic evidence, so like that offered at my own trial, has
now been discredited.'

'Quite so. Quite so.' He looks at her without enthusiasm.
He has been told to expect an uneducated Irishwoman, not
very bright, one who can be jockeyed neatly into position. He
has got Maire instead.

'The thing is,' he continues, 'that you've already been in
prison for nearly thirteen years, counting your months on
remand. That's quite a long time for a lifer.'

'The judge recommended I should serve a minimum of
twenty years,' she reminds him.

'But your record has been exemplary. You wouldn't be
here . . .' he gestures out of the window at the misty Yorkshire
countryside '. . . in an open prison, if your sentence was not
seen to be coming to an end.' He smiles paternally although
he can't be more than thirty-five himself.

'A headstrong young girl,' he goes on, 'a foolish and long-
regretted act . . .'

'I'm not due for my next parole hearing for another two
years,' she points out, 'let alone a release date.'

'You'd be surprised how quickly these things can be done,
Maire. I can call you Maire? You could be out of here in a
couple of months, save the bother of an appeal.'

'You want me to withdraw my appeal.' The penny has
dropped at last. She understands now why 'Mr Robinson' is
here. The government has been seriously embarrassed by the
exoneration of the Guildford Four and the Birmingham Six.
'You've had all the egg on your face you can take.' She begins
to laugh.

'All right, let me spell it out for you.' His voice is cold. 'If
you appeal it will take months to come to court, perhaps a year.
You may or may not be successful. If the appeal is rejected, you

could easily spend another seven or eight years in prison, as the judge recommended. If you fail, the public will be reminded of your terrible crime. They may start asking what you are doing here; we may well be obliged to send you back to a closed prison, perhaps Durham.'

'Oh yes?'

He is bluffing; she can feel the desperation.

'If you succeed, you would want to sue for compensation. That might also take years during which time –'

'In other words,' she breaks in, 'if I appeal and fail, you will make sure I don't get early parole and if I appeal and succeed, you'll make sure my life outside is as hard as it can be.'

'I wouldn't put it quite like that,' he says, smiling an empty smile. 'We would have a duty to see that a mass-murderer was not let loose on the public too soon.'

'So what's the alternative?' She wants to see how far the government is prepared to go to cover its back. He has shown her the stick; now she wants to see the carrot in all its orange gaudy.

He leans over the table and speaks quite quietly and she remembers that this conversation is not taking place. 'A parole hearing within a month, an immediate release date, a – er – a grant to allow you to start a new life.'

'But my conviction would stand? I would still be a mass-murderer?'

'Naturally.'

'And my Licence?' For lifers, even when released, are on Home Office Licence as long as they live and may be recalled to prison at any time, even without committing an offence. They need the Home Secretary's permission to travel abroad, even to marry.

Robinson shrugs. 'A formality. Surely it would be worth it, to be out.' He gestures out of the window again. 'To walk down city streets, to go window shopping, have a drink down the pub with your mates . . .'

Maire stands up a little too quickly and her chair falls over backwards. She leaves it there.

'You took everything I had away from me thirteen years ago, Mr Robinson – or whatever your real name is – everything except my self-respect.'

She turns and walks to the door. Miss Bridges doesn't move, glances uncertainly at Robinson for guidance.

'Let me out please,' Maire says quietly. 'There's no rule says I have to receive visitors against my will.' Miss Bridges hesitates a second longer, then unlocks the door and stands to one side.

Mr Robinson is on his feet again now and coming round the desk.

'But you haven't given me an answer.'

She looks back at him: a mediocre man of middling height and build in a grey suit; a civil servant with a pale face, thin lips and a stripey tie. Come to think of it his name really may be John Robinson – the anonymous name would suit him. They should have sent her someone better. They probably didn't think she was worth it. He has picked up her chair and is standing there holding it against him, looking foolish.

'Oh yes,' she says, 'I have.'

She puts her name down that afternoon for a telephone call to Anne-Marie. She had seen no reason to appeal, any more than she had on first being convicted twelve years ago, but they have talked her into it.

Part Four
Never Wavering

One

Roisin is reluctantly impressed by Steven Hale as her mother was before her. Since he lives in London, they find a middle ground and meet for the first time at Anne-Marie's house in Oxford one night in early May. He greets her with the news that they have already been granted leave to appeal.

'In record time,' he says with his big boyish grin. 'We've got them on the run. They're going to have to bite the bullet.'

He glances round, unimpressed by Anne-Marie's housekeeping, and offers to take them both out for a meal. Rosie protests, concerned at letting him spend his money on her like this, but he waves the objection away. He is a barrister at the peak of his career. His children are grown up; he and his wife have recently parted by mutual agreement and she is about to remarry. He can afford to buy dinner for a couple of accomplices.

Neither woman can refuse him further. He is like a comic-book hero on a mission; he has been given the chance to remedy one of his most grating failures. He rejects their gratitude. It is he, he insists, who should be thanking them.

'Just some pizza or pasta,' Anne-Marie says, 'nothing elaborate.' He agrees to this compromise, helps Rosie back on with her coat and strides out of the door and up the road towards Walton Street with the two women scurrying to keep up.

Rosie is not attracted to older men, has no father fixation, yet she is impressed by his easy power – the way the waiters jump to please him – by his warmth and charm, as he forbids further shop-talk until they are back in the privacy of Anne-Marie's little house. He is over fifty now and his hair is more salt than pepper and his face ripe with laughter lines. But he is a tall, slim and erect figure, casually elegant in his newly refound bachelorhood. She feels Anne-Marie thawing in his company, attempting a little amateur flirtation.

Rosie is staring at Steven all through the first course; she has the feeling that they have met before. Then she has it.

'Fairlawns!' she cries out, interrupting Anne-Marie. 'You came to see me at Fairlawns. It must have been just before the trial.'

Steven nods. 'I thought you'd forgotten.'

'I had forgotten. I can't remember anything much about that time, but little things have been coming back to me recently. You took me into the gardens and gave me sweets and talked to me for about an hour, asking me all sorts of questions.'

'I wanted you to give evidence on your mother's behalf,' he explains. 'She wouldn't hear of putting you through such an ordeal. I might just possibly have got her off if she would only have let me put you in the witness stand.'

'I would have loved to,' she says, bewildered. 'I'm sure I would have done anything to help her.'

'She was thinking only of your welfare, Rosie,' Anne-Marie says gently, 'not of herself.'

Roisin is remembering more and more since that first break-through when she heard her mother calling her name out of the window. One night recently, in a half-waking dream, she had found herself in a room in a tower with toys: building bricks, teddies, dolls. Her mother had been there and another young woman. They had played together. They had built a castle of toy bricks inside that other – more dangerous – castle. She had some idea at the time that it was a hospital, but understands now that it must have been Holloway prison.

Her mother had told her that she was there because people thought she had done a bad thing, but that she hadn't done that bad thing. She, Roisin, had been happy for a little while and then the happiness had turned into anguish and she had forced herself into full wakefulness.

Despite his own prohibition on talking shop, Steven is bursting with ideas as they eat *tagliatelle alla carbonara* and swig warm Valpolicella, crying out at intervals things like 'The policeman, Shaw. He was a decent enough man. I must talk to him some more,' or 'That slimeball she was with in the pub that night. I'd like to see him crawl this time.'

Over profiteroles and ice-cream he leans forward, his face pink from the crowded warmth of the little trattoria. He is not drunk except with eagerness.

'I was an arrogant young puppy all those years ago,' he tells Rosie. 'I believed in your mother's innocence. I was so sure when they briefed me that I was going to win, then it all seemed to disintegrate in my hands.' Rosie listens, enchanted. 'It's not often you get a second chance like this, but this time I'm damn well going to win and win good.'

'Glad you're not still arrogant,' Anne-Marie says, rather acidly. 'I'd put our chances at about fifty-fifty.' Rosie's face falls. 'Do you want the truth, Rosie, or do you want the ano-dyne optimism that Steven is offering?'

Rosie has no answer. Steven frowns. Espresso is drunk in a more subdued atmosphere.

Two

Steven rings Rosie a few nights later.

'I'm not supposed to speak to you except through Anne-Marie,' he says, 'but who cares? Those damn miserable odds of hers just went right up in our favour. Ever heard of the Maguires, the Maguire Seven?'

The name is familiar and Rosie thinks hard. 'One of the Birmingham Six, at their press conference after they were released, called for justice for the Maguires.'

'Right! Well done. Their appeal started this week. They were convicted almost entirely on forensic evidence that they had been handling nitroglycerine, just like Maire.'

'But the appeal is still being heard,' Rosie points out. 'When will there be a verdict?'

'Um. Not for a while. They've already been released, you see, served their time, so there's no rush from that point of view. But the point is, I have it on good authority from someone connected with the appeal that only one verdict is possible and that they'll be completely exonerated. In fact their lawyers are asking for an immediate overturn of the convictions on the grounds that the swab kits might have been contaminated.'

'And you think that will help with my ... with Maire's case?'

'Bound to. I'm going up with Anne-Marie to see her tomorrow. Our appeal date has now been set for late September.'

'So far away?'

'Inevitable, I'm afraid. They break for summer at the end of June and they've got a full schedule until then. The Court of Appeal is made up of old old men and in the summer the South of France beckons, or Tuscany. Watch this space.'

He hangs up.

Steven is over-optimistic, as always. The appeal court rejects the contention that the swab kits might have been contaminated and the case drags on.

But the newspapers are beginning to clamour for a review of the case of Judith Ward, the alleged M62 bomber, and the *Guardian* – whose political editor is a friend of Steven's – raises, for the first time in twelve years, the name of Maire O'Neill.

Three

Steven and Maire shake hands.

'You've hardly aged,' he says.

'I wish I could say the same about you.' She gives him the same sad, sweet smile she last bestowed on him more than twelve years ago.

'It's a hard old world there on the outside.' She groans. 'Sorry, not funny.'

'How are you, Steven? You look . . . prosperous.'

'Life has been good to me,' he agrees.

'And Mr French? What became of him?'

'Oh, he retired a good few years back. Moved to Spain, plays golf.' They smile at each other, at their shared bitter memories. 'Have you forgiven me for that quarrel we had about . . . the line of defence to take?' he asks.

'Whether to put Roisin on the witness stand, you mean?' Steven and Anne-Marie exchange glances. 'It's all right. You needn't be afraid to hurt me, remind me, by mentioning her name. There is never a day when I don't think of her, wonder where she is and if she's well and happy.'

Steven clears his throat. 'I don't think, in retrospect, that Rosie's testimony would have made much difference. I was scraping the bottom of the barrel by suggesting it. It was the forensic evidence which really stitched us up.'

'Either way, I did the right thing. For her sake. But tell me, what about these forensic tests? Won't they still count against me?'

'They've been roundly discredited during the Birmingham Six and Maguire appeals,' Anne-Marie replies.

'That man – that doctor with the Polish name – he was so sure.'

241

'Wrongly so. The May Enquiry showed, beyond a shadow of doubt, that traces of explosive *could* be passed from one person to another via towels, mugs, glasses.'

Maire turns away for a moment, unable to trust herself to speak. How could that scientist have thrown twelve years of her life away with his false and facile certainties? Just because he was a better actor, a better performer in court than the other man. She barely hears the rest of Anne-Marie's words.

'Random testing on hundreds of people picked up off the street has also produced a high proportion of results which could be interpreted as positive . . .'

'So unless the government is prepared to contend that large numbers of people are routinely handling nitroglycerine,' Steven interrupts, 'the floor has fallen out from beneath their feet.'

'Yes,' she says. 'I see.'

She has tried to stifle bitterness, not to let it get the better of her. Momentarily it overwhelms her. Dr Kurowski will no doubt shrug his shoulders and say, 'So, I was wrong. We all make mistakes.' There will be no retribution for him. On the contrary: early retirement, perhaps, on a full pension, on the grounds of 'Limited Efficiency'.

Four

Commander Andrew Shaw is not a bad man. When he sent Maire O'Neill to jail, he did it in the certainty of her guilt. Caught up in the excitement of the bombing, the quick arrest, the unanimous conviction, the praise of his superiors, he did not stop to ask himself if this was the right rollercoaster he had boarded. Not then.

A few years later, by now a Chief Superintendent, he had flown to The Hague to interview an IRA man who was being held by the Dutch police pending extradition. An officer in the Army, not a dull soldier, John O'Malley was educated, articulate, charming and almost insanely courageous. He was the most dangerous man Shaw had ever met; something beneath that courteous manner made the hairs on the back of his neck bristle.

O'Malley was one of a new generation of guerrilla fighters. Born and brought up in Kent of Irish parents, a grammar-school boy with a university scholarship, only later recruited to the Republican cause, he spoke with the middle-class English accent that allayed suspicion. He was a brilliant tactician and could bluff his way in anywhere with his briefcase unsearched. His was almost certainly the hand behind a wave of attacks on British servicemen on the mainland of Europe, but he knew, and Shaw knew, that proving it was another matter.

He had laughed incredulously at the mention of Maire O'Neill.

'The little girl you sent away for the High Wycombe bombing in '78? My, but you must have been proud of yourselves.'

The words had been spoken off the record. Shaw has never repeated them to anyone. The Dutch had not found sufficient evidence to extradite. O'Malley had walked free and disappeared within hours into another name, perhaps another face.

Shaw knows that he has nothing to reproach himself with: it was not as if he had fabricated evidence, fudged the words of a confession. Despite his best efforts, she would not confess – and he'd thought the Catholics just loved to confess. It was the jury that found her guilty, who wanted revenge for the photographs they saw in the paper and the ones they were shown in court of the ruined buildings and the shattered lives. He has let sleeping dogs lie. In a war that has been going on for decades, in a world where O'Malleys are released on a technicality, you can't get too worked up about one civilian casualty.

He is a year from retirement and will get a comfortable pension, although he has not flown as high or as far as he had hoped on joining the force in the first wave of graduate recruits in the mid-fifties. His marriage has survived the unsocial and unpredictable hours, the secrecy. He and his wife have bought their retirement cottage in her native Dorset and get down there as often as they can, looking on it already as home. There is room there for his grandchildren to visit and to play in safety. He will take up fishing. His conscience is clear.

But the Maguire case – not one he was involved in, he is glad to say – is making everyone at New Scotland Yard edgy now. And when he hears on the grapevine that a date has been set for the O'Neill appeal and gets a telephone call from Steven Hale two days later, asking for a private interview, he reflects that he has nothing to lose and only a slightly earlier retirement to gain by talking to him.

Accordingly, he stops off at Hale's Kensington flat one night after work, in time – as Hale had put it on the telephone – for a small glass of sherry before dinner. The sherry is excellent and the respect mutual, and Shaw readily admits – *entr'eux* – that he is no longer satisfied with the O'Neill conviction. Not that he has any evidence to the contrary, Hale must understand that. Hale does understand, perfectly. But, looking back, after all these years, it strikes him that, well, such a young girl, so little really hard evidence; forensic claims which would not, nowadays, convict a dog of pissing against a tree . . .

'You had me on the run in the witness box,' Shaw says without resentment. 'Still, it's all water under the bridge, isn't it?'

'You kept your cool wonderfully as it happens. Not like fat little Barney Winch-Bore, bobbing up and down like a jack in the box, squeaking "Objection!".' They both laugh at the memory.

'I've often wondered,' Shaw says, 'all that anger, all that "innocent girl, political scapegoat" stuff, was it just an act?'

'Of course. Once you lose your temper in court, you've as good as lost your case.'

Shaw is too tactful to point out that he lost it anyway. 'You deserved to win really,' he says instead, 'if only the forensic evidence hadn't been so damning, if only that little Slav boffin hadn't been so cocky and so convincing . . .'

'If only my boffin had been a bit less of a lemon, you mean,' Steven adds.

Shaw sympathises. 'We none of us get the support we deserve. Anyway, he was right, your boffin, and the other chap was wrong.'

Does Hale know what has become of Maire O'Neill? Hale shrugs. She is surviving. There is no hope, naturally, that Shaw will speak up on her behalf at the appeal? Or just the right word, perhaps, whispered in the right ear? Shaw does not answer him; it is not a matter to be decided lightly over a convivial glass of amontillado. Hale does not press him but leaves him to sleep on it.

'You know,' Shaw says as Hale sees him out, 'I'm only surprised that it's taken so long. In a sense, I expected to hear from you, or someone like you, years ago. I suppose everyone just forgot about her. There was no family, as I recall.'

'There is family,' Hale says, 'very close and concerned family. You'll be in touch?'

'We'll see.'

He shuts the door behind Shaw. Shaw is right, of course. Everyone had forgotten about Maire O'Neill. He himself — caught up in the hurly-burly of a successful chambers; of growing children, family weddings and funerals, a crumbling marriage; notions of a political career which had come to nothing — had filed her in the back of his mind under 'Dormant'.

Five

Four men in made-to-measure suits are sitting round a table in a small room in Queen Anne's Gate two weeks later. The first is Somebody Important at the Home Office. The second is Somebody High Up in the Attorney General's Office. The third is an Assistant Commissioner of the Metropolitan Police. They have no names or faces; they represent their offices.

The fourth is younger and has a face, although it is not a memorable one; and also a name, although it is not John Robinson. He seems to have spent a lot of his time lately participating in meetings that are not taking place. He has his gaze fixed on the polished table top, having just been criticised – yet again, and in front of these grave men this time – for not being able to pull the wool over the eyes of someone who is, after all, just a naïve girl and a common criminal.

'All right, Hoare,' SIHO says to him, turning away with a sigh, 'that's water under the bridge. The question is: What now?'

ACMP says that he has been approached, informally, by the officer who investigated the case back in '78 and who is no longer happy with the verdict. ACMP frowns: he does not require that his subordinates be happy. He could do without this. At least there is no question of foul play this time – of forced (or even forged) confessions. He will not be seeing his own officers in the dock; that is a small mercy. He lived through the days of the conviction-at-any-price ethos of seventies policing; Operation Countryman had glanced over him and away.

SIHO asks if nothing can be done to discredit the Doyle woman? She is, after all, just a slightly batty menopausal female.

Robinson/Hoare examines his fingernails in embarrassment at his master's crassness.

She is an active member of the Labour Party, SIHO continues, and of Amnesty International.

ACMP murmurs that these are not exactly proscribed organisations.

SHUAGO explodes that this is not a fucking banana republic.

Robinson/Hoare is relieved by his intervention. He believes, although he has not thought it through in quite those terms, in the cock-up theory of history, rather than the conspiracy theory. If that black-eyed girl – for she looks no more than a girl – has spent most of her adult life behind bars for a crime she did not commit, he wants to believe it is because men are fallible: blinkered, muddle-headed, often silly; not wicked. He does not articulate this thought, even in his mind, but it is there, somewhere below language.

Six

By early June Rosie finds that she is seeing little of Simon, who is swotting hard for his A-levels. After dinner one evening she is feeling tired, has lost some of her buoyant optimism. She calls round at the Lawrences' house.

Barbara opens the door and greets her warmly. Simon, she says, is upstairs in his room, revising. She must go straight up, not stand on ceremony. She is almost part of the family.

Simon's door is closed and Rosie taps on it lightly and hears his 'Come in'. He looks up as she enters and smiles. He is pleased to see her.

'Oh, it's you.'

'How's it going?' She perches on the edge of his desk and he marks the place in his copy of *Macbeth* and closes the book. Real life, she remembers now, is going on elsewhere – a reality where exams are important.

He asks after her cause and she updates him, although nothing much seems to be happening at the moment. She is in a sort of limbo where she waits for news, for replies to her letters.

He asks after her other mother – Betty Mason, that is. She has seen the doctor, Rosie says, has been prescribed some antidepressants, may be referred to a counsellor. She has withdrawn her love – both from Rosie and from her father who is seen as abetting and encouraging her. The house does not get cleaned and food does not get cooked unless she, Rosie, cooks it. Simon is sympathetic and supportive and she feels a little less guilty.

'There's something I have to tell you,' he says awkwardly. 'I've decided I want to go to Sussex.'

'But that's so far away,' she says. 'Brighton. You only had it third on your UCCA form.'

'I liked the place when I went for an interview, though,' he reminds her. 'The course seemed to suit me. I'm not Oxford material, Rosie, and never was – not like you. The chances of my getting the three A grades they've asked for . . .' His hands signal remote, like a fisherman exaggerating his catch.

She is shocked. She had forgotten that he would be going on with his original plans, that he would be leaving home this autumn, in a mere three or four months, while she stays in Nottingham – if that is what she is going to do – and takes her A-levels next year.

Brighton must be two hundred miles away. He will make new friends there, have new interests, meet other girls. Simon: so tall, so handsome, so kind – there will be no shortage of takers.

'I shall be back in the holidays,' he points out. 'Even the odd weekend. You don't think I'd leave Mum all alone after all these years, do you?'

What about me, she wants to ask.

He understands what she is saying without her needing to say it.

'I do love you, Rosie. But you've sort of put me on hold these last three months. You're the one who's really gone away. Maire O'Neill has been the only thing that mattered to you. I have to get on with my life.'

'I thought you understood.'

'I do, in so far as any onlooker can.' He takes her hand. 'And I will wait for you if you will wait for me. If it's real, then it will survive. If it isn't, then it probably wouldn't have anyway.'

But there is a middling reality, she thinks, which thrives on propinquity.

'You will know where I am,' he says, 'where to find me. It just won't be here, that's all.'

She gets up. 'Can't drag you out for a quick drink? Or a walk – it's a nice evening.'

'I'd better not. It's less than two weeks away now.'

'I won't disturb you any further, then. Good luck with the exams.'

'Good luck with your appeal.' He turns his face up for her

to kiss and their lips brush. 'Ring me as soon as you have any news.'

There are the big things, she thinks, the things which have exclamation marks and make the newspaper headlines: OUTRAGE! FREEDOM! UNEMPLOYMENT UP AGAIN! Then there are the small things which are not in the public domain but which are just as important.

She ruffles his hair with affection and leaves.

Steven's telephone rings that same evening. He answers, giving his name. A polite male voice hesitatingly confirms his identity – that it is, indeed, Steven Hale, QC to whom he is speaking – and says, 'You won't remember me I don't suppose, sir. We only met once and it was a long time ago. My name is Jack Carmichael. I was *Corporal* Jack Carmichael then. I was at the Hope and Anchor in High Wycombe . . . that night and I have some information which may be of help to Miss O'Neill.'

Seven

J ack Carmichael is now thirty-eight but looks younger, almost as if he has been trapped in time at the night of the bombing; Steven has no difficulty in recognising him.

He ushers him into his study, offers him a drink. Carmichael accepts a beer. Steven – impeccably polite as always, except when necessarily otherwise in court – joins him, although he is more of a champagne man.

'As I was saying on the phone,' Carmichael begins, sipping, 'I've spoken to the real bombers, recently, to the people who made that bomb and planted it in that bag.' He looks up at the high ceiling, hesitates. 'Then I heard that the O'Neill case was coming to appeal and I thought it might help.'

'But why?' Steven asks. 'I mean, why you?'

Carmichael stirs uneasily in his chair. He has asked himself this question many times over the laborious years he has spent tracking down the real perpetrators. It was not that he was seeking revenge: he had not made foolish and elaborate plans to administer justice to them with his own hands, to make them pay for Scottie's lost leg and damaged mind or for the sleepless nights Carmichael himself has passed over the last thirteen years, the power loud bangs still have to make him shake.

'I needed to know the truth,' he says simply, then adds, 'I've felt bad about her, all these years: Maire O'Neill. I couldn't believe it was her and I felt so bad.'

'You, of all the people mixed up in that sorry pantomime of a trial, have least reason to feel guilty,' Steven tells him mildly.

Carmichael just shrugs. 'I didn't say it was rational, sir.'

Steven is silent; he does not press the ex-soldier, knowing

that he must tell his story in his own way and at his own pace. They sip more beer and Carmichael continues.

'It's taken me three and a half years, you know. It started in 1987, at about the time they began to cast doubt on the scientific tests that sent all those people away in the seventies.'

It had occurred to him, quite suddenly, that he might do something. They always said that you couldn't, not just one man, on his own, that you had to put up and shut up and leave abstract concepts like Truth and Justice to the people whose job they were.

'How did you even set about it?' Steven asks, fascinated.

'I'm a trained soldier, after all. Or I was until then. After I bought myself out of the Army in '79, I went into security.' He pauses and his mouth screws up in disdain and Steven thinks, for a moment, he's going to spit on the polished wood of the study floor. 'Security! Washed-up policemen, ex-squaddies who just want a cushy number. But I gained a few contacts that way, knew how to follow a trail. I've had to do it in my spare time, of course, going to Dublin or Belfast on holidays or at weekends. It's been a slow business. Lucky I never married. I suppose.'

He had talked to A who had warily put him on to B who would mention the name of C who might, possibly, have brought the explosives over from Ireland in his car. Some were in England, some in the Irish Republic, some in the North. Some were still active in the IRA, some long-since retired and wanting to forget their violent pasts. Many had spent time in prison; many others had escaped justice altogether.

'These people didn't object to speaking to you?' Steven interjects.

'Many of them were shifty, guilty, defiant or ashamed, but they had been told to speak to me. It's in their interest, after all, to prove miscarriages of justice. It makes the British judicial system appear inept and corrupt.'

Steven nods. 'Go on.'

Eventually, after almost three and a half years of following a trail that had long gone cold, it had led him to Z.

Carmichael has been all round the houses, literally. After being picked up in a pub in the city centre by a man with a van, he is taken on what amounts to a tour of Dublin city before being dropped at another pub where two more men meet him and tell him they have come to take him to Z.

Z is a man of about his father's age, avuncular, courteous, civilised, living in an elegant square in Georgian Dublin surrounded by oil paintings, Persian rugs and books – history, philosophy, politics. He has a southern-Irish accent although it is not particularly strong and Carmichael has no difficulty in understanding him. He has a well-upholstered but still faintly glamorous wife and there is a boy of about eight whom he introduces as one of his grandchildren. His two men from the pub wait, in case of trouble.

Carmichael reiterates that there will be no trouble. They search him carefully and confiscate his tie.

'You can call me "Volunteer",' the avuncular man says. He knows, as Carmichael knows, that there would be no difficulty in finding out his real name. It is like a game they choose to play.

He takes Carmichael into a room at the back where french windows stand open on to the spacious garden on this warm spring day. He tells the 'boys' to wait in the kitchen and they obey without a word.

'I have been ordered to see you and tell you what you want to know, within reason,' Volunteer says. 'Orders which come from very high up indeed.' He smiles. 'Somebody, somewhere, has a bad conscience about Maire O'Neill.'

'A rather tardy conscience,' Carmichael points out.

'As you say. But you are welcome to my house, orders or no orders and I trust you will not abuse my hospitality, Mr Carmichael.'

'I have made promises and I will keep them.'

'So, what is it you want to know?' Volunteer asks. 'If you ask me anything I don't want to answer I shall say so but I shall tell you no lies.'

'I want to know everything there is to know about the High Wycombe bombing.'

'I shall take you at your word,' Volunteer says. 'I was the commander in charge of the Thames Valley Active Service Units from 1972 to 1978. You have already spoken to both my deputies, I think?'

Carmichael nods. He has met P, who was in charge of intelligence-gathering, and Q who was, appositely, the quartermaster, dealing with mundane matters of finance and actually acquiring the weapons and explosives.

'I had something like thirty people under my command at any one time. They didn't all make and plant bombs, of course. Some just had safehouses to hide men and explosives, some were glorified clerks, some were pains in the arse looking for a bit of excitement.

'We were not, as it happens, all that active,' Volunteer goes on, almost ruefully. 'There were always more important targets. We kicked off with the bombing of the Thameside club in Oxford in '73 and we were summarily wound up after the Hope and Anchor fiasco.'

He pauses as his comfortable wife comes in with a tray of coffee and some biscuits. She smiles her sunny smile at Carmichael and leaves as discreetly as she came in. The coffee pot is silver and, like the house, Georgian.

'We are not monsters,' Volunteer says, following Carmichael's eyes. 'We are not machines. If you cut us, we bleed.'

'Why?' Carmichael asks. 'Why England? Why High Wycombe? Why the Hope and Anchor?'

'Why England?' Volunteer pours coffee for them both, offers his guest milk and sugar and the plate of biscuits. 'What you mean is why don't we paddies stick to killing each other in Belfast, since that's the territory we're fighting over. Is that it?'

'I suppose that is what I meant.'

'Did you ever see an Englishman watching the news, Mr Carmichael? When the announcer says, "And there was another sectarian bombing today in Northern Ireland . . ." they switch off. They switch off their minds even if they don't literally switch off their sets. But when the bombing is in St Albans or Manchester . . . or High Wycombe, then it brings home to them the realities of war in Northern Ireland and, for a few days, they stop ignoring it.

'Why High Wycombe? It was well placed — less than an hour's dash from Oxford along the motorway. It was something of a centre for NATO military, either the Brits or the Yanks. Bomber Command at Naphill, making careful preparations for World War Three. The Hope and Anchor was *identified by my deputy as a place frequented by off-duty soldiers. You were unlucky, Mr Carmichael.'* As they say in the movies: it wasn't personal; it was just business.

'Not as unlucky as some.'

'I was in the British Army myself, you know,' Volunteer says, and Jack Carmichael almost chokes on his coffee. 'Many of us are or were. It's good training and you make useful contacts. It's always handy to know the geography of a British Army base. Yes . . .' He stretches his hand out towards a photograph of an army football team that stands on the desk flanked by kittenish poses of his wife when much younger and a whole gaggle of small children.

'There I am, second on the left in the front row. I was in for eight years. Then I was in Oxford for six years, as I explained. Then my father died and left me this house and I thought it was time I came home. War is a young man's game, Mr Carmichael.'

'That's the pity of it,' Carmichael says.

'Active Service Unit 2,' Volunteer says, tiring of abstract debate and speaking quickly, almost as if in recitation. 'They did the Hope and Anchor bombing. We had two weapons dumps at that time, one in Headington and one in Marston. ASU2 drew guns from the one in Headington, and the bomb, which had been assembled that day in a lock-up garage off the Cowley Road by two other men. It was primed with explosive only when they reached High Wycombe, of course.'

'How many in an ASU?' Carmichael asks.

'Three or four. Four on this occasion.'

'And what has become of them?'

Volunteer scratches his chin, thinking. 'Two have come home to live; one is still active in a mild sort of way. The other – the commanding officer of ASU2 – has become an alcoholic. The Ra has no truck with drinking men, Mr Carmichael, they're too dangerous. Of the others, one is in prison for petty larceny and the girl married an Englishman and is no longer active. But it could have been anyone, you know. Just as it could have been any one of a hundred pilots sent out on a clear night to bomb and kill civilians in Dresden.'

It is no part of Carmichael's self-imposed brief to argue about whether the 'Troubles' constitute a valid war or not; nor to *dispute Z's eloquent attempts at self-justification. Instead he asks, 'And why no warning?'*

'I referred to the High Wycombe bombing a moment ago as a fiasco,' Volunteer reminds him. 'I was not speaking lightly. It was a cock-up from start to finish. The bomb went off forty minutes too early. It was timed to explode after the place had closed for the night, to fire a warning shot across the bows of all you soldier lads, make you a bit less eager to sign up for another tour of duty in Northern Ireland.'

'It worked in my case...' Carmichael gives a sour little smile '... admirably.'

'We had planned to give a half-hour's notice. The bomb went off as my people were entering the phone box to make the call. They'd gone a good distance away from the pub, as usual, in case the police put a dragnet around the area when they got the warning. They scarpered when they heard the bang, as well they might.'

'And where were you while all this was going on?'

'At home, in Oxford, tucked up in bed with the wife, waiting for the confirmatory phone call.'

'And that's it? Six people dead for a cock-up?'

'There was a full enquiry by the Army Council, stopping short only of a court martial. The IRA are as disciplined and unforgiving as any other army, Mr Carmichael. The Thames Valley unit was wound up then, as I said, and I came home under, I suppose, something of a cloud.' He chuckles. 'At least I never denied responsibility for what we did, not like some I could mention.'

'And you are retired now?' Carmichael asks.

Volunteer answers.

'I shall go on fighting for my homeland until the day I die.'

'They saw me out,' Carmichael says, coming to the end of his narration, 'gave me back my tie, dumped me outside the Abbey Theatre. The last thing Z said to me was, "Don't come back. Ever."'

'You know names?' Steven asks.

'I have learnt the names of two members of that ASU and of Z himself.'

'But you won't name them, of course.' It is a statement, not a question.

'Not unless we both want to end up with a bullet in the back.'

'But you will testify at the appeal, if necessary?'

'For what it's worth.' The ex-corporal takes a piece of paper out of his pocket and hands it to Steven. 'Here's my address and phone number.' He gets up and puts his jacket on, preparing to leave. He looks tired, exhausted by his memories.

'He ruined my life,' he says, standing awkwardly with his hands in his pockets. 'If I hadn't been in the bog just at that minute, I'd have been blown to pieces with my mates. Even so, he ruined my life. The army *was* my life, you see, and after that I didn't have the guts to live it any more.'

'You must hate him,' Steven says, 'more than I can imagine.'

Carmichael slowly shakes his head.

'I pity him with all my heart.'

Eight

Betty Mason wants to stop but she's not sure how. It would be easy to make up. She would not even have to say she is sorry – her husband and her daughter are too generous to require that of her. She has only to come out of her room and flush those stupid tablets down the loo and resume her life and it can all be forgotten. Except that then they will think it is *all right* – that she accepts; and she doesn't.

She has nothing against Maire O'Neill. Indeed, she should be grateful to her for giving birth to Rosemary, for allowing her a short-term lease on her. But nothing had been said at the time about her coming back one day to demand repossession. Betty admits a *prior* claim, but is that necessarily a *better* claim? Can Rosemary, whose heart is large and open, love two mothers, or must one give way?

And who is this other mother? She can have no reality for Rosie who, she knows, does not remember her. She is a picture-book mother built up out of Rosie's fertile, romantic imagination. Betty is real: cosy, matronly.

She is bursting with feeling in a way she has never been. She has never had the experience of unrequited love. Her love for Bob was, and is, a gentle, happy thing. He has never made her miserable. A plain and sensible girl with a loving family and many friends and interests, she never knew the heartache of that man who doesn't phone, that idol who prefers another. Bob has never betrayed or slighted her.

She might have learnt, in adolescence or young womanhood, the lesson that most women learn: that broken hearts mend. But she didn't. She lost her heart only late in life, at the age of almost forty, to a tiny girl with black hair and a yearning for affection in her wide, dark eyes. She assumes it was like the moment other mothers experience, when the pain is finished and they hold the baby in their arms for the first time and bond with its helplessness; except that this baby had sprung fully-formed, talking in a sweet, low voice with strange hybrid accents, from the hallway at Fairlawns. She had been shepherded in by a smiling house mother, dressed in a gingham frock which was slightly too small for her and showed the scarred knees which gave the lie to her docile manner. A tattered blue teddy was clutched in one doll-like hand.

'This is Rosie.'

'Hello, Rosie.'

'Say hello to Mr and Mrs Mason, Rosie.'

'Hello.' She observed them but did not smile.

'Mr and Mrs Mason have come specially to see you. Would you like to go out with them for the afternoon? To the park or the shops?'

Betty had held her breath while the infant considered this proposition for a while before asking, 'Will there be ice-cream?'

'Lots of ice-cream,' she had burst out before the house mother could answer with a negative or scold her charge for venality. Rosie had nodded her acceptance. She had solemnly considered the matter of the teddy, then buried it out of sight under a cushion on the hall sofa. Still unsmiling, she had engaged her hand in Betty's of her own accord. There had been no turning back from that.

Betty is mistaken about how much Rosie now remembers.

It is Easter Saturday 1978. There is to be a pageant, a parade, on Wycombe Rye: fancy dress, best Easter bonnet, best decorated egg. Roisin is old enough to take part for the first time and Maire willingly agrees to attend.

All over town women are buying materials for fairy costumes to turn their lumpen daughters into Tinkerbell for the day, or hiring clown suits for sullen boys. Maire has no money to spare for such extravagances but Roisin must not be disappointed. She takes a white sheet which is beyond repair and dyes it an emerald green in memory of home; that will be her dress, her royal robe. A crown emerges from cardboard and scissors and paint and a little glitter. Green felt is fashioned into a pair

of slippers dainty enough for Queen Niamh's feet. The child
clamours for a magic wand and Máire gives in, despite doubts
about its authenticity since it was not Niamh who was the
sorceress, and more gold paint and glitter are employed in
conjunction with half a bamboo pole discarded from a neighbour's garden. Many evenings are spent in painting and sewing
and fitting on a child who will not keep still.

She cannot win in this makeshift but at least she will not be
disgraced. On the day her hair is washed and fluffed around
her face and a little white powder dabbed on to ensure that
winter beauty.

'Is she Snow White's wicked stepmother?' Auntie Sandy
asks, calling for them that morning, and is laughed at for her
folly.

'She is beautiful enough,' Maire replies. She holds her up to
the looking-glass by the door. 'Mirror, mirror, on the wall,
who is the fairest of them all?' and answers with an inept
attempt at ventriloquism, 'Roisin is the beautifullest of them
all.'

Cheryl – a chubby Easter bunny in leotard and ballet tights,
ears and a tail – rocks with laughter at this.

'There's no such word as beautifullest,' she tells Maire kindly.

Roisin remembers a day of spotting rain, her anorak on over
her green gown until the moment the parade starts, sudden
dismay at the realisation that she is still wearing her workaday
plimsolls beneath it. Seeking her mother in the crowd, she
points the error out silently and Maire claps her hand over her
mouth in mock horror, takes the little felt slippers out of the
black shoulder bag where she had stuffed them for safe-keeping
and scratches her head in theatrical perplexity. Roisin begins
to laugh. No one else has noticed their gaffe and she pulls her
gown down long to hide her feet as she trots along in the middle
of the noisy crowd.

The weather clears miraculously by mid-afternoon. The eggs
are pretty in their pastel shades with yellow chicks and fluffy
rabbits. The bonnets are extravagant. She does not win a prize
but each entrant is given a chocolate cream egg and she eats
hers greedily.

There is a Punch and Judy which she has never seen before;
she could happily watch all afternoon. As Mr Punch is hauled

*off to jail by the policeman, her mother and Auntie Sandy haul
her off for tea and Wall's non-dairy ice-cream.*

*She does not envy the little girls in their expensive costumes
– not even the Peter Pan who won the first prize she coveted,
an immense Easter egg. She knows that her own egg tomorrow
will be modest, has already found it hiding at the bottom of
the wardrobe in her mother's room, but Peter Pan's mother
looks snooty and bad-tempered and quite old – at least thirty,
surely – while her own mother is young and loving and almost
silly in her high spirits.*

Happiness is bigger than Easter eggs.

Fight or flight: these are the two possibilities offered by the
adrenal hormone, the two possibilities open, in Steven's view,
to HM Government. They fought Birmingham, as they are
fighting the Maguires, every step. His guess is that they will
fight O'Neill to the last fingernail, the last hair. They deem it
better than the admission of such a gross error. Politicians are
not trained to say, 'I am sorry. I was wrong.'

That's fine by Steven.

He has come to the conclusion that the entire legal system
is more or less of a lottery; but he doesn't say this aloud. None
of his clients ever admit guilt to him, of course, or if they do
he does not hear them; but he has, by weight of eloquence,
caused to be acquitted many of whose guilt he was certain in
his heart. Does he lose as much as five minutes' sleep when a
rapist is put back on the streets because he, Steven, humiliated
the victim in court; because he, Steven, was Gielgud to the
Prosecution's Roger Moore? No, because that is how the English legal system works: each side going all out to destroy the
other, to demolish reputations, to cast doubt on honesty; the
judge acting as a – supposedly impartial – referee and the jury
finally deciding whom it believes.

A wall of silence has been erected between him and the Home
Office, him and the police, him and the Crown Prosecution
Service. He has friends in what ought to be the right places but
even they are being excluded from whatever behind-the-scenes
dealing is going on. For once, there are no leaks – either official
or unofficial.

Steven is taking no more cases for the time being, is giving all his time to this one. He believes his patience will be rewarded. He will never be a judge now, he knows, but he will be remembered.

Maire has noticed this woman in the three days since she arrived, sitting alone at meals, but this is the first time she has seen her venture to speak to anybody.

She is a housewife in her late thirties – a year or two older than Maire herself – long married, with teenage children. Her face is soft and bewildered. She is a stone heavier than she was when she married and grey is visible in her mousey hair. She wears a flowered Laura Ashley frock with a lace collar, which is too young for her. It has been years since anything important happened in her life.

She is serving fourteen days for non-payment of her poll tax. She had not expected this: it had seemed exciting at the time – this act of defiance – a chance to be true to her vaguely left-wing credentials, a legacy of teacher-training college almost twenty years ago. She had forgotten that time had passed and that she was not a resilient twenty-one any more.

She had joined the rallies, binned the final demands, stood confidently in the dock. When the magistrate had said fourteen days without the option, she had almost fainted. She was to be put in prison with criminals, women who had committed who-knew-what appalling crimes. She had seen the horrified face of her husband, the scared expressions of her children, as they had taken her down.

She has not left her room except for meals until now when boredom and loneliness have driven her to the library where she hopes she will be safe.

Maire sits mending the torn pages of a Catherine Cookson paperback with Sellotape as the woman approaches. She looks up and smiles at her.

'Sit down,' she says, nodding to a chair on the other side of the desk. The woman is surprised but obeys. 'My name's Maire. What's yours?'

'Josie.' Surnames are superfluous here. 'I, um, I've read all the books I brought in with me.'

'Time goes slowly, doesn't it?' Josie nods and her eyes fill with tears. 'Much left to do?'

'Over a week still.' Maire laughs, then apologises. She sees that it was not meant as a joke. 'A week can be a very very long time.'

'It may seem nothing to a real criminal,' Josie says, 'but — oh, no offence.'

'None taken.'

'But I never imagined for a moment that I would ever find myself in a place like this. Or what it would be like if I did.'

'It is not within the bounds of imagination,' Maire agrees, 'not for ordinary people.'

'The noise, the lack of privacy . . . I always thought it was a bit of a doddle, you know, somewhere people who couldn't cope went to have their meals cooked for them and a TV supplied to them and no responsibilities. I never imagined what it would feel like just to be caged up.'

'We're not caged up,' Maire points out. 'It's an open prison. You've been lucky. They could have sent you to Risley to teach you a real lesson.'

Josie shudders. 'What would happen if we did walk out of that gate?'

'They would catch us and put us in a closed prison.'

'So the gate is real, after all.'

'Yes,' Maire admits. 'It's real.'

'You take it all for granted outside. If you want to pop down the shops, or just take the dog for a walk, or nip round to a neighbour's for coffee.'

'Yes, I remember.'

'I'm sorry. Have you been here long?'

'Not long, no. Not here,' she replies carefully.

'And some of the women are, well, rather rough. That can be difficult for people like you and me. You're the first person I've spoken to since I got here.'

'I know.'

'I'm . . . well . . . afraid. I don't know what they've done to be here. Do I? They could be murderers and terrorists and all sorts.'

'You can't always tell who the real dirty players are, not just by looking at them.' Maire gets up and walks over to a shelf by the window. 'We have romances and detective novels mostly.

266

Nothing very high-brow, I'm afraid. Oh, there are some Jeffrey Archers. What do you fancy?'

Josie chooses a book and Maire checks it out.

'Try talking to some of the other girls,' she says, as Josie leaves. 'You might learn something.'

But Josie's husband has paid her poll tax and, despite her unconvincing murmurs of protest, he comes to collect her the next morning. The four longest days of her life are over and soon come to seem like a nightmare which is best forgotten.

Simon celebrates the end of exams with the rest of the Upper Sixth and is a little the worse for wear the following morning. He is jubilant, however, since, despite the recession, he has managed to get a job at the Sherwood Forest Visitors' Centre for the summer. It seems that his sturdy Anglo-Saxon blondness and modest success in the school play are just what they need for the annual Robin Hood Festival. In August he will be transformed into a Merry Man for a week.

'Alan-a-Dale?' Barbara laughs. 'Or have they heard you sing?'

He will stay at Andy's in Mansfield during the week and be home only at weekends. He hopes to earn enough to supplement his paltry grant and avoid too large a student loan. The time will pass pleasantly enough while he awaits his results.

It's a long time since Anne-Marie's house had such a cleaning. She has never been one for noticing cobwebs or white specks on the carpet, but it passes the time while she is waiting for news. She has put on her oldest clothes and bound her hair up in a scarf and been out to Sainsbury's for cream cleaner and Windolene and hoover bags, Mr Muscle for the filthy oven.

The telephone rings intermittently. She has a custody case on the go and an adoption appeal where the Social Services will not agree to the stepfather's adopting his wife's children for reasons of their own. Anne-Marie is inclined to agree with the decision – the man is sullen and tough-looking and Anne-Marie does not trust him – but the wife is so tired and sad and helpless that she has agreed to act for them.

Tonight is her night down the Law Centre, advising battered wives, people on the verge of eviction. By then the little house will be spotless. Steven will ring if he has any news, or perhaps even if he hasn't. She will have her nightly chat with Rosie. The telephone lines are humming between London and Oxford and Nottingham.

She toys with the idea of taking a holiday this year. It is eight years since the last one. She has picked up some brochures on her way back from the supermarket and is a little shocked by the prices. Not Italy, since she went there for her honeymoon; France perhaps, or Greece. Maybe a walking holiday where there will be other single people. It is time she opened herself out a little.

She finds herself humming as she scours the sink. She is not naturally musical but the noise pleases her. She feels a sense of achievement.

Bob Mason moves silently about his supermarket. The staff think he is trying to catch them unawares, that some new efficiency drive is underway; but he barely replies to their murmured greetings, does not hear their questions. Once an hour he rings home but there is no reply: Rosie is out and Betty does not bother to answer, has nothing to say to anyone.

It will soon be their twentieth wedding anniversary. Normally he would have booked them into a special restaurant, brought home flowers. Rosie would have come to dinner with them since the family has not been complete without her for the past twelve years or more. The purity of that family circle has been sullied and he is, himself, the violator with his outburst that March Friday night.

There is nothing he can do but wait.

Each of them, this Midsummer's Day, is waiting for something outside his or her control, waiting and hoping. Except for Maire, perhaps, who has learnt to fill time over the past thirteen years, learnt not to hope too much.

Nine

The Maguire appeal finally reports on Wednesday, June 26th. The judges at the Court of Appeal refuse to exonerate the Seven completely. They still contend that someone in that house in Kilburn had been handling explosives but, given that the residue could have been passed from person to person by the towel in Annie Maguire's kitchen, it is not now possible to say who that someone was and the convictions are declared unsafe.

'A new verdict in English law,' Lord Fitt announces on television that evening. 'Not very guilty.' *The Times* suggests satirically that the towel be brought to trial.

'It's good enough,' Steven insists, when Anne-Marie jibes at him that night for his 'good authority'.

At last, it seems he is right in his optimism. The next day he receives an urgent telephone call asking him, on behalf of his client, to present himself at the Court of Appeal at the Old Bailey on Monday, July 1st, when an emergency sitting will be held before the summer recess to consider the O'Neill case.

'This is excellent news,' Steven says on the telephone to Anne-Marie five minutes later. 'To start a case like this at the last minute means that their lordships expect it all to be over very quickly so they can pack their suntan lotion and Bermuda shorts and catch the next flight out of Heathrow to all points south.'

She replies, 'The more likely thing is that they will insist there is still a case to answer and adjourn until October. Alternatively that it will, indeed, be over quickly with the appeal being chucked straight out of court.'

'They can't do that.'

'Within reason, they can do what they bloody well like,' she points out. 'You remember how strong the evidence was in favour of the Birmingham Six as far back as 1987 – much good it did them. What was it Lord Lane said? Something along the lines of the longer this business dragged on the more convinced he was that the original verdict was the correct one.'

'You're just a pessimist.'

'I'm a realist. One of us has got to keep her feet on the ground.'

'That's what pessimists always say.' He begins to quote at her. '"Twixt the optimist and pessimist the difference is droll: the optimist sees the doughnut but the pessimist sees the hole."' Boom Boom!'

'I don't know why it is I like you,' she says and hangs up.

'Bloody woman,' he says affectionately and hangs up too.

It's the night of June 30th and Anne-Marie is staying at Steven's house. She is afraid that she will not sleep for the excitement. Steven feeds her a light meal of pasta and salad and fruit and just one glass of wine and makes her take a long, warm bath. She is now curled up in her demure dressing gown on his sofa, sleepy already. She lights a pre-bed cigarette and Steven pointedly takes the overflowing ashtray away and brings her a clean one. She smiles tolerantly at him.

He telephones Rosie who has elected to stay at home in Nottingham and await the news there. She wants to see her mother for the first time as a free woman. As it happens, Maire has also elected not to attend, as is her right; she does not want her hopes raised, only to be, perhaps, taken back and locked up again when it's all over.

'It's going to be a long day,' Steven is saying to Rosie. 'Several long days, I expect.'

Ten

The Central Criminal Court in the Old Bailey has changed little in twelve years; indeed, in a hundred years. Here are the stiff wigs, the subfusc gowns, the opulence of a gentleman's club with its polished wood and green baize. A gentleman's club is, in a sense, what it is. The main difference from the trial in 1979 is that the jury box stands empty while the bench is rather full.

Even after all his years at the bar, the arrangements for appeals strikes Steven as bizarre, anomalous. You went through all that rigmarole of choosing a jury so that the defendant might be judged by his or her peers, but when it came to overturning (or not) the decision of that jury it was left entirely to the judiciary: which in this case means Lord Justice Dart, Lord Justice Garfield and Lord Justice Smythe – enthroned in majesty on the bench. Lord Justice Garfield is the middle one of the three, the most senior, and he is in charge.

Word has spread quickly, thanks to Steven. The court is crowded with distinguished visitors this first day: the Irish ambassador is here, an Irish bishop, an Anglican archbishop, an observer from Amnesty International, a handful of MPs from all parties. It is not Maire O'Neill who is on trial today but, once again, British justice.

Steven, for the appellant, may speak first. He makes a lengthy opening statement reminding the court, as if they need reminding, of the circumstances of the original conviction. The Crown's case, he says, revolves around the twin pillars of forensic evidence and the merest circumstantial detail. The former, he insists, has been proved in recent years a cracked and flawed pillar.

'The question is posed,' he goes on dramatically, 'whether

among the victims of the High Wycombe bombing – the dead, the maimed and the bereaved – history will count the name of Maire Deirdre O'Neill.'

He explains to the bench the grounds for the appeal which are, primarily, that the forensic evidence was flawed, but also, secondarily, the testimony of ex-corporal Carmichael – a victim of that troubled night, a man with no possible axe to grind.

Jack Carmichael is as simple and convincing as he was the first time round. The Crown, in the shape of a raveningly ambitious young woman – an honorary gentleman – called Mara Needham, QC, is insistent that the ex-soldier is the victim of an IRA hoax.

She is, after all, the champion of the status quo.

'Naturally,' she says, 'it is in the IRA's interest to convince the British public that grave miscarriages of justice have taken place, despite the considered decision of the twelve very ordinary men and women who made up the original jury. It makes it more difficult for the Crown to get a conviction the next time. You tell me, Mr Carmichael, that several high-ups in the IRA have confirmed to you that Maire O'Neill had no connection with that illegal organisation. I put it to you, Mr Carmichael, that, to coin a phrase, "They would say that, wouldn't they?"'

'Pathetic,' Steven murmurs to his junior. 'Not worthy of Needling Needham. She's desperate, knows she hasn't got a leg to stand on. And she's not coining it, anyway. That was no new-minted cliché.'

'Did you say something, Mr Hale?' asks Lord Justice Garfield, who does not like Steven.

'Just conferring with my junior, My Lord.'

'Well, would you mind not doing so while Miss Needham is addressing the witness?'

Steven apologises gracefully.

Carmichael is steadfast in his refutal of Miss Needham's claims. He has spoken to something like thirty people over the last three and a half years, he tells the court, people connected with the IRA in Britain in the late seventies. Many of them are still active; many have retired. Some live in England, some in

Ireland. They have not met each other for at least a decade; some of them have never met at all.

'Mostly,' he adds, 'they only had the briefest notice that I was coming to talk to them. They didn't know who else I'd spoken to or what they'd told me.'

With a couple of obviously mendacious exceptions, their stories tally to a remarkable degree. If it is a conspiracy, Carmichael points out, then it is the most elaborate and long-drawn-out conspiracy he has ever heard of.

Miss Needham next attempts to imply that Carmichael is a coward for refusing to name the real bombers, and Steven shakes his head at her in mock pity. The judges, themselves putative terrorist targets, are on Carmichael's side in this.

Finally Miss Needham respectfully reminds their lordships that ex-corporal Carmichael's evidence is little better than hearsay or, as she phrases it, tittle-tattle. Lord Justice Dart replies ironically that they have noticed that fact for themselves and are bearing it in mind.

'Just going through the motions, Mara,' Steven hisses gleefully as she sits down.

'Oh, fuck off, Steven.'

Steven rises, still smiling, to point out that, if Carmichael has really been hoaxed by the IRA in an attempt to gain the freedom of one its operatives, they have been somewhat leisurely about it since Miss O'Neill has been in prison for more than twelve years.

'The same claims were made about the Birmingham Six,' he reminds their lordships, 'who had been in prison for sixteen years. It would seem, if what my learned friend says is true, that the IRA are content to let their soldiers kick their heels for a long, long time before taking any action to get them out.'

Lord Justice Garfield, who is a fair man, lets slip a faint nod of agreement and adjourns for the day.

Tomorrow the court will hear once more the rival testimonies of Dr Fletcher – surviving, against all the odds, into his eighties – and Dr Pavel Kurowski. They will see if twelve years have made any difference to the latter's cockiness and which of them, this time, will be believed.

Mara Needham and her junior hurry off to seek the advice of the Crown Prosecution Service. Steven and his party adjourn to the nearest pub where Anne-Marie thankfully lights up. Days in court are long for smokers.

'We're very grateful to you,' she tells Carmichael as Steven's junior, a pale young man known only as 'Toby', brings them all their drinks. 'Will you be in court tomorrow?'

'Oh yes, miss. I shall be here every day until there's a verdict.' Carmichael downs his pint of bitter at high speed, commenting, 'Thirsty work, this.'

'When I think of the money you must have spent . . .'

He waves the expense away. 'As I told Mr Hale, it was instead of my holidays. Weekend in Dublin beats a fortnight in Benidorm any day. The beer's better.'

'Have another,' Steven suggests. 'Toby –'

'No thank you, sir. I have to get off.' He hesitates. 'Look, if you really want to thank me what I'd like is to meet Miss O'Neill, you know, once she's out and . . . you know . . . rested and so forth.'

'I'm sure she'll be delighted,' Steven says. 'She's going to need all the friends she can get on the outside.'

Eleven

Mara Needham speaks only to the solicitors at the CPS. It is they who refer the matter back to the men in bespoke suits at the Home Office. SHUAGO had his own shorthand writer in court, sitting unobtrusively among the public, and the transcripts are rushed through, typed and duplicated within two hours of the adjournment. There are discussions far into the night. In the morning, word comes back to Miss Needham that they are not yet ready to throw in the towel. After all, unlike at the original trial, it is now up to Maire O'Neill to prove that she is innocent.

Time has improved Dr Mark Fletcher. Twelve years earlier, shattered by the recent death of his wife after long years of an illness that had left her babbling and incontinent, he had been an old man wearied of life; now, on the threshold of eternity, he is more at ease with himself and the world, determined not to be cowed this time, to have his answer ready to the doubts cast on his competence by Barney (now Sir Barney) Winch-Gore and the late Mr Justice De Freitas so long ago.

Once more he questions the ability, even the integrity, of Dr Pavel Kurowski. He testifies that shortly before the trial he had attended a meeting with the Prosecution scientist at the Metropolitan Police forensic laboratory in Lambeth Bridge Road with a view to questioning him on his tests, examining the results and inspecting his records.

He had on that visit seen a copy of the results of the GCMS test done on the O'Neill swabs by Dr Kurowski at Aldermaston in September 1978. Dr Kurowski insisted both then and at the trial that the result was positive. Dr Fletcher asserts that the blip shown on the oscilloscope was very small, far too small to constitute a definite positive and that he had pointed this out to Kurowski. The copy, like so many useful documents, cannot now be located.

He steps down from the witness box, bridling at the thanks of the judges for his lucid testimony, to make way for a man he has come to think of, over the years, as his enemy. He is glad to have lived to see that enemy fall.

Dr Kurowski is deflated, like a rubber doll with a slow puncture. Steven would feel sorry for him if he had not been the cause of so much havoc. He is less respectful to him than he was the first time round, more brusque. The scientist's certainties are no longer set in concrete. He has seen colleagues effectively dismissed for less after previous successful appeals, although the dismissal is a gentle one and comes wrapped in euphemism and ribboned in pension entitlement.

Dr Kurowski runs verbally through his tests again, almost thirteen years on: Greiss, TLC, GCMS. He says that Dr Fletcher is . . . mistaken . . . when he says he saw a copy of the GCMS test. No such hard copy was made. The doctor asks their lord-ships to take his word for it that the test was positive. The judges look back at him without comment and he licks his thin red lips inside his now grey, pointy beard.

He agrees under cross-examination by Steven that this result takes the form of a tiny blip on a computer screen, rising fractionally and ephemerally and witnessed by none but himself.

'How long does this blip last?' Steven asks.

'Say, half a second. A bit less.'

'And yet you were so positive about a result that hardly had time to flash before your eyes and it was gone?'

'I had done the test many times. I knew what to look for and I didn't so much as blink.'

'And you had the facility to make the computer do what I believe is called a "drop print" of that blip?'

'I did,' Kurowski says sulkily.

'But you say you didn't take one?'

'No.'

'Why not?'

'I can't remember. It wasn't usual practice at the lab. I may have been a bit slow off the mark.'

'Which of those answers are you giving me?'

'I can't remember why I didn't. It didn't seem important at the time . . .'

'Didn't seem important!' Steven echoes, putting as much incredulity into his voice as possible.

'It was just confirmation of the other two tests.'

'But it wasn't a confirmation since Dr Fletcher has told us that, on the evidence of the print-out he saw, which you, Dr Kurowski, claim never existed, the blip was not high enough to be a definite positive.'

'The test was not done until a week after the swabs were taken. You would expect some evaporation of the samples during that time, making a lower blip inevitable.'

Steven knows he has Kurowski on the run now. The scientist is attempting to move the goalposts. The blip was no longer a definite positive but its paucity must be explained another way. He continues.

'My information is that the samples should not have evaporated if properly kept, that is to say sealed and refrigerated.' Kurowski almost shrugs. 'Well? Did you refrigerate them?'

'No. I . . .' The scientist tails off.

'What you are telling me, Dr Kurowski, is that you had made up your mind that there was nitroglycerine on those swabs since the police had told you that was what they expected to find and you weren't going to let little things like facts get in the way. Isn't that right?'

'We all make mistakes.'

'Are you familiar with the results of the May Enquiry, Dr Kurowski?'

The little man says sullenly that he is.

'Do you remember stating very positively at the original trial that it was not possible for traces of nitroglycerine to pass from one hand to another via a medium such as a towel or a glass?'

'I may have said it was unlikely.'

'You said it was *impossible*,' Steven insists. 'Perhaps you would like to have the relevant part of the transcript read to you, if their lordships please?'

'That will not be necessary. I did, um, consider it impossible at the time. I accept now that it is possible, in certain circumstances.'

'A possibility which was proved by the very simple process of trying it to see.'

'So I gather.'

'Simple, but brilliant. Wouldn't you say?'

'Apparently.'

'But it did not occur to you to make such a simple test?'

He repeats, 'We all make mistakes.'

Steven says, 'I have no more questions.'

Lord Justice Garfield regards the witness over the top of his bifocals and remarks, 'It seems extraordinary to me that, in a case of this seriousness, the forensic evidence was handled in such a slapdash manner. You did not seal and refrigerate the samples which even I, ignorant as I am of matters scientific, can see would have been advisable; you did not have a colleague standing by to bear witness to the accuracy of your results, and such records as you kept have apparently been lost if not deliberately destroyed. We would like the prosecuting solicitors to know that we are not impressed by this catalogue of inefficiency, one might almost say of criminal incompetence.'

This outburst is almost unprecedented and the court is stunned into silence. Garfield, unrepentant, adds that it is time to adjourn for lunch, leaving Kurowski in the witness box, looking round helplessly for guidance.

There you have it, Steven thinks. Dr Pavel Kurowski, elevated almost to sainthood by De Freitas, is being judged at his true value at last.

As the court rises, Mara Needham, who has been having a whispered consultation for the past few minutes with a young woman from the CPS who is sitting behind her, asks for an adjournment until the next day while the Crown reviews its position. There is murmuring in the press gallery. Lord Justice Garfield agrees without hesitation and strides out of the courtroom with his colleagues.

'This is it,' Steven says to Anne-Marie. 'This has to be it. We're nearly there.'

'Patience,' she says. 'Don't count your chickens; all the eggs may be duds.'

'You heard what Garfield said. Perhaps he's not such a miser-

able old sod after all. And I always thought he didn't like me.'
   'He doesn't,' Anne-Marie says.

But Steven is right in his optimism at last. When he and Anne-Marie arrive at court at ten the following morning – Anne-Marie neat for once in a dark suit and a blouse that Steven has made her iron – it is to be told that the Crown has withdrawn its opposition to the appeal. Mara Needham states with dignity that the Crown is no longer satisfied with the safety of the conviction and will offer no further evidence.

Lord Justice Garfield confers briefly with his fellow judges, then speaks to a silent courtroom, hanging on his words.

'We have formed the view that no reliance can properly be placed on the scientific evidence which was the cornerstone of the Prosecution's case in 1979 and which will, I trust, come under the closest scrutiny from the new Royal Commission. There exists no other evidence against the appellant: she made no confession – even discredited as such confessions have been in recent years – and everything else raised at the trial is circumstantial.

'We have no hesitation, therefore, in finding Miss O'Neill's convictions on all counts to be unsafe and unsatisfactory and in quashing those convictions.'

At the sound of the verb 'quash' Anne-Marie shouts and punches the air in a gesture of victory which shocks the staid officers of the Court of Appeal. She scatters the white carnations she is carrying – symbols of innocence – into the well of the court. Her loud laughter is a punch in the face for them.

Lord Justice Garfield subdues her with a stare which Medusa would have envied and goes on to say that Maire will be freed as soon as the formalities have been completed, the following lunchtime or thereabouts.

Everyone rises again as the three judges leave the courtroom. They remain standing, ready to go their several ways.

In the public gallery, 'Mr Robinson' smiles very faintly to himself at Anne-Marie's antics before going back to Queen Anne's Gate to report to his masters.

Steven, gathering up his belongings and piling them on to Toby, is a little let down: it is like lighting a firework, stepping back to watch the spray of golden sparks, hear the fizz of adulterated gunpowder, only to have it die on you in the damp November air.

'The great thing about being a pessimist,' Anne-Marie tells him, 'is that I get such a big buzz when things go right for once. You, on the other hand, can only ever be disappointed.'

Steven concedes the point and says he is too old a leopard to change his spots now. He rings Maire at once, then Roisin. Then he calls a press conference; they shall not rob him of his moment of glory.

Twelve

Steven has an early start the next morning.

He leaves Kensington shortly after six and, ignoring speed restrictions on the M40 in the light dawn traffic, is hooting outside Anne-Marie's house shortly after seven. Neighbouring bedroom curtains twitch in annoyance but Anne-Marie is ready and the nuisance is not repeated.

The second leg of the journey is longer and, as they wait in a brief jam on the ring-road outside Leicester, Anne-Marie asks, 'What's the itinerary today, then?'

'Lunch. Champagne, caviar, smoked salmon, fillet steak, good claret . . .'

'You'll make the poor woman sick,' she protests. 'After all these years of prison food. Take it slowly.'

'All right. Porridge, small beer.'

'Whatever she wants.'

'Yes.'

'Then?'

'Leave her alone with Rosie. They need to get to know each other again. We shall be *de trop*, you and I.'

She sighs. 'Yes.'

He takes his hand off the gear lever and squeezes hers in her lap.

'She won't just forget you, you know, not after all you've done for her.'

'You think not?'

'Another eighteen-year-old girl, yes. Rosie, no.'

'It will be a bit of an anti-climax for us.'

'The famous barrister and the concerned solicitor? Winding up the most satisfying case of their careers?' He changes into top gear and accelerates away towards Nottingham. 'Why don't you come and have a celebratory dinner with me on Saturday, just the two of us, at the Manoir aux Quatr' Saisons. I don't call that an anti-climax.'

She is startled. 'You won't get a table at the Manoir on a Saturday. Not at this notice.'

Steven can be forgiven for looking a little smug. 'I booked it as soon as I got that phone call last week.' She is silent. 'Anne-Marie, you can't let a man dine alone at the Manoir. It's just not on. I need someone to argue with about the meaning of life over pudding.'

'No. All right.' She laughs. 'You're still a flash, arrogant puppy, Steven Hale, but thank you.'

They pick Roisin up shortly after nine, and Steven heads north, at high speed, for Yorkshire.

The time of Maire's release has been kept secret but the press has been there all night as if – she thinks – waiting for a bargain fur coat at the January Sales.

Ah, she has forgotten: people don't wear fur coats any more. There are other kinds of terrorists now, not just Irish ones: there are Libyans and Iraqis and Animal Rights activists.

She has one suitcase with all she owns. The governor shakes hands with her just inside the gate and she wants for a panic-stricken moment to beg to be allowed to stay.

She has nowhere to go. Had she been a prisoner being released on Licence after serving a suitable proportion of her sentence, there would have been a place in an ex-offenders' hostel waiting for her, some sort of unskilled job fixed up, social workers and probation officers ready with advice and discreet supervision.

She would have been living in Askham Grange's own hostel for a few months before release, going daily to an outside job. She would have had short home leaves and long home leaves to acclimatise her. But her conviction is to be quashed; unsafe. She is free to go without a stain on her character, to dance on the wire without a safety net.

But she has nowhere to go and no one to go to. Many of her difficulties are just beginning. She will have choices to make, decisions: what clothes to wear, what food to eat, what film to see, whether to go for a walk alone in the rain.

Lights flash. Great phallic microphones are thrust in her face. She barely hears their questions – one word in three, perhaps.

Bitter? No she doesn't feel bitter, exactly; not yet.

She doesn't know what her immediate plans are, she will stay with friends, take a holiday.

What friends? Where holiday?

If only she knew. She tells them she wants to be left alone – fearing, all the while, that that is exactly what will happen to her.

Yes, her solicitor will be starting a claim for compensation.

Write her life story? That's not a bad idea.

Where is her solicitor anyway? Where is Steven Hale? He had promised on the telephone that they would be there to meet her.

Then she sees them on the other side of the road, cut off from her by a moat of braying journalists. They have just got out of Steven's Jaguar. He carries an armful of white carnations. Anne-Marie looks relaxed: younger and happier than Maire has ever seen her, casual in jeans and a tan suede jacket. She waves, beckons, gives the victory salute.

Then a young girl gets out of the back of the car, stands leaning awkwardly against it, staring across the road, shading her eyes from the sun. She is a boyish-looking girl with cropped hair and a cheeky, humorous face, a girl no older than Maire was when Roisin was born.

Maire likes her looks: it could be herself at that age.

'Excuse me.' She pushes the nearest reporter hard in the chest and he stumbles, winding himself up in his electric flex. The moat parts before her like the Red Sea as people scuttle out of his erratic way.

'I have no further comment to make at present. My friends are waiting for me.'

She is watching Maire as she walks slowly across the road – this girl who could so easily be Roisin – not smiling, but with loving curiosity. She is watching Maire as if she believes there is still a human being inside this institutionalised woman who can no longer remember which way you look before crossing a road.

Maire finds that she believes it too.

The girl straightens up and steps forward a pace. Steven and

Anne-Marie fade into the gleaming metal flanks of the car. Her hands go out towards Maire. Then she falters, afraid. Her lips form a word which won't vocalise but which might be 'Mim?'

Maire begins to run.

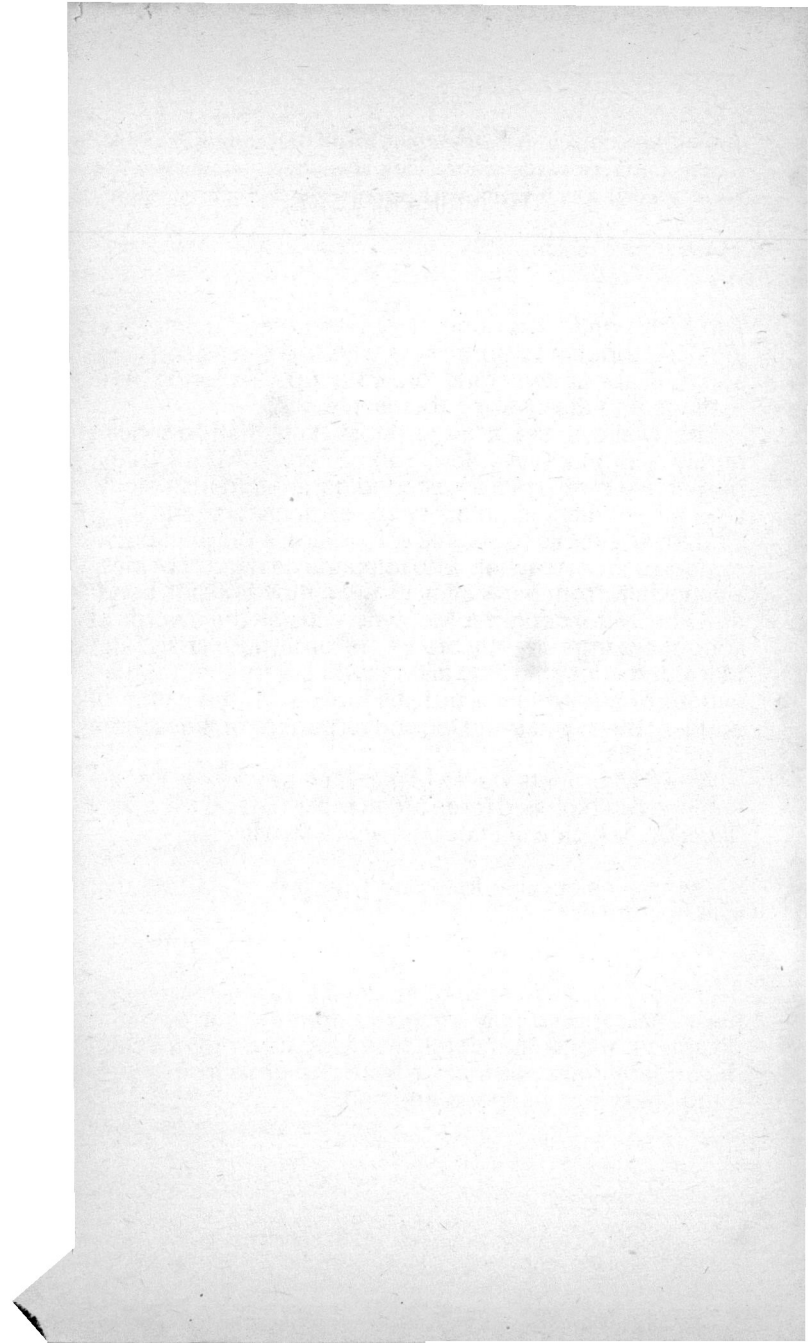

MICKEY CLEMENT

THE IRISH PRINCESS

The Irish Princess is about the pleasure and pain of first love. It's about the warmth of family life – and its sorrows; and it's about two girls growing up, exploring new feelings and discovering themselves.

The Malloys are a large, close knit Irish-American family living in Troy, New York. There is Mike Malloy, one of five brothers from second generation Irish stock, who prides himself on his deep religious faith and iron-clad loyalty to his roots; his wife, Clare, a bright, liberal-minded school teacher, who tolerates no bigotry or piety – especially from her Malloy in-laws; their brilliant, beautiful and wilful daughter Mo, who wins all the awards at school but imprudently draws the family into crisis; and Margie, the lovable little sister, who enters the troubled waters of adolescence but still looks with the clarity of youth at the clashes and the convergences of these three strong wills.

When Mo meets David Markovitch sparks fly. Family feelings run high and force Mo to make a decision, a vital decision, which will affect the entire family.

'Movingly celebrates love and true grit . . . a tale that touches the heart.'

Kirkus Reviews

'Her storyline is so strong, its details so well observed, her characters so fully imagined, that the sorrows and disappointments that come their way never overwhelm the underlying sense that we learn and grow from everything life brings us, good and bad.'

The Washington Post

HODDER AND STOUGHTON PAPERBACKS

BARBARA HALL

A BETTER PLACE

Beautiful Valerie Caldwell was the golden girl, popular and dynamic. She was the one with all the dreams – and the guts to make them happen.

But now, disillusioned with a life in Hollywood that promised glamour and fulfilment, Valerie returns to her sleepy small hometown in search of the comfort and security she left behind.

The comfort of her old friends: shy Tess who only ever wanted a husband and children; Mary Grace who only ever wanted to be slim; and Joe Deacon who only ever wanted to be Valerie's husband and who ended up with Tess.

But Valerie's return causes havoc. And in trying to recapture that special joy she remembers from her childhood, Valerie realises that golden memories are sometimes masks for darker truths . . .

HODDER AND STOUGHTON PAPERBACKS

SUSAN MOODY

HOUSE OF MOONS

Sometimes Tess Lovel dreamed of the house in Spain where she had been born.

Sun-bleached colours and the heavy stillness of noon. A hill town where memories of the Civil War, of blood and betrayal, lay dangerously close beneath the dusty surface of the present day.

In rain-grey England, Tess tried to deny the passion and mystery of her past. But from across the Atlantic, an older woman, revenge-obsessed, was reaching out to ensnare her.

'A complex and often compelling romantic thriller . . . *The* book to take on holiday'
Robert Goddard, *The Mail on Sunday*

'An assured well-plotted pageturner . . . But Susan Moody has also brought to her lush drama a quality of descriptive writing and an attention to characterisation which raises the novel to another level . . . *House of Moons* is a substantial achievement'
The Independent

'A big, enjoyable suspense novel'
The Sunday Telegraph

HODDER AND STOUGHTON PAPERBACKS